D1569022

THE GUILD CODEX: UNVEILED / ONE

THE ONE AND ONLY
CRYSTAL DRUID

ANNETTE MARIE

dark owl
fantasy

Dark Owl Fantasy Inc.
PO Box 88106, Rabbit Hill Post Office
Edmonton, AB, Canada T6R 0M5
www.darkowlfantasy.com

Cover Copyright © 2020 by Annette Marie

Editing by Elizabeth Darkley
arrowheadediting.wordpress.com

ISBN 978-1-988153-59-9

BOOKS IN THE GUILD CODEX

UNVEILED

The One and Only Crystal Druid
The Long-Forgotten Winter King

SPELLBOUND

Three Mages and a Margarita
Dark Arts and a Daiquiri
Two Witches and a Whiskey
Demon Magic and a Martini
The Alchemist and an Amaretto
Druid Vices and a Vodka
Lost Talismans and a Tequila
Damned Souls and a Sangria

DEMONIZED

Taming Demons for Beginners
Slaying Monsters for the Feeble
Hunting Fiends for the Ill-Equipped
Delivering Evil for Experts

WARPED
with Rob Jacobsen

Warping Minds & Other Misdemeanors
Hellbound Guilds & Other Misdirections
Rogue Ghosts & Other Miscreants

MORE BOOKS BY ANNETTE MARIE

STEEL & STONE UNIVERSE

Steel & Stone Series

Chase the Dark

Bind the Soul

Yield the Night

Reap the Shadows

Unleash the Storm

Steel & Stone

Spell Weaver Trilogy

The Night Realm

The Shadow Weave

The Blood Curse

OTHER WORKS

Red Winter Trilogy

Red Winter

Dark Tempest

Immortal Fire

THE GUILD CODEX

CLASSES OF MAGIC

Spiritalis
Psychica
Arcana
Demonica
Elementaria

MYTHIC

A person with magical ability

MPD / MAGIPOL

The organization that regulates mythics and their activities

ROGUE

A mythic living in violation of MPD laws

THE ONE AND ONLY
CRYSTAL DRUID

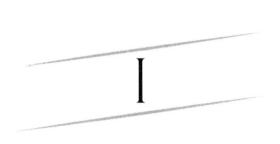

I

AS COLD RAIN pattered on my head, I studied the boy.

"Boy" wasn't the right word for someone who emanated such a menacing, skin-prickling intensity. For someone with a presence that couldn't be ignored, the air around him suffused with an indefinable threat. He was a nameless enigma unlike anyone I'd ever seen before.

But with several more years before "man" could describe him, "boy" was the best label I had.

Broken glass crunched under my boots as I ventured into the narrow gap between buildings, darkness swallowing the orange glow of nearby streetlights. Gang tags and graffiti marked the bricks on either side of me as I cautiously approached.

The boy leaned against the wall in a recessed doorway, a dim security light casting his face into shadow. I couldn't make out his eyes, but I could feel his gaze.

I stopped in front of his alcove, frigid droplets dripping off my chin. A shiver ran down my spine all the way to my toes as a soft stillness enveloped me—an ominous moment of warning I couldn't interpret.

I should have stayed out in the rain.

Stepping into the doorway, I pressed my back against the wall opposite him and swiped my sopping bangs off my forehead. The boy didn't speak, merely observed my presence like I was an unexpected piece of furniture in a familiar room.

We sized each other up. He wore a leather jacket, its hood deep. Sturdy pants. Heavy boots similar to mine. His broad shoulders suggested that, even at six feet tall, he hadn't reached his full height. Stark shadows clung to his face, aging him, but his jaw hadn't hardened yet.

Around my age, I decided. Fifteen or sixteen.

His gaze roved over me, then he lifted his hand toward his mouth, something small pinched between his fingers. A red spot glowed as he drew on a blunt. His shoulders relaxed as he exhaled hazy smoke.

I wrinkled my nose, then hesitated. A cautious, confused sniff as I tried to identify the unfamiliar scent. It had a medicinal tang I hadn't expected.

Silently, he offered the blunt.

I reassessed his features. The dark ring under his lower eyelid: a fading black eye. The shadow on his right cheek: a half-healed bruise. The mark on the back of his hand: an angry red burn. The split in his lower lip … almost identical to the throbbing split in mine.

Without deciding to, I reached out. My fingers brushed his as I took the roll of brown paper. I put it between my lips—where his lips had been moments before—and inhaled its citrus-scented smoke, relieved when I didn't burst into a coughing fit.

As the rain gradually lessened and its noisy patter diminished, we passed the blunt back and forth, saying nothing. What was there to say? We weren't here because we wanted to be. If we could've been somewhere else, we'd already be gone.

In the new quiet, other sounds reached my ears: the low rumble of voices leaking from the building. A deep male tone called out, accompanied by a burst of masculine laughter. A higher-pitched female voice answered, sharp with cutting amusement, and more laughter followed.

The boy's gaze drifted to the door. I wondered which voice went with the fist that had bruised his face and split his lip.

I wondered what my face looked like to him.

And I wondered why it mattered.

I passed the stub of his blunt back to him. Another roar of laughter from the other side of the door scraped my ears.

"Do you ever think about just killing them?"

The question was out of my mouth before I knew I was speaking. The boy's gaze turned to mine. No confusion. No shock. He knew exactly what I meant.

He drew on the blunt, and a swirl of smoke accompanied his reply. "All the time."

His low voice had a raspy edge that I liked. A slight accent tinged it, but I couldn't pin it down from a few words.

An odd, shivery lightness swept up my torso. "Have you ever tried?"

"No." Eyes locked on mine, he dropped the stub and ground it into the pavement. "Not yet."

2

THE MESSAGE on my phone glowed cheerily.

> The Rose Moon is tomorrow. Ritual starts at
> noon. Don't be late!

I reread it, knowing better than to interpret its tone as cheery. Laney was never cheery with me. "Contemptuous," often. "Suspicious," regularly. "Outright hostile," at least once a month. But cheerful? Never.

To be honest, I was more comfortable with contempt than cheer.

Leaning back in my chair, I dropped my phone on the counter beside the microscope. The snow-white cat lounging on the microscope's other side cracked one blue eye open, peered at me, then closed it again. I pinched the bridge of my nose until it hurt, letting the pain clear the fog from my head.

The Rose Moon. No one else considered the pinkish moon of early summer to be bad luck, but it had haunted me my entire life. I'd been born on a Rose Moon, and my mother had even named me after it—Saber *Rose*—ensuring it would haunt me forever.

A hint of leafy, citrus smoke teased my nose, leaking from my broken memories of a long-ago Rose Moon. I squinted, my eyes losing focus as I chased the dim flashes of a dark alley, cold rain, and a faceless figure in a hooded jacket. As my fractured recollection disintegrated into blank nothingness, a suffocating wave of bitter, raging despair rose in its place, clogging my throat until I could scarcely breathe.

My mind might be incapable of recalling that time of my life, but my heart knew what had broken me.

Most days, I was glad I couldn't remember.

Pushing all thoughts of the past away, I positioned my face in front of the microscope's eyepiece and turned the fine focus knob.

"Saber!"

The door beside me flew open and I almost put the microscope through my eye socket.

"*What?*" I snarled.

Kaitlynn hung in the doorway, her green scrubs stained with something wet and her mouth slack at my aggressive response.

"Sorry." My voice rose half an octave as I smiled. "You startled me. What's up?"

Blinking, she recovered her wits. "Oh, actually, I'm just— Dr. Lloyd's last appointment peed everywhere and cleanup took forever, and I have a thing planned tonight. I haven't had time to feed the cats, but I don't want to be late, so I was hoping … if possible …?"

She trailed off, waiting for me to volunteer. The white cat beside me stared unblinkingly at her, but she didn't react to the animal in the lab room—nor did she comment on his unearthly eyes, pale blue and crystalline with no visible pupils. She didn't see him at all.

"Sure, I'd be happy to help out!" I replied brightly.

The cat flicked his tail in annoyance.

Beaming, Kaitlynn gushed, "Thanks. I owe you one. Coffee tomorrow?"

"I'm off tomorrow."

"Oh, then for your next shift?"

"Sounds good!"

She bounced out, swinging the door shut, and my smile dropped.

Utterly authentic. A breathtaking performance.

I shot the cat an irritated look before returning to the microscope. I examined the skin scraping under the lens, identifying the cigar-shaped bodies of demodex mites, and made a note on the requisition beside me. I had two more samples to check—a urinalysis and a white blood cell count—but pushed away from the table. I'd feed the animals first, then finish my lab work.

The snow-white feline sprawled on the counter watched me leave with ten times the judgmental disdain of any mortal cat.

Cutting through the large treatment room, I skirted an exam table, the pervasive odor of disinfectant stinging my sinuses. The steady yowling of a homesick cat leaked through the door ahead.

"Kaitlynn, let's go!"

With thudding steps, Kaitlynn flew out from the hall to the staff room and shot past without noticing me. She disappeared behind the drug cabinet that blocked my view of the back exit.

"I'm here," she panted. "Just give me a second to tie my shoes."

Her impatient companion huffed. "Did you feed the cats?"

"No, I asked Saber to do it."

"Saber?" The disgruntled repetition of my name came from a third voice. "Ugh."

"What's 'ugh'?" Kaitlynn asked.

"Why would you ask *her*?" Though she'd lowered her voice, I still recognized the high-pitched tones of Nicolette, another vet tech. "Don't you get a weird vibe from her?"

"What do you mean? She's super nice."

"Yeah," the third woman chimed in. "She's really nice! Cut her some slack, Nicolette."

The back door thumped shut. I stood in front of the cat room, my reflection in the door's small window gazing back at me. My straight black hair hung to my elbows, thick bangs cut in a severe line at my eyebrows. A tan warmed my fair skin enough that I didn't look like a corpse, and a faint dusting of freckles covered my nose. My cheekbones stood out sharply, my lips turned down slightly at the corners. Classic resting bitchface.

My blue-gray eyes stared, intense and eerily piercing even to me. A soldier's thousand-yard stare.

I opened the door. Feline chatter erupted at my arrival, and I reviewed the feeding instructions for the first cat, a long-haired Himalayan.

People like it when others do things for them. They don't *respect* you for it, but they like you, and that was what I needed. I was *nice*. The nice girl. Nothing more, nothing less.

I'd learned how to be the nice girl while studying to become a vet tech, and I'd perfected it in my four years working at this clinic. The hard lesson that being liked was more important than being honest, genuine, or respected had come much earlier in my life.

Being liked was a survival technique, which was why I would keep doing favors for my coworkers, even when I'd rather tell them to shove it.

I couldn't let anyone realize I wasn't a nice girl at all.

THE EVENING SUN cast beautiful golden light over the narrow road as I drove my pickup truck east out of Coquitlam. I'd left the suburbs behind, and dense, mature trees leaned over the left side of the road, cutting off my view of the sprawling mountain slopes beyond them. On my right, farmland stretched toward the unseen banks of Pitt River.

Quiet tranquility stole over me. The summit to the north was part of a provincial park, and beyond it was the endless expanse of the Coast Mountains. The dense metropolis of Vancouver was less than an hour's drive west, far enough that its hectic bustle didn't disturb my home territory.

The road curved northeast, and as my truck rolled around the bend, a large sign beckoned me:

Hearts & Hooves Animal Rescue

I turned left onto the dirt driveway. My truck's tires rumbled over a metal cattle guard, and I accelerated again, zooming past a long, fenced pasture carpeted in grass. A mixture of hoofed animals—horses, ponies, donkeys, goats, sheep, alpacas, and a handful of cows—lifted their heads to watch my vehicle pass, then returned to their lazy grazing.

Ahead, a dense stand of trees concealed the farmstead. As I drove past the screening foliage and through an open gate, a small house appeared on my left. All the farm's buildings— stable, machinery shed, storage, small-animal enclosures, greenhouse, garden, and more—faced the wide gravel yard. A mixed fruit orchard formed neat rows of trees beyond the greenhouse.

Parking in front of the house beside a rusting first-generation Ford Ranger with pale blue paint, I swung my door open and climbed out. As I turned to close the door, the white cat jumped out after me. He gave me an unreadable look with his ethereal blue eyes, then sauntered off with his tail in the air.

I shut the door, my gaze drifting toward the sunlit forests blanketing the mountain north of the farm, but a brusque greeting interrupted my half-formed thought about going for a hike.

"Saber!" Dominique appeared in the large open doorway of the sprawling stable and jogged across the gravel yard toward me. Several inches shorter and much curvier than my five-foot-nine frame, she didn't look like someone who regularly lifted fifty-pound hay bales. Her tightly curled black locks were cut short, and her bold red glasses stood out against her golden umber skin.

"I'm glad you're back," she said, halting beside me. "The two new geldings are worse than we expected. The vet is coming tomorrow, but can you take a look?"

"Of course," I said quickly.

"The big gray is lame," she told me as we strode toward the stable. "He's got the worst case of thrush I've ever seen. The smaller one is moving okay, but he's underweight and he was quidding half his hay. I suspect serious dental problems."

"I won't be much help with that." Hooves, I could do, but not teeth. "Are these Harvey Whitby's horses?"

"Yes," Dominique growled. "He never should've bought horses for his spoiled-ass daughters. Those girls have never mucked a stall in their lives, so of course they wouldn't know or care about how to keep a horse healthy. But that little prick would rather toss the horses in a field and forget about them than let me take them."

Giving up animals—even ones he'd never wanted—to a rescue organization would be tantamount to admitting he made a mistake. And Harvey Whitby didn't make mistakes.

The crunch of our steps changed to the thud of boots on concrete. Hearts & Hooves Animal Rescue wasn't a high-end facility by any stretch—most of the buildings had needed a fresh coat of paint for decades—but Dominique had poured everything she had into a complete renovation of the stable eight years ago.

On our left, a row of spacious stalls stretched to the back of the building, each one opening into an outdoor turnout twice as large. On the left, windows lined a huge indoor arena, filling the stable's interior with sunlight.

"At least you were able to get them at the auction," I murmured.

"For twice what I should've paid. The meat buyers drove up the price on me again." She smirked without humor. "I returned the favor."

Ears pricked curiously, the stabled horses stuck their heads through the V-shaped openings in their stall doors to watch us stride past.

I frowned. "You said two horses. Didn't Whitby have three?"

Dominique's shoulders twitched angrily. "I was expecting three at the auction, but the third one wasn't there."

"So Whitby kept it?"

"He must've, but I can't imagine why."

At the far end of the stable, two unfamiliar horses stood in the open-front tack stalls, cross-tied between two posts.

Greta, co-owner of the rescue, glanced over as we joined her. Taller than me, rail-thin, and with a deeply tanned complexion from hours spent in the sun, she was different from Dominique in every way except for her uncompromising dedication to the animals they cared for.

She stood next to a light dappled gray, cooing softly to him as she rubbed his forehead. At over seventeen hands, he was on the large side for leisure riding and had at least a bit of draft horse in him—Percheron, I was guessing, judging by his color, thick build, and sturdy legs. The smaller brown was a quarter horse through and through, his ears rotating nervously as he monitored the unfamiliar surroundings.

I assessed the equines on my approach: stiff postures, bony shoulders, protruding ribs, dull eyes. By the time I stood in front of them, a tight feeling had spread through my chest. Not anxiety, distress, or anger, but something cold and brittle. Something hard and sharp. Something tinged red and pulsing like a living thing inside me.

Sweeping into the tack room, I pulled my farrier kit out from beneath the table and tied the leather apron around my waist, its thick panels covering my legs down to my shins. I wasn't a vet—I was a tech, an animal nurse—and I wasn't a fully-fledged farrier either. I was still an apprentice, but I knew enough to be useful.

I loaded tools into my apron's pocket and grabbed my kit. Treating the horses, nursing them back to health, and finding them loving new homes would comfort Dominique and Greta. But that wasn't enough for me.

Neglect. Abuse. Callous mistreatment. Harvey Whitby didn't care about the suffering he'd caused. No one would punish him. No one would disburse consequences commensurate for his crimes against innocent animals.

The red-hazed shards in my chest ground against my lungs as I set my kit down and approached the big gray with gentle hands and soft murmurs.

No one except me.

3

MOTHS FLUTTERED around the stable's fluorescent lights as I hummed to the big gray, now named Whicker. Stroking his shoulder, I slid my hand down his front leg to his fetlock, squeezing lightly, and pulled his foot up. Bright blue goop stained the underside of his hoof, packed into the crevices in his frog and sole where the thrush infection had rotted away the hard tissue. The foul odor of decomposition lingered.

I'd spent the evening scraping, clipping, and filing each hoof, all riddled with infection. I'd scrubbed them with an antiseptic wash, then mixed up the blue copper sulfate paste.

It would take weeks of treatment to heal the damage that basic care could have prevented.

I checked his other hooves, ensuring the paste still generously coated his soles, then grabbed a soft body brush and ran it over his neck and back. He was already clean—Dominique and Greta had pampered both horses earlier—but grooming was comforting. As I sang softly and brushed his side, he slanted his ears back, eyes half closed.

After a few minutes, I moved from his stall to the neighboring one, occupied by the brown quarter horse. His new name was Whinny, and his teeth were so bad he hadn't been eating properly for months. I checked that he'd finished the warm mash Greta had made him, brushed him for a few minutes, then slipped out of his stall.

I leaned on the stall door, watching Whinny nose at the empty feeder. The first meal he'd eaten without significant pain in who knew how long. He wanted more.

The sharp edges in my chest shifted restlessly, scraping my lungs.

It was time for Farmer Whitby's consequences.

I slid my hand into my left pocket, checking for the small fabric case I'd retrieved earlier, then reached for the other pocket and curled my fingers around a comforting aluminum handle. My dark hair was stuffed under a ball cap, and I'd changed into a black jacket, black pants, and steel-toed boots before checking on Whicker and Whinny.

Slipping outside, I locked the stable door. Dark, quiet stillness draped the farm. It was after midnight, and across the yard, the house windows were dark. Low on the horizon, the full moon cast its rosy glow across the pastures.

I took a step, then paused. A few yards away, an owl was perched on a fence post, his feathers a white so pure and unnatural they had the faint blue tinge of fresh snow. He watched me with large, pupilless azure eyes set in a great horned owl's vaguely angry face.

"If you're going for incognito," I told him, "you've failed spectacularly."

I am not incognito, dove. The owl spread his wings to their full span. *I am majestic. It's an appropriate look for a night with such a spectacular moon.*

"Are you coming with me?"

Would I miss such a valorous campaign?

Huffing, I crossed the yard to the equipment shed, which I'd left unlocked. A few minutes later, I was pushing a quad along the long gravel drive. The owl led the way, gliding on silent wings.

Only after I'd pushed the quad across the cattle guard and onto the public road did I climb on and start the engine. It rumbled to life.

The owl landed on a fence post. A faint shimmer of blue light washed over him, and when it had faded, a ferret as eerily white as the owl scurried down the wood. He darted across the road, hopped onto my knee, and clambered up my sleeve to tuck himself against the back of my neck.

I gunned the engine and the quad zoomed down the road. The wind whipped at my face, trying to steal my ball cap.

Is the coven doing a ritual tomorrow? The question sounded in my head, the crisp male tenor unhampered by the noise of the road or wind.

Yes, I answered silently, directing my thought at the ferret on my shoulder.

Soft fur brushed my neck, followed by the prick of tiny claws as he nestled under the collar of my jacket. *May I devour Deanne's familiar this time?*

No, Ríkr, you may not.

Her oversized dragonfly called me a declawed albino rat. I will show her my claws—and the inside of my stomach.

I would've been amused if he hadn't been serious. *If my familiar eats another witch's familiar, I'll be kicked out of the coven.*

A shame that would be, dove. I know you hold those sanctimonious daisies in the highest regard.

I turned onto a dirt road, the black expanse of farmland bordering both sides. *You know why I can't leave.*

Pulling over beside a barbed wire fence, I shut off the engine. Using a post for leverage, I hopped the barbed wire and landed in a field of recently cut plants. If only Farmer Whitby hadn't completed his first harvest yet, I could've ruined his year in an even bigger way.

Ríkr rode on my shoulder as I marched across the uneven ground toward the farmstead, approaching from the back. Navigating by moonlight, I jumped another fence and slipped between two outbuildings. Massive structures surrounded an expansive yard, the gravel churned by the passage of large equipment. My mouth quirked at the sight of the elegant timber farmhouse, several windows lit despite the late hour.

I circled behind the buildings to the machinery shed—though "shed" was misleading. It was more like a warehouse. Keeping to the shadows, I found the door and tried the handle. Locked.

The farmhouse lights felt hot against my back as I pulled the small case from my pocket and flipped it open. Selecting a tiny torsion wrench and a pick, I stuck them into the lock.

Behind me, the warm glow brightened. I glanced over my shoulder. Another window had turned luminescent.

"Watch the house, Ríkr," I whispered as I angled the pick and felt a pin move.

Watching, he replied swiftly.

Ten seconds. Fifteen. More pins shifted.

Door is opening!

I turned the wrench and the bolt clacked. As light flooded the yard, I pushed the shed door open, slid inside, and swung it shut. A quick twist of the bolt and the door was locked again.

The pitch-black interior stank of oil, diesel fuel, and dead plants. I stood silently, listening. Nothing.

"A little light, Ríkr?" I murmured, pocketing my pick.

The white ferret hopped onto my ball cap, and soft blue light radiated off him, illuminating the shed's interior.

My gaze skimmed across a dirt-splattered backhoe and a massive tractor before landing on the largest machine—a green monstrosity with a boxy body, a glass-enclosed cab six feet above the ground, and a wide, spiked rotary header attached to the front.

A forage harvester, relatively new and worth over half a million dollars.

Humming to myself, I strolled past the harvester to the wall where a hose was coiled. I grabbed the end and pulled it across the floor until I stood beside the harvester's front tire, as tall as me with thick treads.

Beside the tire was the fat blue cap for the fuel tank. I reached up. With a few twists, it came free.

"*One more word for signal token,*" I sang as I snaked the hose into the tank, diesel fumes wafting out. "*Whistle out the marchin' tune.*"

I returned to the spigot in the wall and twisted the tap. The hose stiffened with water pressure and an echoing splash erupted from the fuel tank.

"*With your pike upon your shoulder*"—I stepped over to the work bench and selected a hacksaw from the assorted tools— "*by the rising of the moon.*"

At the front of the harvester, a thick bundle of hydraulic lines snaked from the header to the body. As my quiet voice lilted with the Irish folk tune, I set the hacksaw against the first line.

The saw dragged across the line. Fluid spilled down, glopping onto the concrete floor. Still singing, I cut the next line, working my way through the bundle until all the lines were severed. Spotting a few smaller hoses, I cut those too.

With a noisy gurgle, the fuel tank overflowed, water-tainted diesel gushing down the side of the harvester.

"*Death to every foe and traitor! Whistle out the marching tune.*" I crossed to the spigot and turned off the water. "*And hurrah, me boys, for freedom—*"

Light flooded the building's interior.

I dropped into a crouch beside the tool bench, hacksaw in hand and Ríkr clinging to my hat, his faint glow extinguished. Male voices echoed off the walls.

"This is ridiculous, Harvey," a brusque voice complained as the door banged against the wall. "If the wretched beast ran off, just let it go."

"And have some helpful hiker spot it?" a gruff, angry voice shot back.

Two older men had entered the cavernous building, one stocky with a white beard, and the other tall and bald. As they strode across the floor, I slipped silently along the bench until I could duck behind the harvester. The water hose was still hanging from the harvester's fuel tank, but the tractor blocked the men's view.

"Bill was supposed to dump it at an auction in Alberta," the shorter man—Whitby—growled as he headed toward a metal cabinet in the corner. "Now the damn thing is loose and I have to deal with it."

"Why didn't you just sell it with the other two?"

"And let everyone see it at the auction? That persistent bitch at the rescue farm had already been hounding me for months." A keychain rattled, followed by the metallic sound of a lock. "Not my fault the beast sickened like that. Women like her should mind their own business."

I breathed silently through my nose, my grip on the hacksaw too tight. Ríkr's slight weight on my hat shifted.

"Bill texted me ten minutes ago," Whitby continued. "He spotted it north of Quarry Road. It's all wilderness up there."

A clatter reverberated through the shed. Crouching, I peered under the harvester. Whitby had opened the cabinet, revealing a small collection of long-barreled firearms. A gun locker.

Whitby handed his companion a rifle, then checked the time on his wristwatch, the gold band glinting. "It's one a.m. No one will be out. We can lead the beast into the woods, away from the trails, and get rid of it once and for all. It'll be months before anyone stumbles over the corpse."

The taller man grimaced at his weapon. "Fine."

Whitby slammed the locker shut, a second gun in his hands. Both men strode to the door, turning off the lights and locking the bolt on their way out.

"*And hurrah, me boys, for freedom,*" I crooned under my breath, completing the lyrics they'd interrupted. "*'Tis the rising of the moon.*"

Sweeping to the exit, I unbolted the lock and cracked the door open just as a vehicle rumbled to life. A truck peeled out of the yard, spitting gravel behind it. Whitby cared more about his reputation than a horse's life—and he planned to destroy the evidence of his careless neglect before it caused him any more problems.

I wouldn't let that happen.

As the truck's taillights sped away, I broke into a sprint, keeping to the shadows. North of Quarry Road, he'd said. Quarry Road was the next—and last—road to the north. Beyond it was Mount Burke, the same sprawling summit that loomed over Hearts & Hooves Rescue. Chances were the horse wasn't that far from here.

Going back for my quad would take too long, so I would have to rely on my own two legs if I wanted any chance of stopping Whitby before he found the horse. I hoped I wouldn't have to run ten miles.

Ríkr, I called silently.

He sprang off my head, his body glowing. Wings swept out as his shape changed. In the form of a white crow, he zoomed ahead, following the truck. I steadied my pace and controlled my breathing as I jogged onto the gravel drive.

By the time I reached Quarry Road, my calves were burning, but I ignored the feeling. I worked my body all day, every day. My job at the vet clinic wasn't easy, the rescue was even more demanding, and farriery was outright punishing. During my limited free time, I relaxed by hiking, mountain biking, and horseback riding.

I hated sitting still.

Breathing deep and steady, I scanned the treetops for Ríkr's distant form. He'd make sure that, should the farmers find the horse before I caught up, they wouldn't get a chance to shoot it. He might be a small, impertinent, and slightly bloodthirsty shapeshifter with little magic, but he was still a fae. And even smallfae could be dangerous.

The road grew steeper, and as trees overtook the fields, the low-hanging moon disappeared from view. Darkness closed in, the forest crowding the road, towering trees leaning over the ditches. My jog slowed, my breath loud in my ears.

I jolted to a stop.

My lungs heaved as I tried to breathe as quietly as possible. The trees rustled softly in the cool breeze. No other sound—then I heard it.

The distant clop of hooves against asphalt.

I whirled around and squinted down the dark road. Was it Whitby's escaped horse? My skin prickled. Unexpected fear skittered across my nerve endings, and my hand dove into my pocket. I pulled out my switchblade, thumb on the trigger, and shuffled sideways toward the ditch.

Clack-clack-clack. A quick trot. Growing louder. Coming closer.

I slid into the ditch and crouched in the long grass. Trepidation, unfamiliar and unwelcome, simmered in my gut. Jaw tight, I scrutinized the dark road and even darker trees. The breeze had died, and all was silent except for the clack of hooves growing ever louder.

Gooseflesh pricked my arms, and I didn't like the hysterical edge of panic creeping into my thoughts. Why was I afraid? My reaction made no sense.

The sound of hooves was clear now. I should've been able to see the horse.

Unless it wasn't a normal horse.

My eyes widened at the thought, then narrowed. I let my vision relax. The road blurred, and a ghostly white mist washed over the scene as I focused on the ethereal realm instead of the mundane world.

Within the white mist, a cloud of darkness.

Hooves struck the road like gunshots as a beastly horse trotted toward me. It was the size of a draft horse but with a lean build, its obsidian mane floating eerily as shadows eddied around it. Astride its back, a rider moved as one with its mount, black fabric draping his form.

I could almost hear Death calling my name as the rider drew nearer.

Terror ricocheted through me, and I shrank into the long grass like a hunted rodent. I was well hidden, but in another dozen yards, the rider would be close enough to spot me from his high vantage point.

The horse clopped up the road, ten yards away. My switchblade's handle dug into my palm as I squeezed it. Five yards away.

Three.

Two.

Bang!

The distant gunshot rang through the night, and the ethereal steed threw its head up, ears perked. Not fear but focus. The cloud of darkness around it writhed.

The horse launched across the road—away from me. It leaped the far ditch in an easy bound, and I flinched as it landed, expecting a cacophony of snapping branches as its massive weight met the dense underbrush.

It charged into the dark woods without a sound, vanishing from sight.

I sucked in a breath and unclenched my fingers.

Whatever the hell that horse and rider were, I never wanted to cross paths with them again.

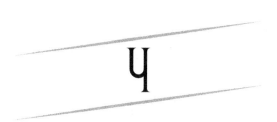

CROUCHED BENEATH the heavy, drooping branches of a fifty-foot-tall pine tree, I peered through the curtain of prickly green needles that surrounded me.

Whitby's escaped horse was dead.

It lay near a patch of lush green grass, its golden coat and cream mane contrasting starkly with the dark leaf litter. The palomino should've been beautiful, but its bones pressed against its skin, its body sunken with advanced malnutrition. It was no surprise Whitby hadn't wanted anyone to see *this* horse. Even his similarly callous peers would have called out his cruelty.

Bright white beams spun and flashed as Whitby and his companion shone their flashlights around the small forest clearing, a hundred yards north of Quarry Road. Rifles in hand, they murmured in low voices.

The razor-edged, red-tinged sharpness under my ribs ground with each slow breath I took.

I didn't know what I was feeling when these icy shards raked my insides. It was darker and deeper than anger. Something more like hunger, like thirst. A base, bestial need demanding to be purged.

My gaze tracked Whitby's steps, his boots crunching over fallen leaves as he circled the dead horse, assessing his handiwork. Would he be walking like the king of the mountain if his feet were rotting out from under him like Whicker's hooves? I'd already planned to make him feel the consequences of his neglect, and now he had killed his victim as well.

With a flick of my thumb, four inches of sharp steel shot out of my switchblade. Whitby's head spun toward the metallic *snap*, his flashlight's beam swinging past the tree where I hid. I hummed a soft note under my breath as I dug my blade into the ground, coating it in mud.

"Did you hear that?" Whitby whispered to his companion.

I clicked my tongue. Stiffening, the two men pointed their lights at my hiding spot, but the pine's branches were too dense, reflecting the beams. I clicked again, and Whitby's brow furrowed as he moved toward me, squinting suspiciously.

"It's just a squirrel," his companion muttered. "Let's get out of here, Harvey."

I rustled the leaf litter, imitating the quiet movements of an animal to lure Whitby closer. As his boots neared the curtain of pine boughs, I shifted forward on hands and knees, silent on the bedding of dried needles.

"Yeah," Whitby said hesitantly. "We should leave before—"

I lunged forward, thrusting my arm through the branches, and rammed my knife into the top of his boot.

He roared with pain and lurched backward, his flashlight falling from his hand. I dropped and rolled out from under the pine's heavy boughs. As I launched upward, a white crow dove from the highest branches of the same tree, flying at the other man's head.

Leaving Ríkr to distract Whitby's companion, I ducked beneath the farmer's rifle and slammed my shoulder into his gut. Precariously balanced on his uninjured foot, he pitched over backward, and I ripped the gun from his hands.

I planted my boot on his throat, cutting off his shout. Tossing the rifle aside, I bore down on my foot. He grabbed my sole with both hands as I sank into a crouch, applying more weight to his neck. His face purpled, eyes bulging.

I spun my knife across my fingers, the bloodied blade flashing.

"Who—" he gasped, his gaze darting from my face to the knife. His arms quivered as he lifted my foot a few inches. I leaned into his grip, my weight forcing his arms back down. The angle was wrong. He couldn't get enough leverage to lift me.

I studied his contorted face, the hungry edges inside me grinding. Coming to a decision, I slapped a hand to his lower face and used my thumb to pull his upper lip up, exposing his teeth.

Many horses' teeth required filing every couple of years, but Whinny's molars had become so overgrown that eating had become agonizing. If Whitby had bothered to provide basic care for either Whinny or Whicker, neither horse's simple, common health condition would've reached the point of constant pain, lameness, starvation, and possible death.

Tightening my grip on his face, I set the point of my knife into his gums between his incisor and first molar. He writhed frantically. I stepped harder on his throat and dug the blade in. Blood spilled over his white teeth.

"*'Tis the rising of the moon*," I sang in a whisper as Whitby's scream echoed through the dark woods.

A bestial roar boomed in answer.

Saber!

At Ríkr's warning, I sprang up. The snapping, crashing racket of something tearing through the underbrush filled the night.

Whitby rolled away from me, a hand clamped over his mouth. "You crazy bitch! What—"

With another ear-shattering roar, the bushes across the clearing flattened as something charged over them—something massive and shaggy, its muzzle ridged and fangs gleaming.

"Grizzly!" the other man shouted in panic.

Oh no, not a grizzly. The man was too human to see the blade-shaped horn protruding from the monstrous bear's forehead or the unearthly gleam of its pupilless topaz eyes.

The fae beast slowed its charge, confused by the dizzying dance of the man's flashlight. As I spun, intending to run like hell, Whitby lurched to his feet beside me, something in his hands. He swung it.

His rifle's stock slammed into the side of my head.

Pain exploded through my skull and I fell onto my hands and knees, my ball cap falling off. My long hair spilled down.

"Run, you fool!" Whitby yelled at his friend. "Don't shoot, just run!"

Footsteps crunched and bodies crashed through the bushes somewhere to my left. I raised my head, my vision blurring.

My fingers curled tightly around my switchblade, somehow still in my grasp.

A low, rumbling growl—and the fae bear charged.

Stunned by the sight of the monstrous creature coming at me, I didn't move. Paws the size of dinner plates hammered the earth, claws as long as my hands tearing through the dirt. Blazing topaz eyes filled my vision.

Ríkr dropped out of the sky, the white wings of his hawk form flashing. He struck the bear's face with his curved talons.

The bear threw its head up, almost skewering Ríkr on its horn. It skidded to a stop a few feet away from me and reared back to swat furiously at the raptor.

Saber! Ríkr growled urgently. *Get to safety!*

I staggered up, then bolted away. The ground vibrated as the bear launched after me, undeterred by Ríkr's raking talons and beating wings.

I couldn't outrun the bear. My gaze whipped across the trees and I veered toward a young Douglas Fir with evenly spaced boughs. I leaped at the narrow trunk and climbed it like a ladder, branches scraping my shoulders and the trunk shaking with my urgent movements.

As I cleared ten feet, the bear hit the tree so hard the whole thing quaked, almost throwing me off it. Clinging to the trunk, I looked down.

Long teeth bared and eyes burning with mindless rage, the fae rose onto its hind legs—and I lunged for a higher branch as its jaws snapped inches from my ankle. Roaring, the bear slammed its weight into the tree. It bent and shook. An alarming *crack* rang out.

I scrambled higher, the trunk bowing with my weight and the branches creaking in warning under my feet.

Too heavy to climb the tree, the snarling bear slammed it again. The branch under my left foot snapped and I grabbed at my remaining hand and foot holds. I couldn't climb any higher. I had no escape.

Ríkr!

No answer. I tore my gaze off the bear to look across the clearing. A white hawk was on the ground, wings splayed and feathers bent as he shook his head back and forth dazedly.

The bear threw itself into the tree again. Another loud crack vibrated the trunk, and the bear leaned against it, bending the young wood with its weight. Snaps ran through the tree. It was only a matter of seconds until the trunk broke.

No way around it, then.

I turned my switchblade in my hand, calculating the best spot to strike: the fae's glaring right eye. My left foot scraped at the trunk, searching for purchase before I attacked. The bear heaved against the tree and it bent a little more. Its jaws gaped ravenously, inviting me to leap down into its waiting mouth.

Quiet stillness stole through the clearing, as though the forest itself were waiting for my next move—then the quiet shattered.

Thundering hooves filled the clearing, and in a swirl of shadow, a horse and rider appeared out of nothingness.

5

FIVE YARDS AWAY from the bear, the dark horse reared, front hooves kicking. Amber light ignited over the rider's hand, and he cast it at the raging fae.

A lasso-like cord of light flew at the bear and looped around its muzzle. The magic cinched tight, and the horse reversed, hooves digging into the earth. The bear snarled as it was yanked off the tree, and the trunk snapped straight, the violent movement almost slingshotting me off it. I grabbed for purchase, the thin branches giving way under my hands.

Fifteen feet below, the horse and its black-clad rider surged away from the bear as it swiped at them with its long claws. The amber magic in the rider's hand lashed out, more like a whip than a lasso, and sliced across the bear's face. The huge equine danced around the attacking beast, as agile as a cutting horse.

Over the racket of their confrontation, I heard the branches I held cracking. My feet searched for another bough, but all the ones in reach had broken.

Jumping was always better than falling. I retracted my knife, quickly glanced down, then shoved hard off the tree, throwing myself away from it for a clean drop—

—right as the evading equine sidestepped into my intended landing spot.

A sharp cry escaped me as I hurtled into the rider's side. We collided, the impact of my body throwing him sideways off his mount. He slammed down on his back and I landed on top of him, my face bouncing off his chest.

I shoved up with one hand—and froze.

Beneath me was not a specter of death but a man. His hood had fallen off, revealing a handsome human face with vibrant, iridescent emerald eyes that weren't entirely human. Those eyes stared at me with surprise almost equal to my own, then flicked past my shoulder.

He grabbed my upper arms and rolled.

A hoof slammed down beside us, barely missing him. The horse reared, kicking with its front hooves as it warded off the snarling bear. Strong hands gripping my arms, the rider spun sideways again, and we rolled together until we were clear of the stomping hooves.

The moment he stopped, I broke free and launched up. He was on his feet just as fast, and amber light spun over his hand as he called on his strange magic. He surged past me without a word, arm whipping out to lash the bear's hindquarters with his spell, distracting it from his mount.

I flicked the blade out on my switchblade, then retracted it. *Ríkr?*

Here, dove.

I looked up. The white hawk was perched on a much sturdier tree than the one I'd chosen, his blue eyes fixed on the battle.

A most interesting matchup, he added, his tone almost gleeful.

I shook my head—and the clearing rocked and tilted. Pain throbbed through my skull. I stepped backward and my heel bumped something.

The palomino.

The fae bear's furious roar rolled through the night air, but the sound was distant and forgettable as I sank down beside the horse's head and touched its thin, bony neck.

I should have slit Harvey Whitby's throat. How dare he allow an animal under his care to suffer this much and for this long? How dare he kill an innocent creature to save himself? How dare he slaughter this horse to …

I frowned, my hand resting on the palomino's forehead. Where was the bullet wound? I'd heard the gunshot, but I couldn't see any blood.

Eyes up, dove.

Ríkr's warning snapped me out of my daze, and I realized the forest had gone quiet. My skull throbbed horrifically, and I wanted to puke. Instead, I raised my head.

The bear fae was gone, the underbrush flattened where it had plowed through the dense foliage to escape. The powerful stallion remained, standing near the splintered tree I'd leaped from. In the dim light, I could see he wasn't black as I'd thought but a magnificent blue roan with a steel-colored coat that darkened to black on his legs. His mane and tail were dark as ebony, as was his face—which made his acid-green eyes even more startling. Pawing the earth with a heavy hoof, the fae equine tossed his head.

I shifted my gaze to his rider.

Fifteen feet away, the man watched me, or so I assumed. He'd pulled his hood up again, deep shadows hiding his face—but I'd already seen his human features, and I wouldn't mistake him for a ghostly wraith again. Instead of a nightmarish black cloak, he wore a long jacket paired with black pants, sturdy boots, and leather gloves.

When my attention landed on him, he strode toward me, his long legs eating up the ground and coat billowing out behind him. Stopping almost on top of me, he reached down as though to take my elbow—and seized the front of my jacket.

I grabbed his wrist as he roughly hauled me onto my tiptoes, bringing my face close to his. Despite the moonlight and forgotten flashlights illuminating the clearing, the interior of his hood was filled with unnatural darkness.

Ríkr watched us from his lofty perch, pale blue eyes gleaming.

"That was quite the scene I came in on," the man rumbled in a low, dangerous tone. "What do you know about that bear fae?"

I stared into his hood.

A rough sound grated from his throat. "You don't seem to be grasping the situation. Tell me what you know before I lose patience."

I smiled, showing my teeth. "Was that a threat?"

"What do you think?"

My smile widened, and I lifted my empty hand toward his face. "It'll take more than a hood and a threat to scare me, especially when"—I pushed his hood back—"I've already seen your face."

The shadows fell away, revealing his countenance again. Inhumanly vibrant green eyes, framed by dark lashes, fixed on mine, his eyebrows lowered with menace. A beautiful face, if I were honest. Striking cheekbones, a strong jaw, full mouth—currently pressed into a thin, angry line. By my best guess, he was in his mid-twenties, maybe a bit older.

My palm brushed against his clean-shaven cheek as I let his hood fall—and with the same motion, I flicked my hand, pulling my switchblade from my jacket sleeve. The blade sprang free, and in an instant, I had the point resting against the corner of his left eye.

But not fast enough.

A cold, thin edge pressed against my left cheek. I didn't break eye contact to see what sort of weapon he had in my face, but the blade felt sharp—sharper than my little knife.

Neither of us moved, his fist tight around the front of my jacket. If either of our hands wobbled, we'd both bleed.

His right eyebrow arched slightly. "How do you want to play this?"

"Let go of me."

"I don't think so."

"I stab you, you stab me," I suggested frostily. "My cheek is more likely to heal than your eye."

"Pass."

He wouldn't let me go and he wouldn't play knife-chicken. What was left? "Then I'll answer your question if you answer one of mine."

His full mouth thinned again, green eyes raking across me. "Fine."

His agreement surprised me until I realized he expected to win this game too. He thought I'd reveal more with my answers than he would with his.

Not likely.

"Who the hell are you?" I demanded.

"Answer my question first."

"*You* first. Who are you?"

He growled under his breath. "The Crystal Druid."

Surprise flushed through me, and I couldn't stop my eyelids from flickering with a single, startled blink. He was a *druid*?

"Now," he rumbled, "tell me what you know about that bear and the other aggressive fae in this area."

"I don't know anything."

His blade pressed painfully into my cheek. "This little game doesn't work if you lie."

"I'm not lying."

"Then you're an idiot. Every fae across the lower mainland is talking about the attacks and disappearances around here."

"Fascinating, but this is the first I've heard of it."

"Aren't you a witch?"

"Yes, but a terrible one."

His striking green eyes narrowed. "Terrible in what way?"

Ignoring his question, I shifted my blade ever so slightly, ensuring he couldn't miss the sharp point in his peripheral vision. "My turn again. Why are you here?"

"The fae—"

"Yes, yes, the attacks. But why do you care about some aggressive fae?" I arched my eyebrows, though my bangs probably hid them. "What are you hoping to gain, Crystal Druid?"

"Does it matter?"

"That's a question, not an answer. You really don't want this blade in your eye. It's already been in a foot and a mouth tonight."

His features twitched with disgust. "What are *you* doing here, if you don't know anything about fae attacks?"

"I'm here because Farmer Whitby was here."

"Why was he here?"

"To kill his starved, neglected horse before it hurt his reputation."

I rather liked the way his eyes blazed at my words.

"And what were *you* doing here, then?" he asked.

I considered how to answer, then told the truth. "I was about to saw Whitby's teeth out of his jaw with this knife."

He stared at me. "How hard were you hit in the head?"

"How do you know I was hit in the head?"

"There's blood all over your face."

Oh.

He shoved me backward, the movement so sudden I didn't have a chance to stab his eye out or brace myself. I landed hard on my ass.

Pushing his coat to one side, he slid his knife into a sheath on his thigh. I watched the ten-inch blade disappear, then watched his hand move up to his belt, where half a dozen test-tube-shaped vials were held in place by leather loops.

Alchemic potions. Was he an alchemist too?

I hated alchemists.

He ran his gloved fingers across the potions, pulled one out, and tossed it to me. Catching it automatically, I glanced at the cloudy brown liquid inside.

"For your concussion," he said shortly. "Drink it immediately. Or don't. I don't care."

Turning, he strode to his fae steed. The stallion arched his neck as his rider seized a handful of dark mane and pulled himself up. He settled into place like he'd spent his life on horseback.

"Stay out of the forest," he called as he guided the horse in a tight turn. "A terrible witch like you is an easy meal for pissed-off fae."

The stallion launched forward. Shadowy mist spiraled around his powerful legs, and as he surged into a gallop across the clearing, he and his rider faded out of reality. The sound of thudding hooves disappeared.

With one hand clenched around my switchblade and the other holding the potion vial, I stared at the spot where he'd vanished.

The Crystal Druid.

Interesting. With a scurry of small claws, Ríkr hopped onto my knee. He'd traded his hawk form for a small vole, sneaking close so he could defend me in case my verbal sparring game with the druid had turned violent. *More* violent.

The fae sat back on his tiny haunches, gazing into the trees. *Most interesting, don't you think?*

I looked down at the potion vial. "Interesting" wasn't the word I would have chosen.

6

FOUR INCHES *of steel flashed as I spun my switchblade over and under my fingers in an endless loop. Rain thundered against the roof overhead, and the only other noise came from below—the rumble of adult conversation, interspersed with sloppy laughter.*

A few feet away, the boy in black sat against the wall. Instead of a knife, he held a small, leather-bound book in one hand. A grimoire, probably—his personal record of magical knowledge. He flipped the pages, his gaze drifting aimlessly across them. He was bored too.

Still, the attic was better than standing in the rain all night.

This was the second time we'd snuck into the attic instead of waiting in the alley. My heart drummed at the prospect of getting caught, but we'd have plenty of time to slip outside before dawn.

I looked at the empty space between us, large enough for another person to sit in, then stretched my legs out, slouching against the wall. The knife started spinning again.

The deepest voice downstairs boomed something, and everyone else went silent. The man continued in a menacing growl, and I strained to make out words, losing track of the precise motion of my hand.

The switchblade slipped from my fingers. Still spinning, it skidded across the floor and bumped into the boy's boot.

He glanced at it. Though he'd unzipped his jacket to reveal a simple black shirt, he'd left the hood up. Only a few locks of his dark hair were visible where they tumbled across his forehead. Tucking his grimoire into an inner pocket of his coat, he picked up my knife and examined the glossy red handle, then the short blade. I fidgeted as I watched him, tugging on my chiffon blouse then adjusting my sleek, sunflower-blond ponytail.

He pressed the switch. The blade retracted with a click. A touch of his thumb and it popped back out.

"Don't cut yourself," I taunted. "Knives aren't toys."

Smirking, he flicked the blade into the air. It whirled end over end, then plunged back down. He caught it by the point. His gaze angled toward me, assessing my reaction.

I pressed my palms to the floor, feigning nonchalance. "Yeah, yeah."

He tossed the blade again and caught it by the handle—then his arm flashed out. The point thunked into the wooden floor between two of my fingers, the edge a quarter inch from my skin.

My lungs heaved with a silent gasp, but I didn't let myself recoil. "Mildly impressive," I drawled.

He arched an eyebrow and released the knife, leaving it stuck in the floor. I snatched it and pointed it at his hand. His eyebrows rose higher.

"Only fair," I told him. "Or are you afraid?"

In answer, he placed his left hand on the floor, fingers spread. I turned the knife over, locking my gaze on the spot between his middle and ring fingers. Nerves twanged in my gut, but I wouldn't be outdone with my own blade.

I bit my lower lip, then snapped the knife down. It hit the floorboards with a dull thud—and the boy lurched back. As he raised his arm, a line of blood ran down his hand.

"Oh shit!" I gasped, retracting the blade. "I cut you!"

He gazed bemusedly at his hand as blood pooled in his palm. Swearing under my breath, I reached for him.

"It's fine," he muttered, dodging my reach. "I don't need—"

I grabbed his wrist. "Let me see how bad it is."

He pulled away. I pulled back. He wrenched his arm, almost yanking me onto his lap.

"Just let me see!" I hissed, digging my fingers into his wrist. Pressed against his side, I yanked his hand toward me and peered down. The slice between his fingers was bleeding freely and I couldn't tell how deep it was. It probably hurt like hell.

"Shit," I mumbled guiltily. "I'm an idiot."

"Yeah, you are."

"Shut up." I glared into the shadows beneath his hood. Abruptly furious, I shoved his hood off. Dim light fell across his face, illuminating his fair skin—and the fresh bruise darkening his cheekbone.

I sat back. He slanted a scowl at me, then leaned against the wall, still holding his bleeding hand up. I pulled out my switchblade again, untucked the hem of my shirt, and cut a strip off the bottom. He said nothing as I wrapped the silky fabric around his hand to form a makeshift bandage, nor when I pulled a small, shallow jar from my back pocket. I unscrewed the lid and scooped white cream onto my fingers.

"What's that?" he asked suspiciously.

I knelt in front of him. "My aunt is an alchemist. She made it. It fades bruises in a couple of hours."

He didn't ask why I carried it around with me. The answer was as obvious as the purple mark on his face.

"Hold still," I warned as I reached for him.

He winced slightly when the cool cream touched his cheek. I spread it carefully across the bruise, massaging it into his skin.

His fingers brushed my wrist, stopping my movement. I met his eyes, surprised by how close our faces were.

"Is your aunt the one you want to kill?" The question was soft, inflectionless.

I searched his unreadable stare. "Yes."

"Is she a buyer or a seller?"

With a glance at the unseen room below, I answered, "Seller."

As if in reply, a deep male voice boomed with cold laughter. The boy didn't flinch, but his pupils dilated with adrenaline.

"Is he the one you want to kill?" I asked.

His chin dipped in a slight nod.

I recalled how that rough voice could silence all the others downstairs. "He sounds dangerous."

The boy's lips pressed into a thin line. His pupils dilated even more. "He is."

"Do you think you can kill him?"

"Not yet." The same words as our first brief conversation. "I'm not strong enough yet."

My fingers slid down and pressed against his jaw in silent sympathy.

"Well, Ruth?"

The growling voice rumbled directly beneath me and I started, falling into the boy. His hands clamped my upper arms, and we froze like that.

"*Keep your voice down, Bane,*" my aunt replied sharply. "*We don't want to broadcast this negotiation.*"

"*It isn't a negotiation,*" the man retorted, an Eastern European accent thickening his words. "*I've already made my offer.*"

"*And I'm not selling to the first buyer to come knocking,*" Ruth snapped. "*Why do you want her?*"

"*My business,*" he leered. "*Either refuse or counter.*"

A short pause.

"*You won't refuse.*" His growling voice went quiet, sinister. "*Keeping the girl will only bring more trouble for you. Get rid of her now. My offer is generous for a magic-stunted runt.*"

The silence stretched again before Ruth replied coolly, "*I'll consider your offer.*"

Bane barked a laugh, and footsteps thumped away. The muffled rumble of conversation swelled as he rejoined the main group.

My fingers trembled as I squeezed fistfuls of the boy's shirt. He hadn't shown pain when I'd cut his hand. He hadn't shown fear when he'd spoken of Bane. But now …

Now he stared at me with such untempered horror that I knew split lips and broken bones had become the least of my worries.

7

I **WAS** going to be late.

Sleeping in wasn't a habit of mine, but getting home last night had been rough. It would've been worse without the druid's concussion treatment, which had begun working within minutes of downing it. By the time I'd returned to the Whitby farm, I'd been walking steadily and thinking clearly again.

Had drinking the druid's potion been stupid? Yes. But if he'd wanted to hurt me, he could've stabbed me and saved his potion. So I'd taken my chances.

It'd been nearly dawn by the time I'd fallen into bed, but despite my desperate need for rest, restless dreams had disturbed my sleep. I'd woken in a cold sweat, unable to remember anything more than a vague feeling of impending doom.

Pushing the lingering feeling away, I focused on driving. I was back on Quarry Road, which divided the land between private properties to the south and wild mountain wilderness to the north. If I continued east, the terrain would descend to the marshes of Minnekhada Regional Park, but Quarry Road curved gently north, carrying me toward the forested slopes of Mount Burke.

Humming under my breath, I steered my truck along the rough asphalt. The police hadn't shown up this morning to arrest me, so I assumed Harvey Whitby didn't know who'd sabotaged his harvester last night. And should he ever suspect me, I was ready. It was remarkable what death threats, blackmail, and a little creative stalking could make people do.

I hoped the stab wound in his foot would develop an infection. That's why I'd smeared my knife with mud first.

Lounging on my passenger seat in the form of a white cat,Ríkr yawned, showing off his teeth. *You're in a fine mood this afternoon, dove.*

"I was thinking about how long I should wait before tormenting Harvey Whitby some more. I didn't do much damage to him last night."

He will not forget you while limping like a lame heifer. It's a shame you did not remove any of his teeth.

"Maybe I can fix that next time."

Ríkr swished his tail in a pleased way. *I adore your viciousness. It reminds me of my impassioned youth.*

"I'm delighted."

Vengeance is the sweetest wine, he went on in a wistful tone. *Are you sure you wouldn't enjoy a charming blood ritual with the farmer's corpse bent backward over your altar?*

"I don't have an altar."

His ears perked up. *We can remedy that easily.*

Ahead, a gravel driveway diverged from the road. I slowed my truck and turned onto the drive. "Try to tone it down, Ríkr. It's awkward when the other familiars hide from you."

He gave me a cat's smile. *If only you would teach the other witches to fear you the same, dove.*

That was the opposite of what I wanted. My whole strategy for my life—my adult life, at least—hinged on making people *like* me, not fear me. The exceptions being human trash like Farmer Whitby, but he didn't know me and never would.

A tall hedge hid the property at the end of the driveway. I steered between the open gates and up to a West-Coast-style cabin with exposed wood beams and grand windows. Though not overly large, it was luxurious and nestled among the surrounding woods like it belonged there.

Half a dozen vehicles were parked in front, and I maneuvered my truck into the line and cut the engine. Climbing out, I inhaled the rich aroma of fir, cedar, pine, and fresh green flora. Ríkr hopped to the ground beside me, back arching in a stretch.

I do not sense the others, he remarked lazily.

They never waited for me. I'd no-showed too many times for them to bother. "Let's go."

We circled the house, crossed the grassy backyard, and started along the dirt path that wound up the mountain slope. The early afternoon sun peeked through the branches, casting dappled light across the path.

Ríkr trotted ahead of me, the shadows casting a bluish tinge over his white fur. He would've preferred to fly, but he always used the same feline form around my coven. I suspected he was waiting for the optimal moment to shock them with his shapeshifting ability. A seven-years-in-the-making surprise. It was so Ríkr.

My thoughts wandered to the surprises of last night. The dark rider and his blue-roan fae stallion. My upper lip curled in distaste. "Ríkr, do you know anything about that druid?"

Of course, dove. He is the Crystal Druid, after all.

"*The* Crystal Druid?"

The one and only. Ríkr hopped onto a fallen log and walked along it. *Most kin in these parts know his name. He is feared by some, coveted by others, and respected by all for his cool head, knowledge of our ways, and uncompromising retribution against any who cross him.*

"Are you a fan of his?" I asked, vaguely irritated. "You aren't usually this complimentary."

Ríkr's tail flicked with amusement. *I merely repeat the accounts of others. For instance, he is rumored to treat well with the Gardall'kin fae—a formidable medley of warriors and beasts who came to this land from across the sea many centuries ago. They won their place among the existing courts through bloodshed and cruel bargains.*

"They sound unpleasant."

Powerful, he corrected. *Which is always unpleasant for the weak. I know of no Gardall'kin here. Their territories lie to the north.*

"Good to know."

If the Crystal Druid lingers nearby, our vigilance should be upon his guardian.

"You mean the stallion?"

No, another.

He said no more as we stepped into an open glade, the warm sun washing over my face.

My coven stood in a loose ring around a clear patch of dirt, upon which they'd drawn circles, markings, and runes. The markings were interspersed with simple pottery dishes filled with dried herbs, fresh leaves and flowers, handfuls of dirt, murky water from the marsh, and bits of fur and feathers shed by the forest's inhabitants. Holding hands, the eight witches sang in Old Gaelic, their voices rising and falling.

I shifted back into the shadows. They were too far along for me to join them. All I could do now was wait.

Lowering my eyelids, I let my vision slide out of focus. A pale mist coalesced around me as the fae demesne, the ethereal spirit world from which fae originated, appeared before my eyes. The trees turned dark and semi-transparent. The ground was solid black, opaque with permanence.

In their circle, the witches were shadowy forms amidst the fog. As they sang, the eddying mist shifted, slowly aligning with the broad curves and gentle loops of the patterns they had drawn on the ground. The fog-like energies of the spirit domain gradually flowed into the same pattern, then spread across the glade and into the trees.

A gentle calm settled over the woods, and the tension slid from my shoulders.

The patterns resembled nothing recognizable. The flow I could see and sense was nonsensical to my conscious mind, but it *felt* right. And I wasn't the only one who felt it.

At the edge of the trees, fae lingered, their dark faces marked by crystal eyes. A short satyr with a goat's lower body and a boy's torso, his head topped with short, prong-like antlers. Something that resembled a large squirrel wearing a woven smock and a tiny crown of flowers. A trio of bucks with silver antlers. A lone wolf with shaggy black fur and scarlet eyes.

I frowned. So few? Normally two or three times that many fae appeared for a large balancing ritual like this one.

The coven's song rose, then trailed off with a final low note. As the eddies of silver mist settled, the gathered fae retreated into the trees.

I blinked away my spirit-vision and focused on the four fae that remained—the other familiars. My coven was made up of nine members, including me, but not all witches had familiars.

Short, plump witch Deanne and her tiny pixie with its transparent dragonfly wings.

Elderly grandmother Ellen and her hob, a smallfae that resembled a garden gnome with very sharp teeth.

Tall, tattooed Pierce and his snake-like familiar, currently looped around his broad shoulders.

And lastly, haughty beauty Laney and her equally haughty fire salamander, the bright orange lizard resting on her crooked arm as she turned away from the nature circle.

Her cool brown eyes settled on me. "Saber, how lovely of you to join us."

I walked out of the shadows. Pierce and Ellen smiled at me. The rest did not.

I'd joined the coven shortly after my eighteenth birthday, and I'd been a member through that shaky first year when I hadn't known what I was doing with my life, then through two years of school to become a vet tech, and on into my career at the clinic. Not to suggest my membership had been a source of support or comfort. I couldn't care less about coven activities, and since I'd never bothered to hide that sentiment, my fellow witches were, at best, ambivalent toward me.

With the exception of Laney, who outright hated me.

"I know there's little you can contribute to these rituals," she continued in a falsely sympathetic tone. "But you need to attend every full moon ritual, or else—"

"I overslept," I interrupted tonelessly.

Her eyes flashed but she held a concerned smile. "Are you feeling well?"

I didn't bother answering. "Arla, can I have a word?"

The coven's matriarch, halfway through collecting bowls of herbs from the circle, looked up in mild surprise. Tucking her short gray hair behind her ear, she rose to her feet. "Of course."

The others eyed us—and Laney outright glared—as the older woman and I moved to the far edge of the glade.

"Are you feeling all right, dear?"

I studied her. Arla Collins. In her early fifties, she was a once-fit woman who'd softened in her later years. Large glasses, chin-length hair, no makeup. She managed her oddly mixed coven with kind words, firm patience, and zero tolerance for bullshit.

She was the complete opposite of her vain, spiteful daughter, Laney. It surprised me that Arla could be such a positive influence on others but completely fail to raise a respectable daughter. But then, I knew very well how nature trumped nurture.

"A fae that resembled a brown bear attacked me last night," I said without preamble.

Her face went slack. "A bear?"

I nodded. "North of Quarry Road, less than two kilometers west of here."

Her mouth bobbed open, then closed with a snap. "Last night? What time?"

"Late." If I told her two or three in the morning, she'd want to know why I'd been wandering the woods in the dead of night—though my evasion wouldn't fool her.

"And it attacked you? Did you provoke it? Are you injured? What about the bear?"

"I didn't provoke it, and I'm fine. The bear was …" I hadn't seen what the druid had done to drive it away, but his whip spell hadn't inflicted much damage. "I think the bear was fine."

"Did you see anything else?"

"Like another fae?"

"Fae … people … anything unusual that might explain the fae's attack."

Did she suspect I might have encountered a druid who had no business being in our coven's territory?

"Have you heard about other fae attacks recently?" I asked.

"No." She stared distractedly toward the mountain's summit. "Hikers found a dead grizzly on Munroe Lake Trail this morning. I got a heads up from Bradley in Parks Management to check it out. The bear was a fae."

A faint chill washed over me. Had the druid gravely wounded the bear after all, or had he hunted it down after leaving me?

"I didn't hurt it," I said sharply. "How did it die?"

"I don't know."

"But you said you checked it—"

"Why are you asking about fae attacks?" she interrupted. "Have other fae attacked you?"

"No. A druid told me there've been incidents of fae aggression around here."

Arla jumped as though the word "druid" had been an electrical shock. "A druid? *Here?*"

"He's investigating the attacks, or so he claimed. He calls himself the Crystal Druid."

She stepped back, her eyes widening. "The Ghost ... is here?"

"The who?"

Her shock softened into an amused, slightly exasperated smile. "Really, Saber, you should socialize with us more. The Ghost is only the scandal of the year. We were all talking about him nonstop a few months ago."

My brow furrowed. "I never said anything about a ghost."

"Look him up and you'll understand." She brushed dirt off her pants. "I've warned you about missing coven events. Full participation is a condition of your rehabilitation."

With that one word, cold fury slashed me.

"As your rehabilitation supervisor, I have a duty to report—"

"My *parole* supervisor, Arla," I snarled softly. "Don't use their bullshit PR language."

"You're not being punished, Saber. I and the rest of the coven are helping you learn how to be a member of the community."

I tightened my jaw so I wouldn't reply.

Her expression gentled. "If you perform your own ritual, I'll count your effort as full attendance. Go on, now, before the others finish packing up."

Spinning on my heel, I marched away from her. The rest of the coven was dismantling the ritual circle and gathering their supplies, and I didn't look at any of them as I crouched and grabbed a handful of dried plant bits.

A furry tail brushed against my arm. Ríkr slunk into my shadow, his pupilless blue eyes on Arla. *A deliberate antagonization, dove. She used language you revile to distract you.*

I glanced over my shoulder, tracking Arla as she strolled toward the path back to her house, Ellen chatting animatedly with her. Ríkr was right. She'd diverted my attention to end the conversation.

She knows something, I told him silently. *Is it something about the druid? Or about fae—*

A shadow fell over me, interrupting my silent conversation with Ríkr. "You missed again."

I looked up at Laney, then rose to my full height so I could properly sneer down at the shorter witch. She smiled at me for the benefit of anyone watching.

"Mother promised to pardon your negligence again, didn't she?" Laney raised her chin as though that would bring her closer to my height. "Well, I won't. I'll make sure they know you violated your conditions again, and this time they'll drag you back to—"

"Laney."

She broke off, her shoulders stiffening.

I curved my lips up, but it wasn't a smile. Not even close. "If you, your mother, or anyone else sabotages me, I'll make you pay."

Simple words, but her face went white.

Hands full of leaves, I walked away. Ríkr trotted beside me, his tail flicking smugly.

You elected to follow my advice, he observed. *She appeared most frightened. Well done, dove.*

I bit the inside of my cheek, unsure if that had been the right move.

Have you other topics of concern upon which I might apportion my wisdom? he inquired. *I am eager to advise you. Have you reconsidered a blood altar?*

Rolling my eyes, I chose a spot at the farthest end of the glade where the movements and voices of the others were easy to ignore. Ríkr sat beside me as I scraped dead leaves off a small patch of dirt, then cataloged the dried sprigs I'd grabbed.

Witches used their spiritual energy to cleanse, balance, revitalize, or manipulate the inherent energies of earth and nature. When I observed other witches performing those rituals, I felt the rightness in them, but when it came to creating them myself, I lacked any instinct whatsoever.

I used a twig to scratch out a basic purification circle. Squinting at it, I tried to imagine how it should be adapted to fit the unique flow of energy around me … but I had no idea. With a mental shrug, I sprinkled herbs on it and closed my eyes. Singing wasn't strictly necessary, but it helped direct my power—the little I possessed. What should I sing?

In the tree above me, an unknown bird let out a series of delicate trills, as though encouraging me to join it. I smiled faintly.

"*Oh swan of slenderness, dove of tenderness, jewel of joys, arise,*" I sang. "*The little red lark, like a soaring spark, of song to his sunburst flies.*"

A soft memory, tinged with sorrow, slid through me. My small hands, engulfed in large, warm fingers. A tall figure on either side of me, our arms swinging. My parents' voices joined my high child's voice as we sang together.

"*But till thou'rt risen, earth is a prison, full of my lonesome sighs; then awake and discover, to thy fond lover, the morn of thy matchless eyes.*"

Long meadow grass swept across our legs as we walked, singing and laughing. My father was tall with medium-brown hair and a reddish beard. My mother was willowy and dark-haired. I'd inherited her coloring and his height.

"*The dawn is dark to me. Hark! O hark to me, pulse of my heart, I pray.*"

A stream paralleled our path, and standing in the knee-deep water was a petite woman with bluish-green skin, dramatically pointed ears, and crystalline eyes. The water nymph's smile enchanted us as she sang too, her voice more beautiful than any human's.

"*And out of thy hiding, with blushes gliding, dazzle me with thy day.*"

She reached toward me, still singing, and touched my chest where a river-stone pendant lay. A shimmer of her blue magic washed over it.

"*Ah, then, once more to thee, flying I'll pour to thee, passion so sweet and gay. The lark shall listen, and dewdrops glisten ...*"

Her cool fingers tousled my hair, then together, the four of us continued across the meadow toward a rustic cabin in the shadow of a towering mountain.

"*... laughing on ev'ry spray.*"

The final note throbbed in my throat, and I cracked my eyes open, unsurprised to find them damp with unshed tears. Though they'd died many years ago, memories of peaceful, laughter-filled days with my parents always struck me hard. I wondered if I could ever be happy like that again, or if carefree joy was no more than a child's innocent illusion.

In the wake of my ritual attempt, Ríkr's sharp eyes had softened with lazy contentment. He sat beside me with his tail curled around his paws—but he wasn't my only spectator.

On my other side, Pierce sat cross-legged in the grass, his serpentine familiar coiled over his shoulders. With his thickly muscled build, bushy beard, and weather-worn face, he was the last person anyone would expect to be a nature-loving witch. But a closer look at his tattooed arms showed depictions of mythical fae intertwined with blooming vines.

"Gleer loves your singing, as usual," he said in his gruff voice. "But you still can't do a proper ritual for the life of you."

Herbs scattered across my sad little circle as the breeze washed through the glade. I sighed.

"You can do what you want, Saber," he added, a deeper growl coming into his voice, "but missing rituals is a risk. Arla will only overlook your absence so many times. Don't blow it."

I said nothing.

"How long do you have left?" he asked.

"Two years."

"That's forty-eight more rituals. Just stick with it, girl. You don't want MagiPol knocking on your door when you're this close."

A slight shiver ran over me. Witches weren't the only magic-users among the human race, and we were all ruled by the MPD, an organization as secret as it was powerful. "MagiPol" not only controlled magic-users—or *mythics*, as we called ourselves—and ensured magic remained hidden, but they were also judge, jury, and enforcer of their own laws. When a mythic committed a crime, the MPD and their agents dispensed "justice."

Pierce had ended up in this coven for the same reason as me—assigned to Arla for his "rehabilitation"—but he'd completed his sentence several years ago and decided to remain instead of starting over yet again. He was the only person here with the slightest idea of what it was like to live under the MPD's absolute power.

"The day I'm done," I murmured, "I'm going to break Laney's nose."

A guffaw burst from him, and he quickly choked it back. "She'll be lucky if that's all you do, but I wouldn't recommend it. MagiPol won't forget you exist."

MagiPol wouldn't forget. They probably remembered better than I did.

I knew what I'd done. I remembered that much. But my memories of that day, and the weeks leading up to it, were fragmented and missing crucial details that I should have been able to recall easily, even after ten years.

"Dissociative amnesia," it was called. A condition where the subconscious mind represses traumatic memories out of self-preservation. At least, that was what the psychiatrist had described when asked to explain why I couldn't testify during my own sentencing. I might remember everything someday, he'd claimed, if I healed enough or if the right trigger brought the memories back.

All things considered, I was fine with the gaps in my recollection.

My thoughts drifted back to my conversation with Arla. I couldn't push her for answers about the bear fae or the druid, not without risking my freedom and future, but like the MPD, I wouldn't forget. I hadn't come here of my own free will, but this place had been my home for seven years now.

And I wasn't about to ignore the inexplicable new danger in my backyard.

8

I PARKED BESIDE a beat-up bronze sedan that belonged to one of Hearts & Hooves' regular volunteers. Dominique and Greta's Ranger was gone; they were running errands this afternoon.

The breeze teased my loose hair through my truck's open windows as I leaned back in the driver's seat, my phone in my hand. On it was the MPD Archives, a website where any mythic with a login could browse information about other mythics, guilds, and bounties set on the heads of the magic community's criminals.

Filling my screen was a bounty listing.

"'Zakariya Andrii,'" I read quietly. "'Also known as the Ghost and the Crystal Druid. Charged with three hundred and forty-five felonies under MPD law. A "dead or alive" bounty of one point three million dollars will be awarded upon his capture or death, pending confirmation of identity.'"

The bounty for killing a demon, the deadliest magical creature out there, was less than half that. I skimmed the list of charges against him. Illegal magic, illegal trading, theft, extortion, blackmail, assault …

Kidnapping.

Murder.

This guy was a dedicated career criminal with a mile-long rap sheet. The bounty information flashed past as I scrolled down to the notes section, used by bounty hunters to share information. A quick scan of the comments revealed that "the Ghost's" real name and his second alias of the Crystal Druid had only been discovered recently.

The commentary also suggested he was the most notorious rogue in Vancouver.

"Why?" I muttered. "If he's an infamous fugitive, why tell me who he is?"

Because you are a witch with a familiar, Rίkr answered, sprawled on the passenger seat beside me. *No fae would mistake him for anything but a druid, and pretending to be any other druid would be a fool's move.*

"Because he's *the one and only* Crystal Druid?" I muttered mockingly, using Rίkr's wording from earlier.

Despite my tone, I could see his point; druids were extremely rare, known for being magnitudes more powerful than their weaker magical cousins: witches like me. They were also known for their extreme power carrying them straight to an early grave.

His energy was exquisitely, savagely delectable, my familiar added. *How does he not have an assembly of drooling fae trailing his every step?*

"Were *you* drooling?" I asked as I scrolled back to the top of the webpage.

I would never drool. Sitting up, he arched his feline back in a stretch. *An august entity such as myself salivates. They are quite different things.*

Snorting, I reread the bounty summary, fitting his name to that enigmatic face and those inhuman green eyes. "Zakariya Andrii …"

Ríkr flicked his tail. *An unusual name, is it not?*

I opened a web search. After a minute of tapping, I shook my head bemusedly. "'Zakariya' is an Arabic form of Zachariah. 'Andrii' is … a Ukrainian given name? I don't think it's normally a surname. Maybe he adopted it."

Remembering his fair skin, I assumed Ukrainian was more likely than Arabic. Pulling up more variants of Zachariah, I spotted a close Russian/Ukrainian spelling—Zakhariya.

I abruptly exited the search. Why was I researching his name? Why was I giving him any thought at all? I wasn't going anywhere near him again, even if that meant leaving the bear fae's death and Arla's secrets alone for now. Where rogues went, bounty hunters and MPD agents followed, and drawing the attention of either was the last thing I needed.

It was better that I hunker down, stick to my usual routine, and wait for "the Ghost" to get lost. Whatever strange fae behavior he might be tracking, he wouldn't risk staying in one area too long. I'd have to refrain from any nighttime wandering—or lawbreaking—but I could resist for a little while. Probably.

"Ríkr," I muttered as I stuck my phone in my back pocket. "Don't let me do anything stupid until that druid is gone, okay?"

He flicked his tail. *That may be difficult, dove.*

I frowned at him as he gave me a catty smile and leaped out the open passenger window.

"Saber!"

I started, whipping toward my window. Colby, our volunteer, stood beside it, and I swallowed a breathy gasp. Why did people keep sneaking up on me?

He grinned. "Thought I heard your truck! You have a customer."

I stared at him without expression. His good cheer faltered.

"The rescue doesn't have customers," I told him flatly. We had donors and volunteers, not *customers.*

"Well, yeah." He rubbed his hand over his shaggy blond hair. "I said you were an apprentice farrier only, but it's a simple job. You can do it. They're waiting in the stable."

Waiting? I looked around the yard. There were no vehicles other than mine and Colby's, and besides that, the city boy didn't know enough about horses or farriery to determine if anything was a "simple" job or not. His main duty around the rescue was cleaning.

He watched me with growing discomfort, and I belatedly remembered he was used to "nice" Saber.

I opened my door with a bright smile. "Let's go see this customer, then."

Relaxing, he fell into step beside me. "You're not mad, are you? I didn't think it'd be a problem, especially since … well, he basically walked his horse into the yard. No idea how he got here and there are no other farriers in riding distance …"

He'd *walked* his horse here? Several farms had horses in this area, but a farmer wouldn't show up out of the blue. "What sort of horse is it?"

His face lit up as we stepped into the cool shade of the stable. "Saber, it's the most gorgeous horse I've ever laid eyes on. Wait 'til you see it."

Suspicion chilled my innards. *Ríkr?*

A quiet snicker answered me. *Have fun, dove.*

That little weasel.

My eyes adjusted to the dim interior, and I gritted my teeth at the majestic blue roan stallion standing in front of the tack stalls.

His ears perked toward me. Nostrils flared. Neck arched with tension. Tail up. If he were a mortal horse, I'd have checked my approach and watched for the first sign of outright aggression—but unlike a mortal horse, a fae wouldn't give me clear warning signs before attacking.

Unconcerned about his mount's behavior, the stallion's escort stood in front of Whicker's stall. The big gray had his head through the door's V-shaped opening, and he was bumping his nose against the man's chest and lipping at his shirt in search of treats while the man rubbed his forehead.

The gentle, confident way the druid touched the horse made me want to carve the bones out of his hands, one by one.

At the sound of our footsteps, he shifted away from the stall and turned. Last night, he'd radiated danger in his black leather and shadowed hood. Today, likely in an attempt to blend in, he'd shed the jacket and belt of alchemy potions, leaving him in a long-sleeved shirt and worn black jeans. His dark hair was tousled, locks falling across his forehead as he observed my approach.

His stallion was an extraordinarily beautiful equine, and I reluctantly admitted that horse and rider were a matched pair for stunning looks.

As I drew closer, the druid's eyes widened. They raked across my face, then flashed down to my boots. His gaze came back up more slowly, following my snug jeans with threadbare knees up to my baggy gray t-shirt.

I added his eyes to the list of body parts I wanted to gouge out of him.

When I halted ten feet away from him, his gaze finally returned to my face. We stared at each other, tension crackling in the air. Colby looked between us, vaguely bewildered.

"Good afternoon!" I chirped, beaming in welcome as I folded my hands in front of me. "And welcome to Hearts & Hooves Animal Rescue. How can I help you?"

The druid blinked, then squinted at me as though wondering if I was the same woman who'd threatened him with a knife last night. "Are you a farrier?"

"An apprentice farrier, yes," I said brightly. "Is your horse in need of attention? We normally provide farrier services only to the animals in our care."

"Can you make an exception? It shouldn't take long."

Very aware that Colby was observing our every word and facial expression, I kept my cheery smile in place. "In that case, I'd be happy to help. Can you please tie your horse in the tack stall?"

"I don't have a halter."

Was the druid a free-riding purist, or did his fae mount not like bits and saddles?

"You can borrow one," Colby said helpfully. "I'll grab it, one sec."

He darted into the tack room. I continued to smile, hands clasped together. The druid gazed at me silently.

Colby reappeared, a halter in his hands. He tossed it to the druid. "That one should be big enough."

The druid caught it with a frown, then turned to the stallion. The fae pinned his ears. The druid slowly approached, and the fae stamped a hoof, then lowered his head. The druid slid the halter on, backed the horse into the stall, and clipped a line to either side of the halter. The stallion tossed his head, the ropes snapping taut.

"Just deal with it," the druid muttered.

My smile widened. I turned to Colby. "Could you please bring Houdini in from the pasture and put him in the small pen? I need to look at him later."

Colby pulled his mesmerized stare off the stallion. "Sure, no problem. I'll be right back."

As he trotted away, I said to the druid, "Let me get my tools."

He nodded, wariness lingering in his eyes.

With a glance to ensure Colby was on his way, I slipped into the tack room. He wouldn't "be right back." It'd take him ten minutes to walk all the way out to the far pasture where I'd seen Houdini on my drive in. And there was Houdini himself: a hundred-pound goat whose favorite game was making humans chase him. Colby would spend the next hour jogging around the pasture while Houdini stayed just out of reach.

I surveyed the tack room. Horizontal posts stuck out from one wall, saddles stacked on them. Halters, bridles, and lead lines hung from hooks. On the other wall was a table piled with random equipment. Beneath it, the toolbox and my farrier kit.

Ensuring the druid was out of sight, I heaved the toolbox out and set it on one side of the threshold. I grabbed a wrench, picked up the pitchfork Colby had left behind, and tucked myself into the corner beside the door, opposite the toolbox.

Bounties and money didn't interest me. But abusers, kidnappers, and murderers did, especially when they were invading my territory. I didn't know whether the druid was here because of our encounter last night or for some other reason, but I didn't care either way. His presence on the farm was far too dangerous in far too many ways, and I wanted him gone.

Or dead. Dead worked too.

I held out the wrench, then let it go. It hit the floor with a loud clang.

Gasping as though startled, I called, "Can I get a hand in here?"

Silence. I waited.

A moment later, the druid appeared in the doorway, cautiously scanning the tack room as he stepped across the threshold.

I lunged for him, pitchfork extended.

He whirled toward me, hands coming up as he instinctively stepped backward—into the toolbox.

He tripped, and as he slammed down on his back, I thrust the pitchfork at his chest. He caught the prongs, the long sleeves of his shirt pulling taut as thick muscles in his arms bulged. He shoved upward, pushing me off. I lunged in again, throwing my whole weight behind the handle.

He caught the prongs again, halting them an inch from his chest.

"*Fuck*," he snarled as he shoved the pitchfork back a second time, twisting the prongs sideways. It tore out of my hands—

and he kicked my shin hard enough to throw me off balance. A second kick caught my other ankle and I pitched over.

I crashed to the floor and he jumped on me with a martial artist's reflexes. I went wild, teeth bared as I attacked with fists and knees. We rolled across the floor and my back slammed down again. Hands caught my wrists, squeezing hard.

With a grunt of effort, he shoved my arms above my head and sat on my diaphragm. The air whooshed out of my lungs.

"Fuck," he said again, panting. "You're strong."

He didn't say "for a woman" but I heard it anyway. "Rot in hell, you bastard."

"Didn't I save your life last night? Nice way to thank me."

"Am I supposed to thank you for stalking me?" I gasped. "What the fuck do you want?"

He glowered at me with eyes that looked more human than they had last night—a striking green with a distinct limbal ring, but not iridescent. "I didn't know you worked here. If I had, I wouldn't have come."

I sneered. "Like I believe that, *Ghost*."

He chuffed in disgust—then froze when a long white snake dropped off the table and landed on his back. The serpent reared up, cobra hood flaring.

Hello, druid, Ríkr crooned, his serpentine tongue tasting the air. *You smell delicious.*

The druid pressed my wrists harder into the floor, half an eye on the snake on his shoulder. "You sure you want to play this game? You'll lose."

Ríkr brought his face closer to the druid's, displaying his fangs.

"Your familiar is tied up," I taunted, trying to hide how breathless I was.

"Tilliag isn't my familiar."

I faltered—and an unearthly chill ran through my bones.

Darkness spilled out from the ceiling overhead, and a shape dropped through the solid wood like a phantom. Shadowy wings spread wide as a massive black eagle dove down. Ríkr bailed off the druid's shoulder as the eagle landed on his back, its wingtips brushing the walls. The raptor fixed its luminescent emerald eyes on me.

Dark, electric power rolled off the fae.

Ríkr coiled beside my head, hissing softly with his hood flared. The druid and I glared at each other, our familiars poised to attack. Since Ríkr wasn't actually a cobra and had no venom, we were doomed to lose, but the druid might not realize that.

"Look," he said, his voice husky with impatient anger. "I don't give a damn about you or your familiar or your job. I came here for Tilliag and that's it."

My eyes narrowed.

"I could tie you up and take care of him myself, but I'm not a farrier. If you have the skill, I'd rather you do it."

My eyes narrowed further. He studied my expression, then growled a curse and looked around for easy-to-reach rope—of which there was a lot, since we were in a tack room.

"I'll do it."

He shot me a disbelieving look.

"Just—" I gasped. "Just get off me before I pass out."

He rose a couple inches off my middle. My lungs expanded and I gulped down air, blinking the stars from my vision.

"Take care of Tilliag's hoof," he said, "and you'll never see me again."

That seemed like the best deal I would get. "Fine."

He pushed up from the floor. As he rose, the black eagle perched on his shoulders flared its wings. Its form softened— and it melted into his back, vanishing entirely. His green eyes brightened into an unnaturally iridescent shade of emerald.

Still on my back on the floor, I stared up at him, scarcely able to believe what I'd seen. His familiar had possessed him.

Possessed him.

That eagle fae was inside his body and mind, its presence and power infecting him. Ríkr had been my daily companion for seven years and I would *never* allow him to do that.

No wonder druids usually died young.

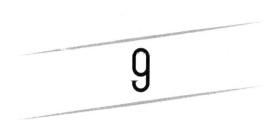

9

"SO," I BEGAN, my voice flat with hostility, "what's wrong with your fae horse?"

With creepily vibrant eyes, the druid watched me tie my leather apron. I was too stunned by his demonstration of fae possession to react properly. Even Ríkr made no comment, his serpentine form curled around my shoulders.

"Tilliag chipped his hoof," he answered. "The broken edge is catching on rough terrain."

Depending on the chip, it might only need to be filed smooth. If it was bad, more drastic measures would be required. I picked up my farrier kit and stepped toward the door, then glanced back.

"Anything I should know about working on a fae's hooves?"

A corner of his mouth lifted. "Don't piss him off."

Helpful.

I strode out of the room. Ríkr uncoiled from my shoulders, and a tingle of magic washed off him as he shifted into a white crow. The bird flew up into the rafters and perched on a beam, his unblinking stare tracking the druid.

Tilliag waited in the crossties, his acid-green eyes burning. Most horses would've been throwing their heads around in agitation, but the fae stallion was alarmingly still. I approached slowly and stopped a few feet away.

Tilliag? I attempted, stretching my inner senses toward him.

A hard mental shove smacked me in the metaphysical face. This fae was as friendly and approachable as the druid.

I exhaled slowly. *I'd like to look at your hooves.*

REMOVE THE ROPES.

His mental voice slammed into me, the equivalent of a full-chested shout inside my skull. Wincing, I set my kit down and reached for the halter. A furious eye watched me as I unclipped the lead lines. I stretched up for the top of the halter to pull it over his ears, and he lifted his head, forcing me up onto my tiptoes.

I dropped back onto my heels. "Fine. Keep wearing it."

His ears flicked, then he lowered his head. I slid the halter off and tossed it aside.

"Which hoof is bothering you?" I asked, picking up my kit again.

He clacked his right front hoof against the concrete floor.

"I'm coming into the stall." Normally, I'd spend a few minutes getting to know a new horse and earning his trust, but I didn't think anything would gain this fae's trust. I slid in beside him, set my kit down, and faced his shoulder. "I'm going to touch you now."

He angled an ear toward me. I lay my hand against his withers, then slid it down. He lifted his leg before I could reach his fetlock. I pulled his hoof between my knees and hooked it against my leather-protected thigh.

"How bad is it?" the druid rumbled from behind me.

I examined the chip in the hoof wall. "Not bad. This won't take long."

Pulling out a curved blade, I dug it into the stallion's sole. He held still as I cut away the jagged edges around the chip. Horses' hooves were like human fingernails; no pain and minimal sensation unless the living tissue was damaged. I exchanged my blade for a rasp and began filing away the roughness.

"These horses aren't in great shape."

The druid's voice came from a bit farther away—near Whicker's and Whinny's stalls.

"They just arrived," I grunted breathlessly, my arms burning and back aching. "Remember the farmer I mentioned last night?"

"The one whose teeth you wanted to cut out?"

"Yeah. Those two were his horses."

"I see." A quiet pause. "Are you treating the gray for thrush?"

"Yeah."

"I can smell it. Must be bad."

"Yeah," I ground out, wondering why the hell he was making small talk with me.

"Are you treating the infection with an alchemic remedy?"

"No."

"Why not? It works better than regular—"

"Would you shut up?" I snapped. "I'm trying to work."

"Does filing require that much concentration?"

I ground my molars together. "Fuck off, asshole."

Tilliag snorted out a breath, sounding amused. Now the horse was laughing at me? Screw them both.

"You're going to disappear, right?" I growled. "Once you do whatever you came here to do?"

The druid's boots clomped closer. "I don't plan to stick around."

"Good. How long?"

"Until I leave? Depends how long it takes me to get to the bottom of the problem I'm investigating."

I resisted the urge to ask more about "the problem." I didn't care. Didn't *want* to care. "Well, hurry up."

"I'd love to, but it isn't easy."

"Why not?"

"You have to ask?"

"Huh?" I gave Tilliag's hoof a final pass with the rasp. "Whatever. I'm done."

Grabbing my kit, I retreated from the stall. The druid was leaning against Whicker's stall while the horse snuffled at his dark hair.

"Tilliag's hoof should be fine." I dropped my kit on the floor and wiped my arm across my forehead, mussing my bangs. "Just keep an eye on it for cracks. You can get lost now."

He pushed off the stall. "Not going to try to stab me again?"

Not while he had a powerful fae literally possessing him. "Just go already."

Giving me an odd, slashing glance, he strode past me to Tilliag as the stallion walked out of the tack stall. He took hold of the horse's fetlock and pulled his hoof up to examine the sole.

"Satisfied?" I asked sarcastically.

"Yes." He released the fae's hoof and turned back to me. "Do you really know nothing about what's happening with the fae in your own neighborhood?"

"Nope."

"You *are* a terrible witch."

I exhaled harshly through my nose.

"There's a coven around here, right?" he asked. "Do *they* know anything?"

"How should I know?"

"You're useless."

"I'm not trying to be helpful!" I snarled.

"You should be, seeing as you work so close to the kill zone. I've found a dozen bodies already and I haven't even made it to the crossroads yet."

Kill zone? Bodies? "Like the bear fae?"

His attention sharpened. "How do you know the bear fae is dead?"

"Did you kill it?"

"No. Tell me how you found out about its death."

My eyes darted between his as I debated whether he was lying. "You're going to the crossroads?"

"Answer my question."

"What does the crossroads have to do with this?"

Impatience ticked in his tight jaw, and he didn't reply, making it clear he'd provide no more answers unless I reciprocated. Which I had no intention of doing.

I bit the inside of my cheek, then let out an explosive breath. "Come with me."

Marching back into the tack room, I reached for the shelf above the table and pulled out a stack of maps marked with horse-friendly trails for our fundraiser rides. I slapped them down on the tabletop. As I flipped through them, the druid appeared beside me. My skin twitched at the invisible buzz of power radiating off him from that damn eagle fae.

And some people thought *I* was creepy.

"What are you doing?" he asked suspiciously.

"You said you haven't made it to the crossroads yet." I spread a map out and pointed to a spot north of the rescue, on the far side of Mount Burke's summit. "The crossroads is in this valley."

"I know where it is."

"But you can't get to it." I met his eyes, waiting for him to deny it, then tapped the map. "This is Dennett Lake. Take Quarry Road up to Munroe Lake Trail. It'll connect to Dennett Lake Trail. Follow that north until you reach the lake."

"I've already been there," he grumbled. "The slope on the north side is too steep to get up without rock-climbing gear."

"I know. You have to go west, around the lake. There's no trail until you get here." I pointed. "Summit Trail. It'll take you up onto the ridge, and from there you'll be able to see the valley. Find a way down and follow the valley to the crossroads."

"Are you sure?"

"I've never gone myself, but I've been to Dennett Lake and the other witches in my coven told me about the route to the crossroads."

Grunting, he leaned over the map to study the route I'd traced, hands braced on the tabletop. Large, strong hands.

"So," I said flatly, "you're going to go there immediately, figure shit out, and leave?"

"That's the plan."

"Good." I whipped my hand out of my pocket. Steel flashed as I brought my switchblade down, slamming it into the tabletop between two of his fingers.

He jolted but didn't yank his hand away.

My knuckles were white around the knife's worn black handle as I looked into his dangerously close fae-bright eyes. "If I ever see your face again, that will be your throat."

He flicked a glance from the knife to my face, his brow furrowed. Instead of angry or intimidated, he seemed disconcerted, almost perplexed—and in response, my gut swooped as though the ground beneath me had shifted.

Then his expression tightened with cold disdain, and I wondered if I'd imagined it.

"With charm like yours," he sneered, "how could I resist returning?"

I bared my teeth. He stepped back—then grabbed the map, tearing the edge where my knife was still embedded.

"Hey! I didn't say you could take that!"

Without a word, he walked out of the room. I sped after him, but by the time I cleared the threshold, he'd reached Tilliag. Grabbing the stallion's mane, he swung himself up. Hooves clopped loudly as the horse pushed into a rolling canter, speeding the length of the stable.

Whicker let out an envious whinny as the fae stallion and his druid disappeared into the afternoon sunlight.

"DINNER IS SERVED!"

Greta set a loaded plate in front of me, and I scooted my wooden chair closer to the table. My mouth watered at the delicious scents filling the eat-in kitchen.

Sinking into her chair, Greta smiled at Dominique. They'd been partners since before I'd met them. Dominique ran the front end of the rescue, Greta ran the back end, and they shared the labor around the farm.

I picked up my utensils and cut into my golden-fried pork schnitzel. "Is this your *Oma*'s recipe?"

"Yes." Greta scooped a forkful of *spätzle* into her mouth. "No more experiments. Chicken schnitzel just doesn't do it for me."

I chewed a perfectly cooked bite of pork, silently agreeing. Not that I would ever complain when they fed me every night for free.

The oak cupboards were faded and scuffed, the patterned linoleum floor curling in the corners, and the floral wallpaper peeling, but I loved this kitchen. I'd started volunteering at the rescue during my last year at vet-tech school, and by graduation, I'd been spending so much time here that Dominique had offered to let me rent the suite above the stable.

I'd lived here for four years now, and every night I ate dinner in this kitchen. I couldn't imagine not eating my next four years of dinners here too.

"Thank you," I murmured, spearing a boiled carrot on my fork.

Dominique sighed. "How many times do we have to tell you that you don't need to thank us?"

"But I'm—"

"Just a volunteer? You always say that, but you also live here, pay rent, spend all your free time helping us, and manage a huge portion of the daily animal care. This rescue wouldn't function without you, Saber."

"But you don't have to feed me."

Dominique muttered something that sounded like, "Talking to a wall."

THE ONE AND ONLY CRYSTAL DRUID ◆ 79

I said nothing, feeling too raw from my encounter with the druid for small talk. I didn't play "nice Saber" with them the way I did at work, but I also never showed them the real me.

The real me scared people. I was creepy. I was crazy. I was the psychotic, violent, vengeful girl with a knife and zero compunctions about using it. If we hadn't been interrupted, I would've sung an Irish folk song as I cut out Harvey Whitby's molars, jagged shards of hate grinding in my chest.

If Dominique and Greta saw that side of me, they'd never invite me into their home again.

"By the way, Saber, I have bad news."

I looked up. Dominique took a slow sip of water, her eyes sad behind her large glasses.

"Harvey Whitby's third horse was found dead in the woods north of Quarry Road. Since it was found inside the provincial park, BC Parks wants a necropsy done just to be safe, but they think it's heart failure due to severe malnutrition."

"Heart failure?" I repeated skeptically.

"I suspect Whitby had something to do with it too." She tapped her fork on her plate. "But the horse had no visible injuries."

I remembered stroking the deceased horse's neck and noticing the lack of a bullet wound. But I'd heard the gunshot. Had Whitby missed the shot but scared the horse to death? Or had that bear fae caused the horse's demise?

After finishing dinner, I helped with the dishes, then bid Dominique and Greta goodnight. My thoughts dwelled on the palomino's mysterious death as I completed my evening routine in the stable, checked on the animals in the pasture, then unlocked the stable's back door and ascended the stairs to the second level.

My suite sat above the tack room, feed room, and tack stalls. Though tiny, it was comfortable, with a squashy sofa facing an old TV I never used, a cramped kitchenette, and the world's smallest table, joined by two little chairs. It looked like playhouse furniture.

I stripped off my clothes and entered the equally small bathroom, fitted with a toilet, pedestal sink, and tiny shower. A few minutes under the shower's hot water washed off the sweat and odor of the barn, but it couldn't wash the questions from my mind.

The bear fae's unprovoked attack and unexplained death. A "kill zone" of fae violence and bodies. The mysterious death of Whitby's palomino. The druid's interest in the crossroads.

Returning to the main room in baggy sweats and a t-shirt, a towel wrapped around my wet hair, I flopped down on the sofa. "Ríkr?"

A moment later, a shimmer disturbed the window. An all-white magpie flew through the glass and landed on the arm of the sofa.

Ríkr's ability to pass through solid objects like a phantom didn't startle me. It was a common fae ability. They could move between their spirit realm and the human world in strange ways, and what seemed perfectly solid in my world was a transparent shadow in theirs. Anything that lacked presence and permanence was insubstantial to them, and human structures lacked both.

When I focused my vision correctly, I could glimpse their domain—a landscape of mist and shadows. If I were to ever fully enter their world, it might look quite different, but I'd never find out.

With a flare of faint blue light, Ríkr transformed into a cat. *You called, dove?*

"Tell me about the crossroads."

He lay down on the sofa's arm. *What would you like to know?*

"Just the basics. I want to know why that druid is so interested."

Dwelling on the druid? he asked coyly. *Ruminating on his—*

I rolled my eyes. "The crossroads, Ríkr."

He swished his tail. *Crossroads are places of power that connect your world to multiple points in my world that are otherwise impossibly far from one another. It is an ancient magic that was used by fae of old to travel great distances with ease.*

"How many other places can a crossroads connect to?"

Some crossroads, only two. Others, a dozen or more. He cracked his lips in a feline smile. *Fae of elder knowledge and power can traverse the world in mere steps if they know the correct route to take from crossroads to crossroads.*

I pushed my bangs up and rubbed my forehead. "How many places does the crossroads to the north connect to?"

He licked his paw and rubbed it over one ear. *Four. You have not asked the most pertinent question, dove.*

My eyebrows rose. "What question is that?"

Standing, he arched his back. *Can a mere human traverse the crossroads as we can?*

I blinked. "Can they?"

He leaped off the sofa and sauntered away.

"Ríkr," I grumbled irritably.

I'm hungry.

"You're not actually a cat, you know. Stop acting like one."

He let out a loud meow. *Maybe I am. You do not know what my true form is.*

"You're a shapeshifter," I scoffed. "Do you even have a true form?"

Of course. Can you not guess it?

I frowned. He favored a cat and a hawk, but somehow, neither seemed quite right for his "true" form. "Give me a hint."

He shot a scathing blue-eyed stare over his shoulder.

"Probably the cobra," I decided.

I am not a cobra!

As he stalked off in a huff, I leaned back into the sofa, chewing my lower lip. Should I have sent the druid to the crossroads? I hadn't wanted to help him, but he would've found it on his own sooner or later, and I'd rather he leave sooner.

Fae aggression. Mysterious deaths. A druid who didn't belong here.

Arla knew something. What was she hiding, and why? I shouldn't have told her about my encounter with the Crystal Druid; I hadn't realized he was a wanted rogue. Had she reported his presence to MagiPol, or did she want to avoid the authorities?

If the druid were to be believed, there was a "kill zone" in my coven's territory—in *my* territory—and I knew only two people who might have answers. One I'd sent to the crossroads, and the other …

I pushed off the sofa and strode into my bedroom, pulling the towel off my head.

Ríkr appeared at my heels. *Going somewhere?*

"To see Arla."

As I opened my closet and pulled out a pair of jeans, my familiar's voice murmured in my head.

Does this count as doing something stupid?

10

THE HUGE FRONT WINDOWS of Arla's house glowed cheerily. Night had fallen half an hour ago and the full moon shone just above the treetops as I parked my truck on the gravel drive. I stifled a yawn as I checked the time. Just after ten. I was usually getting ready for bed around now.

The late hour wasn't an issue for Arla. She had an open-door policy for the entire coven. We could show up at any time, even in the middle of the night.

As I marched toward the door, Ríkr swept away on the silent wings of a screech owl, wishing me a telepathic good luck. Probably for the best. He enjoyed making snarky interruptions too much to include him in serious conversations.

I rang the doorbell to announce my arrival, then punched my code into the door lock. The electric bolt buzzed open, and I let myself in. I waited a moment to see if anyone would greet me, then followed the hall past the formal dining room and into the open-concept main room, a large kitchen on one side and a living room on the other.

"You."

Sitting on the pale gray sofa with a hardcover novel in her hands, Laney shot me a death glare. I gazed back at her emotionlessly. Arla treated coven members like family; we were welcome to show up any time we desired, whether Laney liked it or not.

"What are you doing here?" she demanded, flipping her long, bottle-blond hair over her shoulder. "And so late?"

"I came to see Arla."

"She's busy doing paperwork." She returned her attention to her book. "Including your parole report. I saw it on her screen when I was up there, oh, forty minutes ago? You're too late to stop her from reporting your absence at the ritual."

I started up the stairs.

"Keep it quick. I want to go to bed and I can't sleep with you and your knife around."

At the top of the stairs, I slid my hand into my pocket where my switchblade was nestled. I carried it everywhere, though I'd broken the habit of playing with it years ago. Laney had never forgotten, though.

In the seven years I'd been a member of the coven, I'd seen half a dozen other "parolees" come and go. Laney had hated them all—except the one she'd dated for six months before he'd cut and run mid-rehabilitation—but she hated me the most. Only I was showered with nonstop vitriol.

Pausing in front of Arla's closed office door, I considered how to approach my coven leader. The woman who'd calmly endured my icy attitude and threats when I'd first arrived in her care. Who'd gently encouraged me to participate no matter how many times I'd flung her requests in her face. Who'd given me second and third and tenth chances when I'd failed to meet the requirements of my rehabilitation.

Most people would have given up on me. I would've been sent back to a correctional center, and what was left of my ability to function around other people would have deteriorated to nothing. Arla had probably saved my life.

But she didn't know me. Didn't understand me. Had no idea that I hadn't changed on the inside. I blended in better. I pretended. I played nice. But the real me still wanted to put my knife between the ribs of people who triggered me. The real me still enjoyed seeing them bleed.

I rapped on the door. "Arla? It's Saber. Can we talk?"

When I got no reply, I knocked again, then turned the handle. Open-door policy, after all.

The office had mismatched bookshelves lining one wall and an inexpensive corner desk by the window, two computer monitors facing the room. Arla sat in her chair, her head pillowed on the desk.

"Arla, wake up," I called as I walked in.

My gaze caught on her monitors. One showed the same MPD page I'd perused on my phone this afternoon: the bounty listing for Zakariya Andrii, the Crystal Druid. The other displayed a satellite view of a rugged mountain valley, little red markers dotting it. As I drew closer, I read the label for the only manmade route on the map: Summit Trail.

I sucked in a silent breath—and my hand flew to my face, covering my nose. The room reeked of urine. I looked around, expecting to see a pet-made mess, but Arla didn't have any pets.

I jerked toward the woman. "Arla!"

Her arm lay on the desktop. I grabbed her wrist and shook it. I shook her shoulder. My breath rushed through my throat, quick and frantic. No.

No no no.

Grabbing her shoulders, I pulled her upright. She flopped limply against her chair, arms falling off the desktop, head hanging back. Glassy eyes staring.

Dead. She was dead. Arla was dead.

And the moment I realized it, a single, blinding, all-consuming urge slammed through me: GET OUT.

I needed to get out. Just push Arla back down onto the desk the way I'd found her, walk out, and close the door. Say goodnight to Laney. Go home, go to bed like normal. No one would ever know she hadn't been alive when I'd been here.

But if I left, I'd look even guiltier. Who would believe she'd already been dead when I'd come in? Arla had been alive forty minutes ago, and now she was dead. My word against Laney's.

I couldn't leave. Should I scream? Call an ambulance? Call Laney upstairs myself? But I'd been here too long. A scream now would seem fake. Laney would wonder why I'd stood around for three minutes before realizing her mother was dead.

They couldn't blame me. Arla hadn't been murdered. No injuries. No signs of distress. It looked like she'd simply slumped forward onto her desk and died.

No one would believe I wasn't involved. No one would believe a convicted murderer.

My breath was coming faster and faster. I was doomed. I was fucked.

Better to run.

I spun toward the door—just as Laney walked through, her mouth set in a scowl.

"Are you done talk—" She stared at her mother slumped back over her chair, head hanging unnaturally. "*Mom?*"

Her shriek lanced my ears as she sprinted across the room. I staggered back as she took my spot.

"Oh my god! Mom? *Mom?* Oh my god!"

I backed up another step and stammered, "C-call an ambulance."

Panicked tears streamed down Laney's face as she fumbled for her phone and dialed. I listened to her stutter and sob through her address. "You want me to—p-pulse? Ch-check—"

She almost dropped her phone as she extended a trembling hand toward Arla's exposed throat. Her fingers hovered as though she were terrified to touch the body. As soon as she touched her mother's skin, she would feel that it was too late.

I stepped back again.

Laney's blurred gaze shot to me. Her hand went slack and her phone clattered to the floor.

"You," she snarled hoarsely. "*You!*"

"I didn't—"

"*You killed her!*" she shrieked. "She was fine a few minutes ago!"

I stumbled away. "No—"

"You killed her for reporting you!"

The room spun. "I didn't—"

"You threatened us this afternoon!"

I couldn't get enough air.

"You said you'd make us pay if we screwed up your parole!"

"*I didn't do it!*" My loud voice filled the room. Enraged. Fearful. On the edge of hysteria.

"You're a murderer!" she screamed, her eyes bulging. "You're a psycho killer!"

Her words hit me like blows. I staggered. I spun.

"Where are you going? You can't run away!"

Through the door. Down the hall.

"You're done for, Saber! *They'll execute you this time!*"

Her howling shriek chased me down the stairs. I flew across the house and slammed through the front door. "Ríkr!"

My scream rang through the quiet night. I bolted to my truck and wrenched the door open. A white owl swept out of the dark trees, wings beating fast.

Saber! What's wrong?

"Get in!"

He flashed past me as I jumped behind the wheel. The truck tore down the long drive, and I turned onto the main road at high speed, rubber squealing. Halfway down Quarry Road, flashing lights lit the pavement. An ambulance appeared around the bend, sirens wailing. I clenched my jaw, breathing hard through my nose as it sped past.

Saber? Ríkr asked quietly.

I couldn't speak. I couldn't form thoughts coherent enough to share with him. All I knew was that my life as I knew it was over. Again. My gaze flicked to the horizon.

Fuck the Rose Moon.

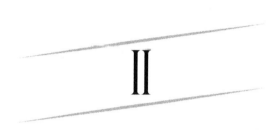

A WHITE CAT landed in my lap, startling me so badly my limbs spasmed.

Saber. Ríkr's piercing blue gaze bored into me. *Snap out of it. This is accomplishing nothing.*

I blinked, and my eyelids dragged over my eyeballs like sandpaper. How long had I been staring at nothing? With a few more blinks, my eyes started to water, cooling the burn, and I took in my surroundings. My tiny living room. I'd returned home. Outside the window, dawn tinged the horizon. I'd been sitting here all night?

Closing my eyes, I focused on the feeling of air moving in and out of my lungs, using it to ground myself in my physical body. Numb disconnection threatened to overtake my mind again.

"I can't go back to prison," I whispered.

As I spoke the words, flashes of sight, sound, and emotion assaulted me—handcuffs, jail cells, sneering faces, condemning voices, barren cots, empty concrete rooms.

You won't. Ríkr stared into my face. *You aren't a child, and you aren't alone. I am with you this time.*

I lifted a trembling hand and stroked his soft back. He wasn't a pet and didn't enjoy being treated like one, but he didn't stop me.

You didn't kill the witch, he said. *Why would the mythic authorities blame you?*

"Because I was there. If they rule it a murder, they'll blame me."

The MPD didn't work like the human police. There were infinite ways to kill someone with magic, and they didn't need to know *how* a murder had been committed if they had a solid case otherwise. I had a criminal record that included murder, no alibi, and a clear motive. I'd recently uttered a death threat, and Laney had caught me standing over the body.

And most damning of all, I was an unsociable, unapproachable, violence-prone woman who gave off distinct "crazy" vibes. When you closely resembled people's idea of a serial killer, they looked for guilt, not innocence.

I'd be convicted again, and the MPD didn't give second chances. Repeat murderers got the death penalty.

"*And if you come,*" I sang under my breath, "*when all the flowers are dying … and I am dead, as dead I well may be.*"

Ríkr's claws unsheathed, piercing my jeans and stinging my thighs. *Enough. What's our next move?*

I raised my head to squint at the window. "We … we could run for it. Disappear. Start again somewhere else."

But if they *didn't* rule Arla's death as a murder, I would have banished myself for nothing.

I pressed my clenched fists to my forehead. *Was* it a murder? Arla had died in a closed room. Laney had last seen her alive forty minutes before I'd arrived, and no one could have gone up the stairs without Laney noticing from her spot in the living room.

Arla hadn't appeared injured and nothing had disturbed the room. She'd probably died of a stroke or heart attack.

Not that magic was incapable of killing someone in a way that mimicked natural causes. But who would want to kill Arla?

I pictured her office. The Crystal Druid's bounty page had been on her computer screen, along with a satellite view of the crossroads' location north of Summit Trail. I hadn't told her about the druid's plan to visit the crossroads; I hadn't been aware he was interested in it when I'd talked to her.

She'd known about the fae attacks the druid was investigating, and she'd known the crossroads was related. If she'd run into him, then her sudden, inexplicable death wasn't quite the mystery it seemed, was it? "The Ghost," as he was known in Vancouver's criminal underworld, had a widespread reputation for cold-blooded murder.

"They'll blame me for Arla's death because I look like a criminal," I told Ríkr. "But what if there were a criminal worse than me who could've killed her?"

He narrowed his eyes. *Are you suggesting the druid engineered her death?*

"It doesn't matter if he did it. It just needs to *look* like he did." I pushed to my feet, forcing Ríkr to leap onto the floor. My stiff muscles ached in protest. "If I can find out what's happening around here and what that druid is up to, I can tie him to Arla's death. What's one more murder charge on *his* record?"

My life was on the line, and I had no issues sending a known killer to the gallows in my place.

Let me guess. Ríkr trotted after me as I headed to my bedroom. *We depart immediately.*

"Yes." I pulled a small backpack from my closet. "We're going to the crossroads."

ON FOOT, the hike to Dennett Lake took about three hours. On a dirt bike, I could cover the same ground three times faster.

The engine snarled as I shifted gears, clumps of soil spraying from the tires as the bike tore up the trail. It bounced over rocks and tree roots, low-hanging branches flashing past, but I didn't let up on the throttle. The trail curved, and I leaned hard into the turn, the wheels skidding across the dirt.

Ahead, the trees parted, revealing Dennett Lake. I sped to its western edge, then cut the engine and dismounted. I wheeled the bike into a dense thicket, hooked my helmet on a handlebar, and pulled a few branches in front of it. I'd rather not walk home if someone stole the bike.

I turned to the west and lifted my long ponytail off the back of my neck, the breeze cooling my skin. Though the mid-morning sky was overcast, the temperature was still rising. It wouldn't get as hot up here near the summit, but I'd be sweating by noon.

Dennett Lake was pretty but small, with a sheer cliff on its far side, the gray rock studded with pines. Barely sparing the picturesque view a glance, I started toward the waiting forest.

No paths connected the lake to Summit Trail, and the quarter mile separating them was too rough for the bike. If I'd ridden a horse, it would've been a different story, but I didn't want to risk another living creature's life when I had no idea what to expect at the crossroads.

I steadied my breathing as a low-level burn settled into my calves. The trees weren't dense but traversing the rocky, uneven ground was a workout. At least I was in good shape.

Away from the noise and exhaust of the dirt bike, my senses attuned to the mountain forest. Fresh, earthy scents filled my nose, the breeze softly rustling branches while birds chirped endlessly. Tension slid from my muscles and I settled into a more relaxed stride.

Would I have to leave this place? Leave the rescue. Leave Dominique and Greta. Leave the animals I'd helped nurse back to health, the pastures and the house, my cozy little apartment above the stable. Leave the woods and the mountains.

My chest constricted at the thought.

I puffed out a relieved breath when I reached Summit Trail, the hard-packed dirt easy to distinguish from the mossy, root-tangled rock I'd been hiking across. As I sat on a fallen log to rest my legs and drink some water from my backpack, beating wings sounded nearby.

A white hawk swooped out of the sky and landed beside me, oozing smugness. *Have a pleasant walk, dove?*

"Screw off," I muttered.

How rude.

"If you were a more powerful fae, you could transform into a bigger bird and carry me."

If I were more powerful, I would have consumed you instead of becoming your familiar.

Fair point. As a talentless witch, I didn't have much to offer a familiar. I turned my arm up to see my inner wrist where, invisible to the naked eye but gleaming in shimmery azure to my witch's vision, a twisty rune the size of a quarter branded my skin. It was my and Ríkr's familiar mark, binding us together.

I tilted my wrist, watching the mark glimmer. "Why *did* you become my familiar?"

He fluffed his feathers. *Boredom, mostly.*

I sighed. He never gave a serious answer to that question.

Ríkr flew ahead as I started up Summit Trail. The path grew steeper and steeper, and my legs started to burn all over again. The temperature rose as the morning wore on, forcing me to strip off my leather jacket and stuff it in my bag. In a loose navy-blue racerback tank, I continued the hike, my swinging ponytail brushing my shoulders.

It took twenty minutes to reach the summit, and another ten minutes of hiking along it before I found a gap in the trees to see north. The Coast Mountains swept away toward the horizon, the forested peaks interspersed with deep valleys. A couple yards beyond the trail, the terrain dropped away into a steep-sided valley overflowing with coniferous trees—and somewhere down there was the crossroads.

A flash of white wings. Ríkr was circling fifty meters farther down the trail.

I hiked to him and found a dry streambed that meandered downward. I followed it into the valley, where it connected to a burbling creek. Soon after, I was deep in the valley, the creek leading me through the forest. The breeze was softer and warmer, the air buzzing with insects and birdsong. Squirrels raucously chided me for invading their territory.

Ríkr landed on a tree branch. He'd switched to the agile form of an all-white jay, and his crest fluffed up as I joined him.

Do you feel it? he asked.

I let my eyes half close. The first thing I felt was the tranquil but aloof energy of the forest. The sluggish aura of the slow-growing pines wove through the bright, urgent life of the summer flora as they raced to bloom and disperse their precious seeds before winter took their lives. The quick, sprightly energy of wildlife flickered among the plants, just as urgently. In the harsh mountain climate, summer was a crucial time of fertile bounty.

Beneath nature's flow of life, I could vaguely sense something else. Something *more*. A deeper power that harmonized with the forest, yet … didn't quite belong.

I turned slowly, homing in on the feeling. "That way?"

Exactly so. He flitted onto my shoulder. *Onward.*

Leaving the creek behind, I ventured into the trees. "What should I expect?"

His feathered head bobbed with my strides. *Difficult to predict, dove. The crossroads is ever changing.*

"What do you mean?"

It is shaped by the power flowing in and out. Some comes from the places to which it connects. Some comes from the beings who tread upon it.

The feeling of alien energy grew stronger until it crackled up my legs with each step, and before I realized I'd crossed the unseen line between the mundane world and the ethereal realm of the fae, I was in it.

Pale mist drifted among the dark, shadowy trees. Draped from their boughs, vines of small blood-red flowers glowed faintly, swaying like eerie garlands. I brushed them aside, my footsteps deadened by the thick carpet of moss and scattered flower petals. Oppressive quiet had fallen, and though it was close to noon, the light had dimmed to the bluish tinge of dusk.

Drenched in the hazy murkiness, pale stone columns rose out of the ground, twice my height and shaped into delicate arches. The unfamiliar architecture, carved with leaves and vines, was ancient and crumbling.

"This is the fae demesne?" I whispered.

An edge of it. He rustled his wings thoughtfully. *This place is to our world as a tidepool is to the ocean.*

Staring around in wonder, I climbed over a fallen pillar and continued on. More stone carvings stood among the trees, wrapped in flowering vines. The mist deepened, and I could barely detect the forest's energies anymore. My senses were overwhelmed with ancient fae power.

With a shimmer of blue light, Ríkr transformed into a furry marten, his front paws gripping my shoulder and his hind legs braced against my back. *This is unusual.*

"What is?"

The crossroads should be lively with my kin. It is too quiet. He canted his head. *But … ah. The druid is here.*

"Where?" I demanded as a knot of anxiety in my chest released. I'd told the druid about the crossroads yesterday afternoon. He'd had plenty of time to investigate and leave, and I'd had no guarantee he'd still be here.

Ríkr leaped off my shoulder. *This way.*

His bushy white tail flashed between trees. I hastened after him, thankful for the moss muffling my steps. Ríkr led me into a cluster of crumbling pillars that had probably been a grand structure in the ancient past. The draping vines, heavy with flowers, grew thicker until I was pushing through them like curtains.

Druid?

The unfamiliar, sibilant drone drifted through my mind. My steps faltered.

Druid?

I looked over my shoulder, unable to see much through the vines. The voice seemed to be calling from that direction.

"Rík̃r," I whispered. "Should we go this way?"

No reply from my familiar. I glanced back but couldn't see anything except endless red flowers. I didn't know which direction he'd gone.

Druid?

A fae was calling for the druid—which saved me the trouble of finding him. Since I couldn't see Rík̃r to follow him, I started toward the call instead, moving cautiously. It wouldn't take Rík̃r long to realize he'd lost me and backtrack.

The pale mist swirled restlessly even though the air was still and heavy. My nose itched with the sweet fragrance of the blossoms as I padded over soft moss. Ahead, the trees parted, revealing a clearing with a small pond, less than thirty feet wide, in its center. A thick layer of reeds surrounded its banks, and ripples danced across the murky water's surface.

Druid.

I paused in the shadow of a semi-opaque pine, scanning for any sign of movement, then ventured into the open. Ten feet from the pond, I stopped. The water rippled as though something were moving beneath the surface. The reeds closest to me rustled.

You are not the one I called.

"No," I agreed. "But I'm also looking for a druid."

The reeds shook as a dark, slimy shape pushed through them, peeking at me. *Why?*

"Why should I tell you?"

More of the creature appeared, covered in wet aquatic leaves and green algae sludge. *Are you his ally?*

"No."

Are you his enemy?

"Maybe."

The shape lifted above the reeds, soggy leaves hanging off it: an arched neck topped by a bulky head concealed in rotting vegetation. What vaguely resembled a horse's muzzle protruded from the slimy mess, except its mouth bristled with jagged teeth.

Do you wish him dead?

I considered the fae. "Maybe."

Its mouth parted—opening like an alligator's—and a long black tongue licked its thin lips. *A bargain, pretty one? I will help you kill him if I may devour him afterward.*

"Do you have a grudge against him?"

A grudge? No, pretty one. I wish only to taste the sweet nectar of his power.

This fae wanted to devour him because his spiritual energy tasted good? Another reason druids rarely reached old age, it seemed.

Lure him to the reeds' edge, the fae hissed in my mind. *And I will strike.*

I slid my hand into my jeans pocket, fingers closing around my switchblade. "What do I get out of this deal?"

I will kill the druid for you.

"Who said I need help killing him? If you want in on this, you need to offer me something I can't get on my own."

A gurgle erupted from the beastly head. The sound resembled a laugh. *What do you desire, pretty one?*

"Make me an offer."

The fae was quiet for a moment. *Do you seek the same answers as the druid?*

Aha. "Interesting question."

I know why Death has come to this mountain. I know of the creature he seeks. I will tell you once I have devoured him.

Hmm. Its offer had potential, but I couldn't blame Arla's demise on the druid if this fae ate him first.

"In that case," I began, "I—"

A hand closed over my mouth from behind.

I jolted violently, and the fae threw his head up in equal surprise. Another hand grabbed my wrist, forcing my fist deeper into my pocket so I couldn't pull out my knife.

Warm breath washed over my ear. "You weren't about to agree to his offer, were you?"

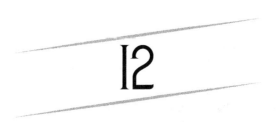

12

THE DRUID'S husky whisper shuddered down my spine, and I threw my head sideways, trying to bash his face. He tightened his hold on my mouth and jaw, forcing my head back into his shoulder.

"I knew you were charming, but plotting my death with a kelpie?" Sarcasm dripped from his deep voice. "And Balligor, I distinctly remember you saying only a few hours ago that you had no idea what was killing fae around here."

A wet grumble rolled off the slimy fae among the reeds. *You offered me nothing of value. But if you give me the pretty one, I will tell you.*

"Treacherous, isn't he?" the druid murmured. "He would have killed you once I was dead, you know."

As though I hadn't expected as much. I grabbed his wrist with my free hand and tried to wrench his hand off my mouth. His fingers dug painfully into my cheeks.

His lips touched my ear, his whisper almost soundless. "Keep struggling and I'll let him have you. You're way too close to the water."

My gaze darted to the fae's dark head. We were only a step away from the reeds, though I could've sworn I'd stopped ten feet away from the pond.

The fae opened its mouth, displaying rows of jagged fangs pointing in every direction.

"Don't even think about it, Balligor," the druid barked, pulling me harder into his chest. "I have business with this one."

Then do your business with her quickly. I hunger.

"Tell me what you know about the fae deaths, and I'll give you something tastier than a weak witch."

Balligor gurgled another laugh. *Foolish druid. Knowing of Death will not protect you from it. Too many know your name.*

Water erupted as the fae launched itself out of the pond, a huge mass of seaweed and slime. The druid flung us both sideways, and we crashed to the ground as the fae's clawed feet slammed into the earth where we'd stood. It lunged at us, its fanged mouth gaping. We had no time to move.

Vicious snarls erupted.

Out of nowhere, two shaggy canine shapes charged past us and leaped at the kelpie's throat. It reared back, front legs kicking.

The druid rolled to his feet and whirled toward the kelpie. As the two black dogs darted around it, a golden glow lit his arm. The light filled his hand, and he snapped it out. A golden whip flashed, cutting across Balligor's face.

The fae squealed and lurched back. Snarling throatily, it fled into the pond. A muddy wave splashed across the ground as the creature disappeared under the surging water. I pushed silently to my feet as quiet fell across the small clearing.

The druid lowered his arm, the golden light of his magic fading—and the moment it was gone, I stepped up to his back, wrenched his head back by his hair, and laid my switchblade against his exposed throat.

He went still.

"Send your dogs to the far side of the clearing," I ordered, pressing against his back to limit his movements.

"Really?" he muttered.

"*Now.*"

He sighed, and though he said nothing out loud, the two black dogs retreated across the clearing, their scarlet eyes glaring hatefully at me.

"Is this necessary?" he growled. "I just saved your life *again*. Clearly, I'm not planning to hurt you."

"You said you had business with me."

"I was bluffing, idiot."

I pulled harder on his hair. "Did you kill her?"

"Who?"

I kicked the back of his knee hard enough to buckle his leg. Slamming him from the same side, I knocked him to the ground and leaped on his chest. He caught my wrist as I aimed my knife at his throat for a second time.

"Did you kill her?" I yelled, shoving downward with both hands.

He grabbed my other wrist, halting my motion, and shouted back, "Who are you talking about?"

I rammed my knee into his groin. His eyes glazed with pain, and my knife dipped toward his throat. Swearing, he heaved his body sideways, throwing me off. I rolled away before he could pin me and pulled my legs under me to leap up.

Curved fangs in a dark snout snapped at my face. I froze. A black dog hovered in front of me, its muzzle ridged furiously. The second one was behind me, judging by the sound of its snarls. My fingers tightened around my switchblade, but the odds were impossible. They'd rip me apart.

Heaving a rough breath, the druid sat back, legs sprawled in front of him, bracing himself with one arm. "What the hell are you going on about?"

Aware that I was moments from death, I surveyed him. Locks of dark hair had tumbled over his forehead, and sweat dampened his black t-shirt, sticking it to his muscular chest. Leather ties hung around his neck, each one holding a rough-cut crystal of a different color. Black fingerless gloves glinted with steel on the knuckles. His alchemy belt was back in place, loaded with potions, and that big knife was strapped to his thigh.

He was well armed even without two guard dogs. And all I had was a switchblade, a missing familiar, and a mean disposition.

Locking my stare on his, I asked again, "Did you kill her?"

"I kill a lot of people. You'll have to be more specific." The irritation in his eyes didn't falter as he spoke. He had no idea who'd died or why I cared.

"My coven leader is dead."

Surprise flickered over his features. It seemed genuine. "How?"

"Don't know. She was found dead in her home last night. No sign of foul play."

"But you suspect me anyway? If I'd known you'd hold this much of a grudge against me for saving your life, I wouldn't have bothered."

Scowling, I retracted my switchblade. "Call off your dogs. I won't gut you ... for now."

"They're vargs, not dogs. A type of wolf fae."

As he spoke, the shaggy canines trotted over to him. I crouched on my heels, not willing to rise while he was sitting. I wanted a good view of his eyes—vivid green but human, meaning the dark raptor fae wasn't possessing him right now.

"Are they your familiars too?" I asked. "Where's your eagle?"

"Nearby. Where's your familiar?"

"Also nearby." I hoped.

A knowing smile ghosted over his lips. "The crossroads is a strange place. It's easy to get lost or separated."

"And you're an expert?"

"Not even close, but I know more than you, the terrible witch. You must have a death wish to come out here, especially now. And don't pretend it's because you think I killed your coven leader."

"That's exactly why I'm here."

"To accuse me of murdering a woman I've never met, let alone had an opportunity to kill, before you even know *how* she died? Sure." He pushed to his feet. "I'll show you the way back. Your little shapeshifter will find us soon."

I shot up to my full height, hand clenched around my switchblade. "I don't need your help."

"I'm not helping you. I'm getting rid of you. And I'll be sending a varg to ensure you don't sneak back in for another attempted stabbing."

I gritted my teeth so hard my jaw ached.

"Speaking of which …" He moved toward me, and I braced defensively. He extended his gloved hand. "Give me that knife."

I stared down at his forearm. Rough pink scars ran from his inner wrist up to his inner elbow, as though he'd been raked by razor-sharp claws. They cut through a dark tattoo I couldn't make out under all the damage.

He flicked his fingers expectantly and I refocused. "Huh?"

"I'm not walking anywhere with you while you're armed. Give me your knife."

"Fuck you."

"Charisma oozes from your every pore," he observed dryly. "Give it to me, or I'll take it from you."

I was strong—*for a woman*—but his total muscle mass still outstripped mine by a dangerous margin. Plus the two guard dogs. Growling under my breath, I slapped my switchblade into his palm.

He pocketed it. "I'm going to pat you down for hidden weapons."

"Like hell you are."

"Again, you can cooperate or we can do it the hard way."

What choice did I have? I lifted my arms straight out to the sides and raised my chin, glaring with every ounce of my loathing. Stepping closer, he swept his large hands down my sides to my waist, then around to the small of my back and over my back pockets. My molars crunched together.

Crouching, he ran his hands over each leg, poked his fingers into the tops of my hiking boots, then straightened to his full height. I craned my neck back. At six-foot-four-ish, he had over half a foot on me and I didn't like it.

His gaze dropped, fixing pointedly on my chest. "Are you one of those women who stash things in their cleavage?"

I slapped my hands to my breasts, cupping them roughly through my tank top. "Do these look large enough to hide weapons in?"

"No." He raised an eyebrow. "But I'm sure they're very nice."

"I'm sure your tiny prick is real fucking nice too."

"Murderous *and* foul-mouthed. You're seduction in motion, sweetheart."

I snarled, arching up onto my toes to get in his face. He stared down at me, lips curving with cool amusement and eyes locked on mine.

"Got a name?" he asked.

"Not for you."

"'Sweetheart' it is, then."

"Saber," I spat.

His eyebrows rose slightly. "Fitting."

"I already know your name," I sneered. "Zakariya."

"Zak. No one calls me Zakariya."

"The MPD does."

A muscle in his jaw twitched. I leered. He scowled.

Realizing we were standing inches apart, our faces indecently close and gazes fixed on each other, I dropped onto my heels and stepped back.

He cast me a brief, assessing glance, then turned. "This way. See you later, Balligor."

The latter statement, which he'd directed toward the pond, sounded more like a threat than a farewell. The reeds rustled in answer, but no dark, slimy head appeared.

I followed the druid away from the water, keeping a few steps behind him, my hand opening and closing as I wished for my switchblade. Would he give it back? And what should I do next? Going straight home, possibly into the waiting arms of the MPD, wasn't part of my plan. Not that I had much of a plan.

I couldn't see or sense Ríkr, but I knew he was nearby. He was lurking in the shadows or hiding up in the trees like the cunning little ambush hunter he was.

Zak—*the druid* waved at me. "Hurry up. It's easy to get separated in here."

He'd mentioned that before. I glanced around at the shadowy trees and curtains of flowering vines, looking for a likely place to—

Reaching back, he grabbed my wrist. I jerked my arm as he pulled me forward again.

"Forget it." He pulled me to his side. "There are nastier fae lurking around here than a kelpie. Do you *actually* have a death wish?"

I snorted.

"From where I'm standing, it's starting to look like it. You were chatting with a kelpie like he was a toothless hob, and you barely flinched when my vargs were in your face."

"I told you when we first met that I don't scare easily."

"There's a fine line between brave and stupid. You fight like a cornered lynx, but that doesn't make you a match for a grizzly bear."

"Are you the grizzly bear in this analogy?"

"I'm saying you're not as tough as you think you are."

"How the fuck would you know?"

He rolled his green eyes toward the misty forest canopy. "Has anyone ever told you you're excessively prickly?"

"I thought I was charming, according to you."

"In your own special way," he retorted, sarcasm returning in full force. "Do you threaten to disembowel everyone you meet?"

"Only the people I really like."

He barked a short laugh, and I bit the inside of my cheek, tamping down the urge to shoot off another combative remark. I wasn't normally conversational … though I supposed this wasn't much of a conversation.

Tugging my wrist, he detoured around a crumbling pillar. "Is there a particular reason you want to slit my throat so badly?"

"Do you really need to ask? I saw your bounty listing."

"That's it? So your hobbies include volunteering at an animal rescue, a farrier apprenticeship, and bloodthirsty vigilante justice?"

That was hitting a little too close to the truth, though I wouldn't call my compulsive acts of vengeance a "hobby."

"Or are you after the bounty itself?" he mused. "That cold million tempts a lot of mythics."

"I don't give a shit about money. You're a kidnapper and a murderer."

"The rumors of my abduction activities have been greatly exaggerated."

"Let me guess. You aren't responsible for dozens of murders either."

"I don't keep count, but that part is probably accurate."

My eyebrows scrunched. Why would he deny one but not the other?

His grip on my arm tightened, and he yanked me toward him. I thumped against his hard chest as he looked down at me with cold eyes, the strange dusky glow of the ethereal forest highlighting the angles of his face.

"You came after me for a reason." His deep voice, rough with threat, rolled down my spine in a shiver. "Tell me what you really want."

I bit my lower lip until pain stung my senses. "I haven't decided yet."

"What?"

"I'm considering a few options."

His menacing aura faded into confusion. I gazed up at him, my teeth worrying my lower lip—and he slapped his free hand against mine, stopping me from slipping my fingers into his pocket in search of my switchblade.

He pulled my hand away from his pants, now holding both my wrists—and his mouth shifted into a rueful, half-exasperated grin. "You're something else, Saber."

An odd, weightless twist in my lower belly caught me off guard. I bared my teeth at him.

He pushed me in front of him, keeping a hand on my shoulder so I didn't run off, and I breathed a silent sigh of relief that his face was out of my line of sight and couldn't keep messing with my head.

Because he was *really* messing with my head, and I didn't understand why.

13

THE DRUID AND I marched through the crossroads as the mist faded and the trees grew more solid. By the time the last of the flowering vines disappeared, daylight had returned, the sun peeking through the scattering cloud cover.

I glanced back. The woods looked completely normal.

Zak—*the druid* steered me to the creek that bisected the valley and stopped. I chewed the inside of my cheek, frustrated that I still had no plan. I waited for him to speak. When he didn't, I craned my neck to see him.

He was staring downstream, his jaw tight. "Shit."

"What's shit?"

"Since you're going that direction anyway, you'll find out." He glanced around. "Has your familiar returned yet?"

Rikr? I silently called. No answer, but that didn't mean he wasn't here. Telepathic communication wasn't always private, as Zak—*the druid* had demonstrated with the kelpie. It worked much like speaking aloud: the closer and quieter our communication, the harder it was for another fae, witch, or druid to eavesdrop on it.

On the other hand, Ríkr and I "shouting" to each other from a distance would be easier for the druid to listen in on, which I was certain my familiar had realized.

"He'll catch up," I told the druid dismissively. "What am I going to find out?"

Strangely grim, he started forward. This time, he didn't hold on to me, and though I was tempted to bolt into the woods, I could sense a fae presence nearby—one of his two guard dogs. Plus, I was curious to see what lay ahead.

We crunched along the creek's pebbly bank for a few hundred feet until it curved. I hadn't seen this section of it—I'd swerved into the woods before coming this far—and I scanned the towering conifers and dappled shadows for signs of movement.

But that wasn't where I should've been looking.

Zak came to a quiet halt, and I stopped beside him. Scattered beside the burbling water, four dead bucks with half-grown, stump-ended antlers lay on the ground. The fifth body resembled the others, except its broad antlers were pearly white and sharply pointed, as though it were rutting season instead of mid-June.

Zak—*the druid*, I reminded myself—approached the buck with white antlers and knelt. He touched its withers. Its pupilless amber eyes stared lifelessly.

"This is what you've been talking about?" I asked. "Dead animals and fae?"

"Larger animals, yes. In the last four days, I've found deer, moose, a few elk, coyotes, two black bears, and an adolescent grizzly. Plus a dozen fae. All dead within the past two weeks."

I crouched beside a buck. He lay as though his legs had buckled where he stood. "What's killing them?"

"Since there are no wounds, I thought it was a disease, but ..."

"But there are no signs of illness. Their coats are in perfect condition." I brushed a hand across the buck's neck. "They don't appear underweight, and their knees aren't scraped as though they were staggering or falling before dying. What disease could make a healthy animal drop dead with no warning?"

Zak nodded. "And this group died at exactly the same time. A disease wouldn't do that. A poison could, though."

I glanced at his alchemy belt as my distaste for that particular arcane art welled in my throat. "Did you test any of the bodies for poison?"

"Everything I could think of that can be tested for."

I sat back on my heels. "I could try doing a necropsy," I said skeptically, "but I don't know if it would tell us much without being able to send tissue samples for histology."

"Are you a vet?"

"Veterinary technician."

"Hm. Full of surprises." He ignored my irritated look. "Are you offering to help?"

"No," I snapped reflexively. "I mean ... I don't know."

"Haven't decided yet?" he asked, half mocking, half amused.

"Shut up. I'm thinking." I stared down at the buck. "This is how Harvey Whitby's palomino died. The horse was just ... dead. The park authorities are having a necropsy done, so if he was killed by the same thing as these bucks and the fae ... a full necropsy by a vet will reveal more than anything I could do out here."

"Cutting a dead animal open and making a bloody mess this close to the crossroads would be a bad idea." Zak rose to his full height. "Can you get a copy of the necropsy report?"

"I'll try." I stood as well, staring down at the bodies. "This is how my coven leader died too."

A moment of silence. "Are you sure?"

"I saw her myself. She was slumped over at her desk as though she'd fallen asleep. She had no health problems that I know of. No one besides her daughter was in the house."

"I can think of a few poisons with a delayed activation, but none of them are an easy death." He rubbed the dark scruff on his jaw. "Why target her? All the other deaths appeared to be random—fae and animals in the wrong place at the wrong time."

I squeezed my temples. Arla had known something about the fae deaths. Had she gotten too close to the killer? "If I'm going to help, I want the truth. What's in this for you?"

His gaze weighed me. "If I can stop all this senseless death, every fae on the mountain will owe me. And"—he raised his left arm, turning the underside of his wrist toward me—"I could use some fae favors."

His right forearm was scarred, ruining whatever tattoos he had, but on his left, five precisely wrought circles were tattooed from his wrist up to the crook of his elbow—magic circles. The one on his wrist held a spiky green rune, and the second-to-top one contained a vaguely squarish golden rune.

That gold rune was the source of the amber whip spell I'd seen him use. The magic wasn't his own, but power a fae had gifted him. The green rune was another fae gift, while the other three circles were empty.

So that's why he was here. He was hoping the fae in this area would gift him with powerful magic once he eliminated the danger lurking on the mountain.

"I see." I tugged my tank top straight. "I'm going now. I'll see what I can find out about the palomino's necropsy and my coven leader's death."

"And you'll share that information with me?"

I looked across the dead bucks and the fae body. There were several white-antlered fae in this area. I'd seen them at the coven's rituals many times. Much like their animal counterparts, they were shy and skittish, more likely to flee than fight. The energy they exuded was always peaceful.

Something was killing fae and animals in my territory, and I couldn't stop it. But maybe Zak could.

"Yes," I said quietly. "I'll tell you what I find out."

"Then we should set the parameters for how we'll split any fae gifts. Since you're helping."

"I just want my knife back."

He slipped it from his pocket and turned it over in his hands, studying the black aluminum handle. "How long have you had it?"

"A long time," I snapped. "Hand it over."

He tossed it to me. I caught it, momentarily comparing its cool weight to my first switchblade with its glossy red handle. I'd bought this one within a few weeks of joining Arla's coven, despite my parole conditions forbidding me from possessing a weapon. Arla had never reported it. Maybe she'd understood how much I needed the small blade to feel in control of myself and the world around me.

Pushing away thoughts of my dead coven leader, I stuffed it in my pocket, circled around the dead bucks, and strode toward the towering summit. The skin on the back of my neck prickled.

The druid watched me until a bend in the creek carried me out of his view—and no sooner was I out of sight than a tiny white sparrow flittered out the canopy and alighted on top of my head.

Rejoice! Ríkr exclaimed. *For we are once again united, my beautiful dove.*

I waved my hand above my head, forcing him to take flight again. "Where've you been?"

First, I attempted to lead you to the druid, only for you to gallivant off alone. So, while you occupied the druid in the company of a pernicious kelpie, I explored the crossroads to learn what the druid has been meddling in.

"And what's he been meddling in?"

Ríkr landed on my shoulder. *Thus far, the druid has questioned the fae who live near the crossroads, and he has extracted promises from several to gift him magic if he ends the killing.*

"He's arranging favors in advance?"

A wise bargainer. Ríkr flitted into the air and landed on my other shoulder. *Your plans for the druid have changed, it seems.*

I cursed under my breath. "I might have a chance to turn the MPD's attention on him later, but if Arla was killed in the same way as the other deaths Zak is investigating, I'd rather expose the real killer than fabricate something."

Zak, Ríkr crooned. *You speak his name with such familiarity.*

I'd been trying *not* to use his name, but somehow that had happened too.

Spotting the dry streambed I'd followed down into the valley, I angled toward it. "We don't have much to go on to catch the killer. All we know is that fae and animals have been inexplicably dying in this area. The palomino may have died the same way, and possibly Arla too."

Death is not the only symptom of this danger, Ríkr mused. *Unusual aggression has plagued some fae as well.*

"Like the bear fae," I murmured, recalling its unusual attack. "It probably died like the others. So we have a killer who murders mostly at random, but seems to have targeted Arla. The deaths are instant and don't involve physical harm, and some fae have been infected with unusual aggression that may or may not be directly related to them dying."

And the crossroads seems to be the focal point, Ríkr concluded. *Somehow.*

I pushed my bangs off my sweaty forehead, puffing as the slope grew steeper. "I don't even know where to start."

Hmm. Blue light shimmered over Ríkr, and his hawk's talons bit into my shoulder as his form changed. *First, we must ensure the mythic authorities do not detain you. Then we can ponder over the rest.*

Right, that too. I'd find out soon what awaited me on the other side of the mountain.

AT THE BASE of Mount Burke, I pulled my dirt bike off Quarry Road and into a small gravel parking lot for hikers. I cut the engine and, still astride the bike, fished my cell phone out of my backpack.

Half a dozen notifications filled the screen. I checked the first one—my supervisor at the vet clinic replying to my text about missing my shift due to a family emergency. The rest of the texts were from Pierce, the only witch in our coven who had my personal number aside from Laney.

I tapped the call button. The phone rang in my ear all of once before Pierce's voice boomed down the line.

"Where have you been?"

"Hiking. I needed some space."

"*Space?*" he half shouted. "My god, woman. Are you trying to look as suspicious as possible?"

Cold slid through my gut. "What do you mean?"

"You shouldn't need an explanation," he growled. "*You* found Arla's body last night. You're the first person the MPD wanted to talk to, and no one could find you. If you'd had any chance of not being the primary suspect, your little 'hike' blew it."

"Primary suspect of what? I found her dead in her office. It looked like a heart attack."

"Well, MagiPol disagrees." He exhaled harshly through his nose. "They're cagey as always, won't even say how she died or if it's a murder investigation or something else, but they've talked to every member of the coven now—except you."

I squeezed my eyes shut. It was most definitely a murder investigation.

"And Laney …" Pierce let out another rough breath. "She's out for your blood, Saber. Dished every bit of dirt and gossip about you she could think of. She's absolutely convinced you killed Arla."

Opening my eyes, I gazed at the shadowy woods. "Do *you* think I killed her?"

"No," he grunted without hesitation. Surprise flickered through me, then he added, "You'd never get caught this easily."

Ah. Of course he wouldn't doubt whether I was capable of murder.

"But you might go down for this anyway, Saber." His phone crackled. "Those agents are gonna come knocking on your door soon, and you need to be real careful how you handle them."

"Yeah," I agreed softly. "I need to go."

A pause. "Goodbye, Saber. Good luck."

The line went dead. He'd uttered his farewell like it might be our final one.

Pocketing my phone, I kicked the bike back to life and sped onto Quarry Road, desperate to be home while simultaneously dreading what I might find.

My throat tightened uncomfortably as I rolled down the long dirt drive of Hearts & Hooves. I named each animal in the pasture as I passed. Dunkin, the donkey with horrendously overgrown hooves who still limped a year later. Hippy and Funko, two former racehorses we'd saved from slaughter. Fluffball, a sheep who hadn't been sheared in years and could barely walk when we took him in. Pip, a draft horse who'd been so aggressive his owners had planned to euthanize him, but who'd actually had a painful abscess in his mouth, causing him to act out.

And more. Animals I'd helped. Animals we'd saved. And I might have to leave them all.

In the yard, Dominique and Greta's Ranger was parked beside mine, no other vehicles in sight. Ríkr, still in hawk form, was perched on top of the stable, watching me. Humans couldn't see him unless he allowed it, and he only ever allowed it while in cat form so as not to confuse the human owners of the rescue with a myriad of albino wildlife visiting their property.

No strangers lurking? I asked him.

The only beast on the prowl in these fields is me, he replied loftily. *And should I encounter a stranger of ill intent, I will smite them down for you, my beloved dove.*

I sighed. *Attacking MagiPol agents won't help my case, Ríkr.*

Nonsense.

Bringing the bike to a halt in front of the shed, I dismounted and pulled off my helmet. The house's front door flew open.

"Saber!" Dominique grinned cheerfully as she hastened across the porch, a flower-patterned tea towel in her hand. "Did you have a good day on the mountain?"

I'd left them a note this morning saying I was taking a personal day. I hadn't wanted to panic them when they realized I wasn't at work.

"It was good," I said noncommittally. "A bit hot, though."

"You had visitors while you were gone." An anxious shadow dimmed her good mood. "Two men in suits? They said they'd try to catch you another time."

An uncomfortable shiver ran down my limbs. I'd expected it, but knowing my home had been invaded by my worst enemies set me on edge. A dangerous, savage edge. My fingers twitched, longing for my knife.

"Did they leave immediately?" I asked. "They didn't wander around, did they?"

"They left right after talking to me." She hesitated. "But I didn't hear their car arrive, so I'm not sure how long they were here before coming to the house. Who are they?"

"I'm not sure," I lied. "Dominique, have you heard anything about the necropsy on Harvey Whitby's palomino?"

Her brow furrowed. "No, why?"

"Is there a way to see the necropsy results?"

She nudged her glasses up her nose. "I'm not sure. I can ask around."

"Could you do that for me, please?"

"Sure, but why?"

I pressed my lips into a thin line. "I have suspicions."

Her eyebrows rose at my vagueness, but she merely said, "Dinner will be ready in an hour."

"I'll be there."

Behind the stable, I tested the rear door that led up to my suite. Locked, as I'd left it. That didn't mean anything. Unlocking it, I cautiously ascended the stairs. I wasn't worried about agents lying in wait—Ríkr would've warned me—but apprehension still sizzled through my bones.

I unlocked and opened the door to my suite. The familiar, comforting scent of coffee and laundry detergent filled my nose. Everything looked normal and undisturbed. Closing the door and toeing off my shoes, I began a slow, careful pass through the entire apartment. When I finished, I returned to the center of the small main room.

Rage sawed at my chest.

They'd been here. Probably before going to the house to speak with Dominique. The signs were subtle. I always left my closet door cracked open so my clothes didn't smell musty, but it'd been shut tight. There were smudges in the dust on my veterinary reference texts, and the old laptop I'd used for school was turned the wrong way. The used coffee filter I'd tossed in the garbage yesterday, the last thing I'd thrown out, had been flipped over.

Those bastards had looked through my *garbage*.

Dread laced my fury. They wouldn't search the garbage of a witness. Pierce was right. I was a suspect.

And that meant talking to them wasn't an option. Not until I was certain an interview wouldn't become an arrest.

I'd die before allowing the MPD to arrest me again.

Showering calmed me down enough to act normal when I returned to the house for dinner. Greta's roast chicken and *bratkartoffeln*—pan-fried potatoes with onion and bacon bits—was absolutely delicious, and I tried not to think about how many meals I might have left with her and Dominique.

After cleaning up the kitchen, I headed out to the pasture, checking on the animals and giving extra pats and attention. Despite my best efforts, I couldn't stop myself from checking the horizon every few minutes, searching for approaching vehicles or strangers in suits. Ríkr would detect intruders long before me, but logic wasn't helping right now.

Gloom settled over me, accompanied by that familiar grinding sharpness in my chest. Hatred-laced, frigid, wrathful. An icy, burning need to make someone pay. Pay for *what*, I wasn't sure. For the dread hanging over me? For the inescapable threat of MagiPol's "justice"? For the unfairness of it all?

The crushing feelings spiraled through me until numbness cooled them, and I lost all sense of time as I wandered the pasture in a daze. By the time my awareness of my surroundings returned, the setting sun had stained the clouds pink and orange.

I returned to the stable. One by one, I checked on each horse, singing softly as I gave nose bumps and forehead rubs. All the real work had been done already, either by Dominique and Greta or by the afternoon's volunteer.

Whicker stuck his head through the opening in his stall door as I approached. I breathed on his nose, a polite horse-style greeting, and he puffed against my cheek. I rubbed his forehead, then opened his stall door and led him out. Setting him up in crossties in the open-fronted tack stall, I spent a few minutes checking his hooves. The odor of infection had diminished.

As I ducked under the crossties, he lipped at my t-shirt for a treat.

"You're quite the friendly fellow," I murmured, smoothing his pale gray forelock. "You've been dying for attention, haven't you?"

Fetching grooming brushes from the tack room, I stacked them on the half-wall between stalls and started working on his dappled gray coat with a dandy brush, skipping the currycomb since he was already fairly clean.

"*The minstrel-boy to the war is gone,*" I sang quietly, the mournful tune suiting my mood. "*In the ranks of death you'll find him.*"

I switched to a soft body brush. Whicker slanted an ear toward me, lazy contentment written all over him.

"*His father's sword he has girded on, and his wild harp slung behind him.*" I reached up to run the brush along the horse's broad back. "'*Land of song,*' said the warrior-bard, '*though all the world betrays thee, one sword, at least—*"

Whicker's ears perked forward, and I broke off. The crosstie clips jingled as he raised his head.

An intruder, Ríkr warned me, his voice coming from somewhere outside. *But not a stranger.*

The dull *clip-clop, clip-clop* of a horse trotting across the gravel yard reached my ears. The sound grew louder, and I leaned out of the stall to peer at the open doors, filled with the golden glow of the setting sun.

A horse and rider trotted into the threshold and stopped, silhouetted by the sunlight. I couldn't make out any details, but I didn't need them to recognize the long, sturdy limbs, elegantly arched neck, and powerful build of a certain fae stallion.

And I didn't even need that much to know who was dismounting in front of the stable.

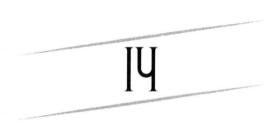

14

"THE MINSTREL FELL," I sang under my breath as footsteps clomped toward me. *"But the foeman's chain could not bring that proud soul under."*

Whicker let out a loud whinny in happy greeting.

"The harp he loved ne'er spoke again," I half-growled even more quietly as I tried to contain my anger. *"For he tore its chords asunder."*

The footsteps halted. I moved the brush across Whicker's back, refusing to look up.

"Why are you here?" My voice was soft. My temper was not.

Whicker's head bobbed as he greeted the druid. Reacquainted with his equine pal, Zak ducked the crossties to join me. "If you didn't want me to show up, you should've given me your number."

Reluctantly, I shifted toward Whicker's flank to make room for the druid beside me. He selected a wide-toothed comb, and

I watched him out of the corner of my eye as he combed the horse's mane. He looked exactly as he had nine hours ago, but more tired and dirty.

"You stink of sweat," I informed him.

"You stink of horse."

"The horse stinks of horse."

"Which means you do too." He worked the comb through a knot, the thick muscles in his arm flexing with the movement. "I found two more dead animals, but no more dead fae. I talked to a few, but they didn't know anything. The locals who are aware of the killings have either hidden or fled."

"What about the kelpie? He seemed to know something."

"Balligor was probably bullshitting to lure you in close enough to eat, but I did try to talk to him again. He's avoiding me, and I'm not desperate enough to force him to show himself." Zak was quiet for a moment, the motions of his comb slowing. "I've never seen anything like this, and I deal with darkfae on a regular basis. An entire fae populace scared of the same thing …"

I ran the brush over Whicker's rump. "But *what* thing? What kills animals and fae by making them drop dead? What makes fae turn aggressive? What killed my coven leader without entering her house?"

"That's assuming no one entered her house. A fae wouldn't use the door." He resumed combing. "If this is a fae killer, I can't find any sign of it, even around the bodies."

I circled Whicker's rump to brush his other side. "Is tracking a fae possible?"

"There are a few methods, but none of them are working."

"So you have a bunch of dead bodies and no leads whatsoever."

He growled something under his breath. "My leads are the bodies. I've marked them on your map, but I'm not sure how accurate it is. Translating the locations from my memory to the map is difficult."

"Show it to me."

"If you want."

I finished brushing Whicker, then returned him to his stall. As I latched the door, Zak picked up a black, dirt-smudged backpack leaning against the wall and slung it over his shoulder. I hadn't noticed him carry it in, and he hadn't had it at the crossroads.

My attention turned to the tack room door, which had a table we could use for viewing the map ... but there were no chairs in there. My legs were aching from a long day of exertion and I didn't want to stand anymore.

With a silent sigh, I waved at the druid. "This way."

He followed me outside and waited while I locked up the stable. He still didn't speak when I led him around the back, through the rear door, up the stairs, and into my small suite.

"You live here?"

I instantly regretted my choice to reveal where I slept at night. "Give me the map."

"Where—"

"Give me the map," I repeated sharply, "and take a shower before you sit on my furniture."

His eyebrows climbed. He opened his backpack's front pouch, handed me the folded map, then kicked off his boots and went straight into the bathroom, taking his bag with him. The lock clicked.

I waited for the water to start up before heading into my room to change—my clothes *did* smell like horse, and I'd need to shower again before bed. Pulling on sweats and a baggy t-shirt, I returned to the main room and lowered myself onto the sofa with a tired sigh.

Just as I was spreading the map out on the coffee table, a hawk shimmered through the wall and landed on the sofa's arm with a sweep of snow-white feathers.

The druid is in your bathroom, Ríkr remarked, folding his wings.

I studied the red notations on the map. "I know."

And a lovely black eagle is perched on the roof. He clicked his beak. *I lavished her with compliments, but her response was not favorable.*

A number and date accompanied each mark on the map. Zak had been thorough. "How did she respond?"

She suggested I prostrate myself in the dirt before speaking with her, as that was my proper place.

"Hm."

To be fair, he mused, contorting his neck to preen his back feathers, *she is well powerful enough to join a court, though not enough to rule one.*

"Yet she's a druid's familiar. Seems like a demotion."

Not a familiar, dove. He uncontorted himself to fix me with his crystal-blue stare. *The druid's relationship with the Lady of Shadow is quite different.*

"The Lady of—"

The shower shut off with a clunk, and I abandoned my question for another time. Ignoring the rustles and clatters from the bathroom, I focused on the map and the scattered markings that dotted the mountainside. The map on Arla's computer screen had been marked as well, and I canted my head as I tried to remember where the icons had been. I'd only glimpsed it for a moment.

With a click of the lock, the bathroom door opened and Zak emerged, wearing a clean sleeveless shirt and jeans—both black—with his damp hair roughly combed back from his face as though he'd dragged his fingers through it. His backpack hung from one hand.

Eyeing his face, I demanded, "Did you use my razor?"

"I used my own razor." He ran a hand over his smooth jaw. "I borrowed your toothbrush, though."

"*What?*"

"I'm joking." He hefted his bag. "Do you have laundry in here?"

"In the closet."

He opened the closet near the entryway and started loading his garments into the washer—not only what he'd taken off before showering, but at least one more change of clothes. Did that bag contain all his supplies for his mission to earn fae gifts?

I waited to see if he'd ask how the machine worked, but he figured it out. As it started up with a hum, he closed the closet door, set his backpack against it, and strode toward me.

Watching him approach—over six feet of broad shoulders, muscular arms, and dangerous magic—I wondered why the hell I'd brought him into my space. This was my sanctuary, and it'd already been invaded once today. I didn't know how to handle a second invasion, even one I'd invited in.

Good evening, druid, Ríkr crooned silkily. *Welcome to my witch's humble abode.*

Zak's eyes narrowed. He didn't buy the shapeshifter's sincerity any more than I did.

May you find it rife with female temper and sharp blades, Ríkr concluded with a taunting tilt of his avian head.

"I appreciate the well wishes," Zak replied dryly, sinking down beside me. "Do you care to share a name?"

Ríkr, my familiar offered. *By the way, you smell luscious.*

"I get that a lot. From fae," he added pointedly, as though I might've forgotten I'd recently informed him that he stank. Post-shower, he smelled like pine-scented soap that reminded me of mountain forests on cool, crisp evenings.

Ríkr shuffled his talons on the sofa's arm. *I suppose your dark lady on the rooftop would be opposed to sharing a taste of your power.*

"I'm very sure she would. So would I."

Annoyed at my familiar's blatant schmoozing, I cut in, "Are all the bodies marked on here?"

"Yes." He leaned back against the cushions. "Figure out anything?"

"Lines."

He blinked. "What do you mean, 'lines'?"

I pointed to several animal deaths. "These bodies all fall near an old trail that was closed two years ago after a landslide."

As he sat forward for a closer look, I indicated another few bodies. "I think there's a streambed here. And here—these ones are in a ravine. I've seen it from Munroe Lake Trail."

"So ..." He stared down at the map. "You think the killer traveled along these paths, slaughtering all the animals they encountered along the way?"

I nodded. "These routes are easier than cutting through the forest. And all of them move down the mountain, suggesting the killer was traveling away from the summit. That makes more sense than zigzagging aimlessly across the slopes."

"Maybe the killer isn't lurking *around* the crossroads but coming out of it. They appear from the crossroads, go on a killing spree, and retreat into the crossroads again."

"Seems plausible." I tugged on a lock of hair hanging over my shoulder. "The lines are less clear here and here"—I pointed to individual clusters—"but there could be more bodies you didn't find."

Zak said nothing, and I glanced at him. Brows drawn down, elbows braced on his knees, he was studying the map intently. With a quiet thought to tell me he was going to keep an eye on the eagle fae outside, Ríkr took flight, disappearing through the wall.

"Do you see the other pattern?" I asked the druid.

"Yeah," he muttered. "On each 'line,' there are multiple animal deaths, but only one fae death."

I combed my fingers through another lock of my hair, then absently split it into three pieces and started braiding it. One fae death per "excursion" by the killer. Did that mean the killer was seeking out those fae, or was it coincidence? And, I noticed, the fae body was usually the farthest point from the summit. Did the killer return to the crossroads after murdering a fae? Why? What did it all mean?

"What song is that?"

I started. "Huh?"

His gaze slid across my face. "You were humming."

The tune of the old Irish ballad I'd been singing to Whicker was still running through my head. I shoved to my feet. "We're done here. You can get out now."

He leaned back, head resting on the cushions. "You were actually semi-pleasant for a while there."

I turned back to the sofa and leaned over him. Bracing my hand on his shoulder, his body heat warming my cool fingers, I smiled. "Don't misunderstand, druid. I'm working with you to find this killer, not because I enjoy your company." Bringing my face closer to his, I made sure he couldn't miss my animosity. "Everything you are is everything I utterly loathe."

"And what is that?"

"A powerful man who abuses those weaker than him."

I didn't see his hand move, but suddenly, his fingers were clamped around my wrist.

"Then what are you, witch?" he asked, his voice dark and dangerous. "When you wanted to cut that farmer's teeth out, were you a switchblade angel dispensing righteous justice? Why are you allowed to pass judgment on others, but I'm not?"

He shoved my hand off his shoulder and stood. Trapped between the sofa and coffee table, we faced each other, toe to toe, glaring into each other's eyes. His palm pressed against my upper thigh, pushing on the switchblade hidden in my pocket, silently telling me he knew it was there.

"I've never pretended to be the good guy," he growled softly. "So quit acting like you're so much better than me. You might not be as deep, but you're down here in the dark right along with me."

My breath rushed out and I shoved away from him. "Get out."

He moved into the center of the room. "My clothes are in your washer."

"Not my problem."

"I'm not leaving without them."

I swore and turned away from him. "Then leave when they're done."

"And go where? I'll be back in the morning anyway."

Bristling, I spun back. "Why?"

"Finding a killer, remember? Or has your commitment fizzled out already?"

My teeth clacked together. Maybe I should tell him the MPD was investigating me for murder; the prospect of agents knocking on the door would get him out of here. But revealing that information meant handing him a weapon he could use against me.

"Fine," I snarled. "Do what you want. I'm going to bed."

"Got anything to eat?"

"In the kitchen. Help yourself." I stormed to my room. "But don't touch anything else!"

Slamming my bedroom door, I gulped back the urge to pull my knife.

Down in the dark, he'd said. I didn't want to understand, but I knew exactly what he meant. The dark … the violence. We were people who lived with and in violence. Around us and inside us.

But what had he meant when he'd asked why I could pass judgment on others, but he couldn't?

My breath rushed through my nose. I stomped to my closet, stretched up for the top shelf, and grabbed a clean bedsheet, a spare pillow, and a fuzzy blanket I used on cold winter nights. I stomped back across my room and whipped the door open.

The druid looked up. He was standing in front of my fridge, one hand on the open door as he examined its contents.

I threw my armload onto the sofa, marched back into my room, and slammed the door for a second time. Leaning back against it, I rested my head on the wood. *Ríkr? How do you feel about guarding my room all night?*

His reply was instant. *I will protect your virtue with my dying breath, dove.*

I grimaced as I pushed away from the door. My virtue wasn't what I was worried about.

15

"ARE WE REALLY *going to do this?"*

The boy didn't answer as he paced back and forth, his boots crunching on the gravel-strewn asphalt.

We were in the alley behind the "den," as my aunt called the place where she did business once a week. I didn't know if the building was a gambling den or something else, but it's where she and other mythics went to make secret, illegal deals—like selling their nieces to terrifying men called Bane.

She was in there right now. So was Bane. If I had gone up to the attic, I might have been able to eavesdrop again, but the boy and I were out here for the same reason. We didn't want anyone overhearing us.

Leaning against a graffiti-marked brick wall, I watched him pace. Should I finally ask his name? But then he'd ask mine. Names were dangerous.

"Well?" I prompted.

"I plan to kill him." He growled the words without stopping his restless movements. "I will kill him. But I'm not ready. I'll only get one chance so I have to be certain."

His words echoed my reservations. Killing someone shouldn't be that difficult. I had a knife and Ruth had a carotid artery. But walking up to her and stabbing her in the throat wasn't as easy as it sounded. If she guessed what I was about to attempt ... if I missed ... if she survived ...

I shuddered.

"He has a sixth sense for threats," the boy muttered. "As soon as I make a plan, he'll suspect it."

"Poison his food?" I suggested.

"He'd notice. Besides, he's practiced mithridatism for decades."

I nodded, familiar with the method of building up a tolerance to poisons by ingesting small doses. "Can you ambush him?"

"Unlikely. If it was that easy, I'd have done it already."

Then we should just run away. On a night like this, we could do it. As soon as Ruth and Bane went into the den, we could run for it.

But I didn't suggest that. If my aunt was alive, I'd never escape her no matter how far I ran. I'd always be looking over my shoulder, always watching my back. I wanted to be rid of her forever, and I'd bet the boy felt the same way about his guardian.

Spinning on his heel, he swept over to me and stopped a couple feet away. His hood shadowed his features, the darkness in the alley clinging to us both.

"What about your aunt?" he asked. "How would you kill her?"

Grimacing, I tugged roughly on my blond ponytail, hating the color she had chosen. Hating that she controlled everything about my life, including my body. "She locks me in a room at night, so I can't sneak up on her while she's sleeping. If she's awake, she's on guard."

"What about poisoning her?"

"She's an alchemist. She carries a universal antidote with her everywhere, and—"

"That doesn't work on everything."

"And," I finished, "she has antidotes for almost everything else."

The boy leaned against the wall beside me, then sank down to sit on the damp pavement.

I lowered myself beside him, my hands tightening into fists. "It's impossible, isn't it? She's gonna sell me to Bane, and he's going to ... what?"

"Feed you to a fae, probably."

A fae? So Bane was a witch? Did that make the boy, his apprentice, a witch too?

Just like me.

"What if ..." He glanced at me. "What if I could get you a poison with no antidote?"

I scrunched my face skeptically. "Where would you get that?"

"It's one Bane doses himself with for his mithridatic training." He fidgeted with his sleeve. "I could steal it."

A thrill of fearful anticipation ran through me. "Really?"

"What will happen to you if your aunt dies?"

I shrugged. "My parents are dead, and if I have other relatives, I don't know them."

He considered that. "Bane might try to take you anyway, depending on how bad he wants you."

"So we have to kill them both. Especially if you're going to steal from him."

He bit his lower lip.

"What's the biggest thing stopping you from killing him?" I asked softly.

His eyes darted around as though he expected a monster to materialize from the darkness. "His fae. They're always there.

Always watching my every move. He knows I'd murder him in a heartbeat, so he always has one shadowing me."

"Even right now?"

"Not now. My familiars are keeping his away, but that won't work if he's nearby. He'd notice right away."

He had multiple familiars? I didn't even have one.

My hand drifted to the collar of my jacket. "If you could get past his fae without them noticing you, could you kill him?"

"Yeah, but it's impossible to sneak past those fae."

"Actually, you can. With the right magic."

His attention fixed on me, intense and piercing. *"What magic?"*

"I have a ... an artifact. It hides the person wearing it from fae senses. I could lend it to you."

"Something like that exists?" He sounded breathless, as though my words had hit him like a punch to the gut. *"You'd let me use it?"*

"Borrow it," I clarified emphatically. "It was a gift from my parents. It's the only thing of theirs I have left."

"Borrow," he agreed quickly. *"For one night. Just long enough to ... Are you sure that's how it works? It will hide me from any fae?"*

"My parents said it doesn't matter what kind of fae or how powerful. As long as I'm wearing it, no fae will notice me."

"That's ... that's unbelievable." He raked his hand through his hair, pushing his hood off with the motion. *"I could test it with my familiars, figure out exactly how it works ..."* He looked up, his eyes burning into mine. *"If the spell does what you say it does, I can do it."*

"You can kill him?"

He nodded. *"He relies on them to watch me. I can slip away using your artifact, and while they're searching for me, I can kill him."*

"And I can kill my aunt with your poison." My brief grin faded, and I added haltingly, "And after they're dead, we could …"

He canted his head toward me. "We could what?"

"We could … band together?" I blew out a breath. "Better than going at it alone, right? I mean … if you want to."

"Like … long-term?"

I forced myself to nod, my shoulders hunching with uncertainty. Why would he want to saddle himself with someone like me? What did I have to offer? We barely knew each other. We hadn't even exchanged names.

"I …" He rolled his shoulders. "I like that idea."

A sharp edge of hope embedded itself in my lungs. "You do?"

"Yeah."

My cheeks flushed. I hastily looked around for a distraction, then grabbed his wrist. "How's the cut?"

I turned his hand over, surprised by how much bigger it was than mine, with long, strong fingers. I peered between his ring and middle fingers, finding a rough, pinkish ridge where I'd cut him. A scar.

"Sorry," I muttered guiltily.

He laughed. "A memento, I guess."

"You don't need a memento of me. We're going to stick together, right?"

"Right."

I looked up at him. "We are … aren't we?"

His lips curved, a small smile that struck me like lightning, electrifying my nerve endings. "Yeah. Together."

My fingers tightened reflexively around his hand. "Then I guess we should, you know, introduce ourselves. My name is—"

"Wait." His free hand came up, fingers pressing against my lips to stop me. "Not yet."

"Then … when?" I asked in confusion.

He hesitated, his eyes moving across my face. "After they're dead. A reward."

My brow furrowed.

"I need something to look forward to," he whispered.

His fingertips drifted from my mouth to my cheek. My heart drummed against my ribs as I tilted my face up. He leaned down, his breath warm against my lips. A shiver of anticipation rolled over me, and I closed my eyes.

16

MY EYES FLEW OPEN as Ríkr's telepathic voice pierced my consciousness.

There is an intensely conceited bird on my roof, he complained loudly. *There is an unduly imperious horse in my pasture. There are two fractionally less overbearing canines in my yard. And there is an extravagantly tempting druid asleep on my sofa.*

I squinted blearily, the fading dregs of my dream swimming through my head. "Tempting?"

The heady scent of his power is making me dizzy with thirst. I am a dormant shrub in the driest desert, and he is the first rain of the monsoons. His allure is like the kiss of summer sunlight after—

"Get a grip, Ríkr," I groaned. As my vision cleared, I spotted the shapeshifter—sitting on my nightstand in cat form, his ears bent sideways in displeasure. "Or are you practicing your druid pickup lines?"

His back arched with irritation. *You have no concept of how delectable druid power is.*

"You're right, I don't." I yawned good and long, then grabbed my phone. The clock read 4:58 a.m. and I switched off my five o'clock alarm. "What's so special about druid power? He's just an extra powerful witch, right?"

Ríkr grunted crankily, and I rolled my eyes. He wasn't a morning fae.

Witches, he began in an impatient, lofty tone, *possess a well of spiritual energy that they can harmonize with the energies of nature. They then attempt to manipulate the latter by shaping the former.*

"Yes, I know all that." He was describing witch rituals. The witch patterned her power to match the flow of the earth's energy, then shifted her energy to a new pattern, causing the other energies to move with it. It required a lot of "instinct" and "natural ability," which I lacked. The witch bloodline must not run strong in my family.

I pulled my hair free from the topknot I'd slept in and combed my fingers through it. My nose wrinkled as a distinctly equine musk perfumed the air. I'd intended to shower before sleeping, but after Zak had taken over my living room, I'd gone straight to bed. Now I'd have to change my sheets.

Druids, Ríkr continued, *are the opposite. Their power is so intense and commanding that nature's energies seek to harmonize with them.*

My hands paused, fingers tangled in my hair.

A druid's aura is infectious to the very land. All that exists around him harmonizes with his energy, spreading outward, multiplying his presence. If he is calm, serenity blankets the pastures. If he is angry, restless energies cascade across the fields.

"Wait, across the *fields*? That far?"

The longer he is here, the more his presence spreads. Ríkr's tail lashed. *Nomadic druids are rare. Usually, they choose a territory and allow the land to harmonize deeply with them, increasing their influence over it and the fae who flock to them.*

I lowered my arms. Was Zak nomadic, or merely … on a business trip?

Ríkr bared his sharp feline teeth. *I want to devour his energy as much as I want to chase him out of my territory before it becomes his.*

"No devouring," I muttered. "I don't think his bird, horse, and dog pals would like that."

Ríkr grumbled wordlessly.

Swinging my legs off the bed, I stretched my calves, the muscles tight after yesterday's hike, then pulled my sweatpants on. With a selection of clean clothes tucked under my arm, I cracked my door open and peeked out.

Predawn light cast a bluish tinge through the main room, illuminating the druid stretched out on my sofa, one leg hanging off. He was too tall for it and probably painfully uncomfortable, but with an arm slung over his face to block out the slowly increasing light, he seemed to be fast asleep.

I tiptoed to the bathroom and locked myself in. My shower was quick but hot, and as I massaged shampoo into my scalp, I tried to recall the dream Ríkr had interrupted. Jagged flashes of a dark alley assaulted me, coming on a wave of anguished fury that left me breathless, and I abandoned the attempt.

Out of the shower, I blow-dried my hair. My thick bangs needed trimming, the severe line falling below my eyebrows, and I squinched my eyes in a vain attempt to lessen the intensity of my pale blue-gray stare.

Zak was still sleeping—or attempting to sleep—when I exited the bathroom. I debated waking him up and kicking him out, but he'd looked so tired yesterday that I wondered how much rest he'd gotten in the past few days.

Leaving him be, I slipped out of my suite, down the stairs, and out into the chill dawn air. I might have a druid in my living room, a killer on my mountain, and MagiPol agents lurking around my coven, but I also had responsibilities I couldn't ignore.

By the time I finished my morning chores, the sun was properly up and I had less than fifteen minutes to get ready for work. I stumped back up the stairs to my suite, and when I opened my front door, the rich aroma of coffee met me like a warm embrace. Zak leaned against the tiny stretch of counter in my kitchenette, the percolating coffeemaker and two mugs beside him. Ríkr was perched on the back of the sofa, now in hawk form with his feathers ruffled grumpily.

"How do you take your coffee?" the druid rumbled, his voice rougher than usual from sleep.

"Black."

"Fitting."

As he poured two cups, I hastened into the bathroom to plug in my straightening iron, then brushed past him into my bedroom. Emerging again dressed in pale blue scrubs, I accepted the mug he offered and carried it into the bathroom, leaving the door open.

"So, what's the plan?" I asked, taking a steaming sip.

"It looks like you're going to work."

I tugged my hair out of its messy bun and swiftly brushed it. "I faked a family emergency yesterday. I can't miss again."

He leaned against the doorjamb. "Then see if you can find anything about that dead palomino, or stories of people's pets dying unexpectedly."

Wielding the straightening iron, I smoothed the kinks out of my hair. It didn't take much; my hair was deeply opposed to any form of curl. "What about you?"

"I'm interested in your coven leader's death and what that might have to do with—"

"Don't even think about going near my coven," I threatened. My original plan to sic the MPD on him for Arla's death was no longer viable. If he went anywhere near my coven, and the MagiPol agents investigating it, I'd end up sent to the gallows right along with him, mistaken for his accomplice. I never should've let him in my home.

He watched me run another lock of hair through the straightening iron. "I can head back up the mountain to check out the trails we think the killer followed, but I'm running low on supplies. Do you have a vehicle?"

"The white and teal truck is mine."

"Can I borrow it?"

"I need it to get to work."

"I'll ride with you to your clinic and return the truck by lunch."

I unplugged the iron, then squinted at his reflection in the mirror. Tilliag could carry him most places, but a horse galloping through city streets would attract attention. And while the fae stallion seemed capable of vanishing at will, he was actually crossing into the fae demesne when he disappeared. That wasn't a place he could take his rider—at least, not for longer than a few minutes, as Ríkr had once explained.

"You're a fugitive," I pointed out. "You can't just walk around grocery stores like a regular person, can you?"

"The chances I'll run into a bounty hunter or MagiPol agent in Coquitlam are minuscule. Even if I did, they aren't likely to recognize me, especially since the MPD is convinced I'm in Victoria."

"Victoria? Why?"

He smirked. "Because that's what I want them to think."

Ire tugged at the corners of my mouth. "If you leave my truck at the clinic, how will you get back out here?"

"I'll manage."

He was less likely to draw attention driving my truck than hitchhiking, stealing a vehicle, or riding his fae horse down the highway. Grunting my permission, I grabbed my mug and gulped down my coffee.

A few minutes later, my old truck was speeding down Cedar Drive toward Coquitlam, Zak in the passenger seat and Ríkr sulking on the floor behind my seat in feline form. It was that or sit on Zak's lap. The druid and I discussed our incomprehensible collection of information again, but we were just going in circles. The killer was probably a fae. That was all we had.

My vet clinic was part of a small strip mall on the west side of Coquitlam. I warily scanned the parking lot for signs of lurking MPD agents, but the only vehicles belonged to the staff. Pulling up in the front, I left the keys in the ignition and instructed Zak on where to park when he returned.

As the clinic door swung shut, I realized Ríkr hadn't followed me inside. Had he stayed in the truck to snoop on the druid? I wished he'd stayed, just in case MagiPol made an appearance later.

"Morning, Saber!" Kaitlynn greeted brightly. "Missed you yesterday. Not feeling well?"

It took me a moment to pull up my cheery smile. The expression felt more fake than usual. "No, I had a family emergency, but everything is under control now."

"Oh." Her expression softened with sympathy. "Glad to hear it's nothing too serious."

"A family emergency?" Nicolette appeared from the back hall, her hair done in a neat bun and makeup thick on her face. She stared at me as though waiting for me to elaborate.

"Good morning, Nicolette," I said warmly. "You look good today."

"Thanks," she muttered as I passed her, heading for the staff room.

Falling into my usual routine was difficult, and I twitched every time the clinic door jingled. Would the MPD show up here? They didn't like making a scene in front of humans, who had no idea that magic or magical police existed.

My morning disappeared in a fast-paced blur as I dove into my first task—prepping a young female cat for a spay. I monitored her throughout the surgery, got her into recovery, then rushed straight into anesthetizing a big, leggy Great Dane puppy and shaving his belly for a foreign body surgery to remove half a teddy bear he'd eaten.

With my stomach complaining about how long it'd been since dinner last night, I hurriedly cleaned the surgery room and scrubbed the instruments down, my last task before my lunch break. Voices rumbled through the wall, coming from the reception area, and I hoped my one o'clock nail-trim appointment wasn't early.

The door behind me burst open, and Kaitlynn hung in the threshold, her eyes wide. "Saber!"

Tension slammed through me. "What?"

She leaned farther in and lowered her voice to an emphatic hush. "Who is the absolutely *divine* male specimen asking for you at reception?"

I blinked.

"He's gorgeous. *Gorgeous.* Are you dating him? Can *I* date him?"

My brow furrowed. "Don't you have a boyfriend?"

"For that man, I could very quickly not have a boyfriend."

Frown deepening, I set my bottle of disinfectant on the counter and followed her down the short hall. Together, we peeked around the corner into the rectangular reception area.

Nicolette, two other techs, and one of the female vets were crammed behind the long counter, smiling like idiots. Nicolette and the vet had flushed cheeks.

Zak waited near the door. He wore the same sleeveless black shirt and jeans he'd slept in, and if his dark hair had been combed, it'd been with his fingers—but his rumpled, slightly disreputable air wasn't affecting the women's opinions of him.

Well, at least it wasn't an MPD agent.

I stepped out of the hall. He turned to me, his green eyes arresting in their intensity, and I felt the women's gazes swing toward me as well. Acutely aware of my audience, I forced my scowl into a welcoming smile as I walked over to him.

His eyebrows shifted upward at my warm expression.

"Hi!" I greeted him. Unless I whispered, there was no way my voice wouldn't carry across the room. The others weren't even pretending not to listen in. "Get your errands done?"

"Yeah." He held out my keys, and I took them, still smiling. His eyebrows crept even higher, and I felt a muted rush of heat in my cheeks. I'd been playing "nice" Saber for years, and this was the first time I'd felt stupid doing it.

"Wasn't sure if you needed lunch," he added, lifting his hand. A white grocery bag hung from his fingers. "Hopefully there's something in here you'll like."

My smile slipped with surprise, and I hesitated before taking the bag. "Uh … thanks."

"I'll be back later tonight," he murmured, his gaze flicking to our audience. He didn't ask if he could spend the night again, but I heard the question.

"Okay," I said, hitching my bright smile back into place. "See you later."

His eyebrows rose again, their movement corresponding to my level of cheeriness—the more chipper I was, the more dubious he looked.

He abruptly leaned in close. His warm breath stirred my hair over my ear as he whispered, "Am I the sole recipient of your real temper, then? Not sure if I'm flattered or disappointed."

"Go fuck yourself," I whispered back in a sugary tone.

He laughed as he straightened. "That's more like it. See you tonight."

Holding my "nice Saber" smile in place had never been so difficult as he crossed to the door. I watched through the large front windows as he strode through the parking lot to the street.

Behind me, female sighs filled the reception.

"Saber, Saber," Hailey, one of the techs, chanted reverently. "Spill the beans. Please. I'm dying here."

I turned to her. "Sorry?"

"Where did you find him and how long have you been together?" She pretended to swoon. "Oh man. So rugged and, like …"

"Bad boy, except he's *all man*," Kaitlynn finished, appearing from the hallway. "So? What's his name?"

"He—he's not my, uh, partner." I struggled to pull my thoughts together. "He's … a volunteer at the rescue."

They all knew I was a longtime volunteer of Hearts & Hooves Animal Rescue. I waited for their curiosity to evaporate.

"Not your man *yet*," the vet laughed. "He's all eyes for you, hon. And that kiss on the cheek may have been chaste, but it was a lot more than friendly."

"He didn't—"

Hailey fanned herself. "If you aren't sure about him, I volunteer to take him for a test ride. Several test rides."

The others laughed.

My smile had fallen away and I couldn't bring it back. "He's not a rollercoaster."

Hailey froze. "Huh?"

"Would you like it if a man came in here and talked about you like that?" I snapped.

The five women stared at me.

"Sorry," Hailey said quietly, her amusement gone. "I was just joking."

"It's not funny." I swept to the exit. "I'm going for lunch."

The door swung shut behind me, and I stood on the sidewalk for a moment before marching away from the clinic. At the far end of the strip mall, a tiny patch of grass surrounded one lonely tree. I sank down, using the trunk as a backrest, and closed my eyes.

In my four years at the vet clinic, I'd never broken character, but one visit from Zak had me lashing out over pointless banter about a good-looking man. How much damage had I done to my reputation as a cheerful, good-natured helper?

I exhaled slowly. As I relaxed against the tree, a discordant twist of energy rubbed across my senses. Man-made structures, concrete, pollution. They stifled and contaminated natural energies. It's the reason fae rarely ventured into cities.

Eyes opening, I started humming, a gentle tune that reminded me of green meadows and soft, warm breezes. The tree's welcoming shade sheltered me from the noon sun as I opened the plastic bag and peered inside. A vegan salad full of veggies and nuts, a ham and cheese sandwich, and a cup of broccoli cream soup, all from a nearby grocery store.

Saving the soup since I had no way to warm it up, I ate the sandwich and salad. It was a better lunch than I would've picked out for myself.

As I scooped vinaigrette-coated nuts from the bottom of the salad container, a white sparrow landed on my knee, snagged a cashew, and gulped it down.

A fascinating encounter, Ríkr declared, fluffing his feathers.

"What did Zak get up to?" I asked.

He went to the shop where you often purchase items for hiking, and to the grocer. He also refilled the fuel in your truck.

Why was a notorious rogue with a million-dollar bounty on his head so damn considerate? It was bewildering.

"That doesn't sound fascinating," I muttered.

It wasn't. The encounter at your clinic is what fascinates me. He fluttered down to the grass and transformed into a cat. After peering at the lonely tree behind me in an oddly critical way, his piercing blue eyes turned to my face. *What do you think of the druid, Saber? Your true thoughts.*

"He's ... not what I expected." I stirred the last few nuts around with my plastic fork. "I suspect I haven't seen his full power yet. He's more dangerous than he lets on, but he's also ... not ..."

Not evil. Not heartless. Not unnecessarily violent—at least, not that I'd seen. He genuinely cared about the deaths of wildlife and fae, and he'd gone out of his way to protect me without asking for anything in return.

How did a man like that end up with a one-point-three-million-dollar bounty on his head?

"I think there's another side to him," I finally said. "So far, I've seen the Crystal Druid, but he's also called the Ghost—and that's the alias that earned all the charges against him."

Ríkr's tail lashed from side to side. *That's my clever dove.*

Snorting quietly, I shook my head. "Were you worried I was going soft on him?"

I was concerned a deceptive and alluring manipulator was spinning a hidden web that you could not perceive.

Packing my recyclables into the grocery bag with my uneaten soup, I rose to my feet. I couldn't be sure whether Zak was spinning webs, but I did know there was much more to the Crystal Druid for me to unveil.

THE CLINIC was closed and the others had gone home for the night. One vet remained, completing paperwork in her office, while I finished the last of the cleaning. No MPD agents had made an appearance, and I wasn't sure whether that was a good thing. They were in the area. Maybe they were collecting more evidence before arresting me.

I didn't dare hope they lacked sufficient evidence to arrest me.

My thoughts all afternoon had fluctuated between MagiPol paranoia and pointless analysis of Zak and his true nature, whatever that might be. It hadn't helped that every time I'd walked into a room, the other techs had been whispering about "Saber's hot boyfriend."

Hot. Gorgeous. Rugged. Hunk. Man-candy. All words they'd been tossing around.

I chewed my lower lip as I tidied up the cleaning supplies. They weren't wrong. His features were striking. Beautiful even, and he exuded a magnetism that was difficult to explain. Plus, he was tall, broad-shouldered, and muscular, with a commanding physical presence almost as strong as his druidic aura.

My phone buzzed in my pocket. Grateful for the distraction, I pulled it out, glanced at the caller ID, and answered, "Hi Dominique."

"Saber." She sounded troubled. "You know how you asked about the necropsy for Harvey Whitby's palomino?"

I shut the storage room door, enclosing myself inside. "Yes."

"The vet doing it called me. He was tracking down the new owner of Harvey's other horses."

"He was? Why?"

"He'd just finished the necropsy, and ..." She gulped as though to steady herself. "He said the horse's heart was ... gone."

Adrenaline spiked in my blood.

"The vet opened the horse up, and the coronary arteries and veins just ... 'shriveled up to nothing,' is what he said. The heart was missing entirely. But that—that's *impossible*." She laughed shrilly, then cut herself off with a cough. "He swears the horse's chest cavity was intact, with no damage or anything that would suggest the heart had been removed."

I stared at the wall, seeing the small herd of dead bucks in my mind's eye. Seeing Arla slumped over her desk.

"The vet wants me to bring the other two horses in for chest x-rays. He's theorizing about some sort of crazy new virus that attacks heart tissue, but he probably just messed up the necropsy somehow. Maybe he missed a wound or ... something."

How could an experienced vet fail to notice a wound large enough to extract ten pounds of muscle and arteries from the horse's chest?

"Anyway," she said weakly, "thought I'd fill you in since you were asking about it. Were you expecting something like this?"

"No." My voice was almost as thin as hers. "I wasn't expecting this at all."

A short pause. "Will you be home in time for dinner? Greta is making *maultaschen* dumplings."

A shimmering flash of white in my peripheral vision. Feline-form Ríkr trotted through the closed door, probably sensing my distress. His gaze lifted questioningly.

"I can't," I replied, my voice hoarsening. "There's something I need to do this evening."

"All right. I'll save you some, so just grab it out of the fridge when you get home."

"Thanks. By the way, did those men in suits come back today?"

"No, no one was here except Colby for a few hours."

"Okay. See you later, Dominique."

"Take care, Saber."

I disconnected the call and my arm fell to my side. My pulse thudded in my ears, blood rushing. Dread roiled through me, wavering dangerously close to outright fear.

*Saber?*Ríkr prompted.

"The killer is stealing hearts," I whispered. "The palomino's heart was gone. That's how all the animals and fae have died."

He was silent for a moment, then concluded, *And that is how Arla died.*

"Yes, and the MPD knows it. That's why they're investigating ... and that's why they haven't tried to interview me yet. They think I killed her with some kind of dark, heart-vanishing magic, and they'd don't want to set me off. Maybe they missed me on purpose yesterday."

They are dancing around you, Ríkr mused. *Keeping you in their sights without cornering you.*

How could the MPD be so naïve as to think a *witch* could wield magic capable of stealing someone's heart from their chest without inflicting a wound? That wasn't the kind of magic fae gifted to anyone.

Was there any way to prove my innocence? How long until the agents moved against me? Zak and I still had no clues, no strong leads.

But we knew the killer had targeted Arla. Had she known something significant enough for them to consider her a threat? If she had, I needed to know what.

Lifting my phone again, I pulled up the new listing in my contacts called "CD." Crystal Druid. We'd exchanged numbers before he'd taken my truck, and I was now glad we had. He was back out on the forested slopes of Mount Burke, searching for more clues, and he needed to know what we were dealing with sooner rather than later. I typed a brief message.

```
I found out how the palomino died. The
killer is definitely a fae. Contact me as
soon as you have reception.
```

I hit send, stuffed my phone in my pocket, then paused. Jaw tightening, I yanked my phone back out, typed two more words, and sent them before I could overthink it.

```
Be careful.
```

Jamming my phone into my pocket again, I swept out of the storage room, Ríkr trotting at my heels. We had no time to waste.

17

I DROVE THROUGH the privacy hedge around Arla's property, and my shoulders stiffened with new tension. A row of cars was parked in front of the house, bathed in the golden beams of the evening sun.

The coven had gathered—and no one had told me.

A bad sign.

Coven meetings always took place outside unless the weather was poor. The witches were probably in the trees somewhere. I might have enough time to get in and out before they returned.

I backed my truck up behind Laney's silver Prius, ensuring I could make a quick escape. "Ríkr, can you find the coven and warn me when they head back this way?"

The white cat on my passenger seat slanted his ears sideways. *Leave it to me.*

I opened my door and he leaped over my legs, landing on the gravel drive outside. He took two bounding leaps, then transformed into a screech owl and flew toward the trees. As he disappeared, I reached under the driver's seat and pulled out a small lock-picking kit. I suspected Laney had deleted my access code for the lock, but even if she hadn't, I didn't intend to use it.

Calm quiet lay over the property as I went to work on the front bolt. I twisted the tiny wrench, the bolt turned, and then I was inside.

The house was dead silent. I stood in the entryway for a long moment, listening, then ghosted down the hall. The kitchen and living room appeared empty; no one was home. My boots were silent on the carpeted stairs as I headed up. The door to Arla's office was closed. I'd half expected it to be barricaded with police tape.

I tugged a handkerchief from my pocket and covered my hand before trying the handle. Locked. It took two seconds to pop the lock, then I swung the door open. A wave of reeking air hit me in the face. Laney hadn't cleaned up.

My gaze skimmed the room as I stepped inside. As far as I could see, nothing had been touched. Had the MPD been through here? Or were they waiting for a future stage of the investigation?

The empty desk chair drew my focus like a magnet. Despite the countless times I'd seen Arla sitting in that chair, alive and well, all I could see now was her limp body slumped in it.

I nudged the chair out of the way and faced the desk. A framed photo from last summer, Arla's large glasses slipping down her nose and Laney's natural brown hair curly with a perm she'd hated the moment she'd gotten it done, sat beside the monitor. Using my hanky to keep my fingerprints off any surfaces, I wiggled the mouse to wake the machine. The screens blinked awake, revealing a login screen.

Her computer was locked? When I'd found her body, the screens had been glowing with a map of the crossroads valley and Zak's bounty listing. I clicked in the password box, the cursor blinking expectantly, but I couldn't even guess.

Giving up on the computer, I shuffled through the items on her desk. There wasn't much—bills, reminders, MPD paperwork, and an agenda book. What had I expected? A folder labeled "Suspicious Fae Activity"? Pushing my loose hair off my shoulders and fighting my hot frustration, I stepped back. Should I check the closet?

Using my hanky, I rolled Arla's chair back into the spot where I'd found it. The wheel caught, grinding on something.

I crouched. On the stained floor beneath the chair, a gold chain was caught under the wheel. Lifting it, I slid the object out. A heart-shaped locket. I pried it open and squinted at the two tiny photos inside: Laney and a vaguely familiar man.

Tension prickled through me. I didn't know why, but I was suddenly certain that I needed to leave. I slid the locket into my back pocket, then sped across the office and closed the door, ensuring it was locked as I'd found it. Back down the stairs. Along the hall. I slipped out the front door and locked it as well, glancing over my shoulder for any sign of Ríkr.

Three steps away from my truck, I pulled up short as a voice spoke.

"Returning to the scene of your crimes, Saber?"

Around the corner of the house, the entire coven stood in the shadows, watching me. Short, heavyset Deanna held a shimmering green orb the size of a beach ball in her hands, and inside it, a snow-white owl glared with furious blue eyes. Her pixie familiar sat on top of the orb, her dragonfly wings fluttering for balance and her tiny hands glowing as she maintained the magic that had captured Ríkr.

Laney stepped to the front of the group, glowering at me with unmitigated hatred.

"Trying to clean up the crime scene?" she asked venomously. "Or did you come to rob me now that you've killed my mother?"

"I didn't kill her," I said automatically.

Laney's features contorted with rage and grief. "I found you standing over her body!"

"Why would I kill—"

"Save it, Saber." She drew herself up, her tone shifting to one of command. "As acting guild master of the Coquitlam Coven, I am detaining you on suspicion of killing Arla Collins."

"*You* are detaining me?"

"If you didn't do it"—her lip curled in a skeptical sneer—"then you have nothing to worry about. You can stand trial in front of your fellow witches and prove your innocence."

A sharp, twitchy feeling rolled down my back and through my limbs. "Stand trial? What the hell are you talking about?"

"The coven is putting you on trial for murder," Laney said coldly. She gestured at the witches standing with her. "We've all agreed that we deserve the truth. You'll stand before us first, then we'll present our findings to the MPD."

Scarcely able to believe what I was hearing, I scanned the coven's faces and realized Pierce wasn't with them. *He* wouldn't have agreed to this insanity.

I flicked a glance over my shoulder. My truck was right behind me. I could leave—but I couldn't abandon Ríkr.

"Let my familiar go," I said flatly.

"You were hiding his powers." Laney waved at the green sphere trapping him. "You never once said he could shapeshift."

"Why does that matter?" I looked to Ellen, the most senior coven member. "You can't seriously support this. A witch trial?"

The elderly witch, who'd always been friendly before now, peered down her nose at me like I was grimy slug in her garden. "I'm wondering why an innocent witch is protesting the chance to show her coven that she isn't responsible for a heinous crime."

My hands curled into fists. I was innocent, but I couldn't prove it. I couldn't prove anything. I couldn't even explain why I was here. They'd probably watched me pick the front lock and enter the house like a thief.

With that thought, I realized nothing I said, now or during their "trial," would convince them I wasn't a killer.

People knew. They could sense that I was dangerous. That I was capable of violence. No matter how nice I acted, the best I could do was make them second guess what their instincts were telling them—and at the slightest confirmation, they always turned on me.

Seven years as a member of their coven, and this was all it had taken for them to label me an enemy.

"You killed your aunt ten years ago," Laney declared, a faint tremor tainting her words. "And you killed my mother. You'll stand before the coven and confess your crimes, then the MPD will convict you—and execute you."

My chest filled with shards of bloody glass, shredding my lungs with each breath I took. Shards. Shattered pieces. The broken remains of who I might've been had life been different. The sharp, gouging remnants of a functioning human being.

The snap of my switchblade extending rang through the silence. I didn't recall drawing it from my pocket.

"I didn't kill Arla." My voice was low, husky. "But if you don't release my familiar, you'll find out what happens when I actually want someone dead."

Laney's face went white. "You wouldn't dare—"

My feet moved. I was walking toward her. Gliding. The air shivered around me, and a soft hum escaped my lips—the first notes of a haunting old Irish melody.

They were backing away. They were afraid. Finally, they were afraid. I didn't have to play at being someone else. I didn't have to hide my teeth, pretend, fake every word and expression.

I smiled, and it wasn't the "nice Saber" smile. It was my real one. The one that found its way across my lips when the blood rushed in my veins and I felt alive. I felt powerful. I felt like *myself*, not a stupid, vapid, declawed fake.

"Release him," I suggested, the words crooning.

Laney lurched back into Nina. "Ungel!"

At her cry, a bright orange lizard the size of an iguana appeared on her shoulder. His bright yellow eyes flashed as he raised his head, his throat bulging. He spat a mouthful of flame.

As the sparks scattered through the air, they swelled into the shape of fiery butterflies. Tiny wings fluttering, the swarm rushed toward me. I coiled to dive beneath them—and the air beside me shimmered as a waist-high shape appeared.

Ellen's stocky hob slammed into my side, grabbing hold of my left leg. He wrapped his thick arms around my thigh and squeezed. I tried to wrench away, but despite his size, he was powerful and heavy. His pupilless brown eyes stared up at me as he crushed my leg, holding me in place as the swarm of burning butterflies closed in. Heat washed over me, fast growing painful.

As the fluttering, flaming wings formed into a fiery dome, Laney called shakily, "You *will* stand trial in front of this coven, Saber. We aren't giving you a choice."

Spinning my knife in my hand, I coiled my arm to drive the blade into the hob's face.

The writhing swarm of flaming butterflies rushed toward me, their heat scorching my skin—and a gust of wind blasted over me, snuffing out the fiery insects. Unnatural gloom dimmed the evening sun, drenching the yard in deep shadows.

The air cooled, the darkness thickened, and power buzzed across my senses—familiar power. The flow of energy through the earth twisted as a fae moved from the ethereal demesne and into the physical plane.

Shadows coiled in front of me, then solidified into a … a woman.

Around my height. Porcelain skin. Silky raven hair that swept down her back to her knees, the locks drifting around her as though a gentle breeze were caressing her. Silky garments clung to her curvaceous figure and left her smooth midriff and flat stomach exposed. The layers in her long skirt revealed glimpses of lean, graceful legs.

Her inhuman emerald eyes moved across my face, then turned down to the hob clinging to my leg.

"Move," she commanded in a throaty purr.

The hob released me and scrambled backward, his thick features contorted with fear. Her full red lips curved into a pleased smile. Her hands floated up, the movement dripping grace.

"Stop!" Laney shouted. "You can't—"

The fae woman lay cool hands on my shoulders.

Power rushed over me, a tingling weightlessness, and the world dissolved into mist and shadow. Laney and the rest of the coven turned to dim silhouettes that kept fading. The house and trees shimmered into dark semi-transparency, and pale fog swirled and eddied around me. A soft rushing noise filled my ears.

Holding my shoulders, the fae asked, "Are you harmed?"

"No." My voice sounded oddly deadened, as though I were in a soundproof room.

"Excellent." The corners of her mouth lifted into a wider smile, and she leaned so close our lips almost touched. "Then I have no need to waste energy punishing pathetic witches over an even more wretchedly pathetic witch."

I stiffened, but she was already leaning back. Her hand slid down my arm in a caressing touch, and she entwined our fingers. As the world dissolved into deeper mist and shadows, she pulled me into a leisurely walk.

The coven and the house had disappeared. My shoes made no sound on the gravel drive; I couldn't see my own feet, eddies of mist hiding everything below my knees.

As we walked into the shadows of the trees, they grew solid again—but not like I had ever seen trees before. Their bark shone iridescently, as though dusted with fairy powder, and their leaves, electric green with bluish undersides, glimmered and winked as a faint breeze teased them.

I wasn't merely *looking* into the fae demesne. I was walking in it.

The beautiful fae woman led me deeper into the trees, then halted and again faced me. Still holding my hand in hers, she reached up with the other to touch my cheek, her finger tipped with a curved black talon.

"This should be far enough. You may escape under your power from this point." Her talon pricked the underside of my jaw as she tipped my face up. "Though I would find it more entertaining to slit your pretty throat instead."

My switchblade was still clenched in my hand, but I didn't raise it. "Then why did you help me?"

She leaned in again, bringing her face obscenely close. Her mouth touched mine, but I held my ground, not giving her the satisfaction of recoiling.

"My druid bid me to find you after reading your message. He suspected you would be in danger." Her wet tongue brushed over my lower lip. "Your power is sweet, little witch, despite the pitiably scant amount you possess."

With a flash of white wings, Ríkr landed on my shoulder. *Taste her again, vulture, and I will shatter your flesh into a thousand shards.*

His voice rolled through my mind in a savage, frozen snarl that sent a shiver across my skin. In the white mist of the fae realm, swirls of pale blue light radiated from his feathers.

The female fae laughed softly. She pulled her hand away from my throat, and I felt a sharp sting. A drop of my blood clung to her talon, and her pink tongue appeared, licking it away. Then she released my other hand.

Sunlight plunged through the mist-shrouded trees, evaporating the haze. The heavy weight of my body returned in a rush and my ears popped, sound filling them as the bizarre hush of the fae demesne lifted. I swayed dizzily, taking in the solid trunks of old pine trees around me.

The Lady of Shadow was gone, leaving the soft scent of night-cool wildflowers behind.

I turned with careful steps, Ríkr perched on my shoulder. The glow of the evening sun lit Laney's house, fifty yards away. Voices drifted to my ears, raised, emphatic. Laney's piercing shout erupted, the words unintelligible.

Zak's eagle familiar had pulled me into the fae demesne, out of reach of humans or witches, and led me into the trees where I could escape without being seen. It was similar to how Tilliag could disappear with Zak, but I doubted the fae stallion took his rider as far from human reality as the Lady of Shadow had taken me.

I couldn't see my sturdy old truck through the foliage, but that didn't matter. I wouldn't be reclaiming it. At least I'd taken my lockpicks, the only condemning item in it, with me. I was done with the vehicle—and I was done with my coven.

Turning on my heel, I headed deeper into the woods.

18

LALLAKAI.

According to Ríkr, that was the fae woman's name. She was also known as the Night Eagle and Lady of Shadow. An old, powerful fae, and one I didn't need threatening to slit my throat.

Deep shadows lurked in the forest as I cut cross-country toward home, navigating by the evening sunlight streaking through the forest canopy. Ríkr, now in ferret form, rode on my shoulder.

I apologize, dove, he murmured. *I was careless, and the pixie surprised me.*

"Not your fault." If there was blame to assign, it was mine.

As I walked, I watched my hands swing in and out of my peripheral vision. These hands. Was there anything they wouldn't do? If Lallakai hadn't come, would I have killed Ellen's familiar? Would I have hurt or killed my fellow witches?

I half closed my eyes, searching my emotions for ... *something*. But all I could feel were the broken pieces inside me grinding, grinding, grinding. I wanted to go back. I wanted to hurt Laney for turning the coven against me and I wanted to hurt the rest of them for believing her.

Even though their accusations and suspicions were logical, and I'd done nothing to change their minds, I still wanted to hurt them.

I was so fucked up.

Moisture clung to my eyelashes. Why couldn't I be normal? I tried to fit in. I tried so damn hard.

Golden light bloomed as I stepped out of the dense woods and into Hearts & Hooves' orchard.

Wait here, dove, Ríkr told me as he transformed into a speedy white starling. *I will check for unwelcome visitors.*

He zoomed away, and I waited obediently, my lower lip caught between my teeth. Had Laney told MagiPol that I'd broken into her house and attacked the coven? Or did she not want the agents knowing she'd attacked me first? Did she want a chance to condemn me herself before I was arrested and whisked out of her reach? How important was my confession of guilt to her?

As long as Ríkr deemed it safe, I wanted to maintain my usual routine. However guilty I might look to Laney and MagiPol, I was innocent. The best thing I could do for myself right now was act like an innocent person. Suspicious behavior would only work against me.

You may come, Ríkr called to me from somewhere near the house. *Only Dominique and Greta are here.*

I hastened between apple trees, my gaze dragging across the house on the far side of the yard. Dominique and Greta had saved food for me, but I couldn't go in there right now. Not in this kind of mood.

Swerving, I strode to the rear of the stable and up to my apartment. It took me a few minutes to freshen up and change, then I was jogging back down the stairs, dressed in jeans and a black t-shirt several sizes too large, with my hair roughly tied in a high ponytail. Ríkr, perched on the stable's roof, watched me head toward the fields.

An hour later, I was lying on my back in the far pasture, cool grass beneath me and the sun hanging low in the west.

Houdini the goat was lying beside me, vapidly chewing a mouthful of grass. Two more goats wandered nearby, and Fluffball the sheep was nosing at my boot. Hippy and Funko, our rescued racehorses, were grazing off to my left.

A butterscotch-brown muzzle appeared above me, blocking my view of the sky. Pip, a sorrel draft horse, snuffled at my bangs, wondering why the silly human was lying on the ground. I rubbed his nose, then closed my eyes. The animals' energies drifted around me, calm and peaceful as they entwined with the softer energy of the pasture. I might be weak and incompetent, but nature and its creatures calmed me as much as any other witch.

Pip ruffled my bangs, then lipped at my nose. Eyes still closed, I gently pushed his head away. "If you bite my nose, we're gonna have words, Pip."

He blew hot, stinky grass breath over my face, then his shadow moved away. I heard his hoof scraping at the ground, followed by a grunt and a thump. Opening my eyes, I tilted my head back to see him. He was rolling enthusiastically in the grass. Well, if the human was doing it, why not him?

I patted Houdini's side and relaxed again. Once you earned an animal's trust, it was yours until you betrayed it. Often, it was yours even long after you'd betrayed it—and that was why I loathed animal abusers so deeply.

This place was my haven. I couldn't let Laney and the MPD take it away from me. Somehow, I had to keep hold of it.

The setting sun was staining the scattered clouds pink and gold by the time I felt centered again. As I sat up, the animals lingering around me stiffened with alertness, all looking in the same direction—toward the forested mountain to the north.

A dark horse and rider cantered toward the pasture fence. The stallion jumped the barrier in an easy bound, then stretched into a pounding gallop toward me. The rescue animals scattered, but I glimpsed the shape of a white bird in a distant tree—Ríkr keeping watch.

I pushed to my feet, brushed the grass off my jeans, and straightened my shirt, which was hanging off one shoulder.

Tilliag slowed his headlong gallop, then thundered to a halt a few feet away. His rider, still in a sleeveless shirt that displayed his muscular arms, looked down at me with vividly green, human eyes, his backpack hanging off his broad shoulders.

"Are you okay?" he asked sharply.

I gazed up at the druid. "I'm fine."

"You were on the ground."

"Yeah. Relaxing. I do that once in a while."

His eyes narrowed. "Lallakai said she found you in trouble with your coven."

"I didn't need help."

"That's not what she said." He gave his head a slight shake. "What did you find out about the palomino's death?"

THE ONE AND ONLY CRYSTAL DRUID ◆ 171

My serene—sort of serene—mood soured. "I'll tell you back at my place. I haven't eaten anything since lunch."

The lunch he'd brought me. It seemed like days ago, not hours.

I started walking toward the distant orchard that concealed the farmstead. Tilliag's hooves thumped up behind me, then beside me—then an arm looped around my back and hauled me into the air.

I swore furiously as Zak pulled me onto the stallion in front of him.

"Get your leg over," he told me, holding my back against his chest.

I swung my leg over Tilliag's neck so I was straddling the horse properly. The view of the stallion was quite different from his back, and my stomach dropped when his ears swiveled toward me and his neck arched.

"Tilliag," Zak began warningly.

The stallion's muscles tensed, and he reared.

Zak released my waist as he pitched backward—letting go so he didn't drag me off with him. Clutching a double handful of mane, I scarcely noticed him slide off Tilliag's rump, my legs clamped around the horse's sides.

His front hooves slammed into the ground and his head dropped. I leaned back sharply as he kicked out with his back legs, trying to throw me—and when that failed, he launched into a full-blown rodeo routine. Rearing, plunging, bucking, he spun in circles, and I hung on through sheer stubbornness— but with each violent lurch, I lost my balance a bit more.

"Asshole!" I yelled as the stallion reared so high his body was vertical. My weakening grip gave out and I fell. Landing on my feet with my arms windmilling, I stumbled backward and fell on my ass.

Zak hastened in my direction, but I shoved to my feet before he could reach me, breathing hard and glowering at the fae horse.

Acid-green eyes studied me calmly, then the stallion turned, presenting his side.

"Tilliag," Zak growled.

She may ride me. The fae's rough voice scraped inside my head, his tone decisive.

Oh, so I'd passed his little test, had I? How nice.

His ear turned to me, and I could read the small gesture so easily. He was wondering if I was too chicken to get back on him now.

I surged toward the stallion, grabbed his mane, and launched myself up. He was so damn big that I ended up sprawled on his back before straightening myself out. Settling into place, I gripped his mane and glared ferociously at his ears.

"She's right." Zak appeared at my knee. "You're an asshole, Tilliag."

I wished to know if she was worthy.

"You've carried passengers for me before without bucking them off."

She is different.

Zak cursed under his breath, then swung up onto the horse with a lot more grace than I'd managed. His warmth pressed against my back as he reached around me to grip Tilliag's mane—the only handhold. "Let's go."

Neither he nor the horse apologized for the impromptu rodeo, but I hadn't expected them to.

Tilliag went straight into a bouncy trot, then pushed into a rolling canter. As a cool wind rushed over me, my temper slipped away. I rocked with the stallion's smooth gait, his run effortless, strength flowing through his powerful body. I'd ridden more horses than I could count, and none had ever felt like this. Power, grace, and an absolute freedom that came from the complete lack of control I had.

We were halfway across the pasture before my overwhelmed senses remembered Zak. He was pressed against my back, arms on either side of me, and he moved with his mount and with me. The three of us were in perfect harmony, and as the fence between the pasture and yard rushed toward us, I instinctively leaned forward and braced my legs. Tilliag jumped it easily, his hooves clattering on the gravel on the other side.

He slowed to a walk, and as the exhilaration of our short ride quieted, I let out a long, soft sigh. The stallion stopped.

I didn't know what made me do it, but I leaned back— leaning into Zak, my entire body relaxing, my head resting against his shoulder. I closed my eyes, breathing Tilliag's equine musk and the druid's pine scent.

Why did this feel so good?

Zak's legs flexed, subtle guidance for his mount, and Tilliag moved into an easy walk. I didn't shift, slumped against the druid, hips swiveling with the horse's steps. Gravel crunched, then Tilliag halted again. I opened my eyes to find him standing a few yards away from the stable's rear door.

Zak swung off the stallion's back, dropping to the ground. I lay a hand against Tilliag's powerful neck. Thanking fae was always risky; some took it as an admission of debt.

That was a magnificent ride, I said instead, hoping only the fae would hear my silent words and not the druid.

Tilliag's ear slanted toward me, but he didn't reply. I slid off his back, and pain twinged through my thigh where Ellen's hob had nearly crushed my leg. Tilliag tossed his head, then trotted away, leaving his two riders where they stood. He disappeared in the direction of the fruit orchard.

Shaking off my strange mood, I patted my pockets for my keys. My fingers pressed against the shape of my switchblade.

"So?" Zak rumbled from behind me.

I pulled my keys out of my other pocket.

"The palomino's death," he prompted. "You said you found out how it died. And what happened with your coven earlier?"

Had Lallakai told him about Laney's "witch trial"? Inserting my key in the lock, I shot an icy look over my shoulder. "The second one is my business."

His eyes narrowed. "We're in this together, aren't we?"

I went rigid as his words triggered a visceral surge of emotion that hit me in the chest like a runaway draft horse. I was suddenly, inexplicably vibrating with rage, grief, and a sickening terror—and I had no idea why.

"You should have waited for me," he continued. "Instead, you … what's wrong?"

My chest heaved as I struggled to contain the emotional onslaught. "We're not in *anything* together."

"What?"

Leaving my key in the lock, I pivoted to face him, my fingernails biting into my palms. I didn't understand why I was choking on rage right now, but neither could I turn off the emotions that had me in their grip.

His mouth thinned. "Did I imagine that conversation where we agreed to pool information to stop the killer slaughtering animals and fae all across the mountainside?"

"That doesn't make us partners or some shit," I spat, my clenched hands shaking.

"When did I say that? We're working together for a mutual goal, not getting engaged." He raked his hand through his hair. "But going to the coven leader's place alone was stupid. You should have—"

Surging toward him, I grabbed the front of his shirt. "I don't answer to you! I can do whatever the hell I—"

He grabbed my wrist, ripping my hand off his shirt—then shoved me back into the stable wall.

My switchblade was in my hand in the next instant. The blade snapped out and I pressed its edge to his throat, my teeth bared.

A sharp prick against my side. I hadn't seen him draw his knife, but I didn't doubt the feel of it just below my ribs.

He bared his teeth too, his face inches away. "So we're back to this, then?"

"This is more fun," I retorted viciously.

His eyes darkened, pupils dilating. His warm weight pressed into me, his chest rising and falling with each deep breath. "Do you get off on near-death experiences?"

"I get off on giving other people near-death experiences."

"I can't decide if you're a hell of a bluffer or actually a scary, bloodthirsty savage."

My voice went husky. "You think I'm scary?"

"Not if you're bluffing."

I tilted my face up, pushing into him. Pain stung my side as I leaned into his knife. "I don't bluff."

"No?" he rasped. "Are you going to slit my throat?"

"If you piss me off any more"—I twitched the knife against the soft skin under his jaw, making sure he felt it—"I might."

His warm breath teased my lips. Our faces were too close.

"*Everything* pisses you off." His voice rumbled from his chest to mine. We were both breathing a bit too hard, a bit too fast. His eyes filled my vision. Intense, unafraid. Challenging.

Hungry.

My lips parted.

My knife was at his throat, but he leaned down anyway, closing the scant buffer space between us.

Then his mouth was crushing mine.

My head thumped against the wall as he kissed me hard. I gasped, my nerves lighting up with adrenaline that drowned the emotional storm inside me. His hot tongue met mine. Kissing me even harder. Even deeper. A shudder ran through me—and I bit down on his tongue.

He jerked away with a curse. Our eyes met.

I grabbed the back of his head and yanked his face down again. As his mouth covered mine, he drove me into the wall. Our lips moved urgently, hands grabbing at each other, and heat pierced me like knives, plunging through my core and gathering between my thighs.

His fingers dug into my upper arms. He had both hands on me. Where was his knife? I didn't know.

Both my hands were in his hair. Where was *my* knife?

My fingers fisted, pulling his mouth down harder. He tilted his head, changing the angle of our kiss, his tongue stroking aggressively across mine. He was devouring me, and air rushed through my nose in short pants.

This wasn't kissing. It was too primal, too rough, too violent.

THE ONE AND ONLY CRYSTAL DRUID ◆ 177

And every moment his mouth was on mine felt like being shocked awake after years in a coma.

The harder he pushed me into the wall, the harder I pulled his hair. The more forcefully he kissed me, the more sharply I bit his lower lip. He yanked my ponytail. I raked the back of his neck with my fingernails.

And the fire inside me burned hotter.

My arms coiled around his neck, and I rocked my hips, rubbing against his erection through the rough fabric of his jeans. A growl rasped his throat as he thrust against me, flattening me against the wall.

"*Fuck*," I gasped, tearing my lips from his. "I'm gonna stab you in the goddamn jugular."

He laughed huskily as his mouth latched onto the side of my throat, his teeth stinging across the fragile skin over my pulse. My hands spasmed in his hair.

"I'm not joking, you bastard," I panted.

He raised his head, his eyes meeting mine. "I know."

My pounding heart lurched, and suddenly there was no strength in my legs. Those eyes. Ravenous, relentless, on the edge of violence.

His mouth brushed over mine, almost gentle—then he caught my lower lip between his teeth and bit down. Pain stung me, and I sank my fingernails into his scalp in retaliation. His tongue pushed back into my mouth, and a faint moan escaped me as my head fell back, my legs going limp. He pressed me into the wall, hips grinding against mine.

Oh hell. I could feel him, hard and ready, and I burned for him. My hands dragged down the back of his neck, then grabbed fistfuls of his shirt, ready to tear it off him and—

"Saber?"

Breaking apart, we both spun.

Dominique stood on the path that led to the stable's rear door, a covered casserole dish in her hands and her eyes wide behind her glasses. Those goggling eyes ran over me as though assessing my condition, then snapped to Zak and scanned him from head to boots.

"Everything okay, Saber?" she asked.

Did she think he'd been assaulting me? Considering how rough we'd been, I could see why she'd make that mistake, but I'd hurt him more than he'd hurt me.

"Fine," I replied shortly. My shirt was hanging off one shoulder again, and I debated straightening it.

"You didn't come in for your dinner," she added, hoisting the casserole dish higher as though I might not have noticed it, "so I brought it out for you. It, ah, should be enough for two?"

She snuck another glance at Zak, then hastened forward and pushed the dish into my hands. Giving me an exaggerated wink that he couldn't see, she flashed a grin, then spun around and practically ran back to the yard.

I gazed down at the white dish, catching my breath. My extremities tingled. My core burned. Beside me, Zak was breathing deep. A trickle of blood ran down the side of his neck from a nick just under his jaw, courtesy of my knife.

Said knife lay on the ground, blade retracted. Balancing the casserole dish on one hand, I scooped up my weapon, then turned toward the door where my keys still hung.

I needed to move, to put distance between me and the man behind me, to focus on something else, *anything* else—before the voice in the back of my head demanding that we resume where we'd left off won out over my better judgment.

19

THE MOMENT I was inside my suite, I escaped into the bathroom, locked the door, and started up the shower. Tearing off my clothes, I stepped under the stream without waiting for it to warm up. Cold water blasted me and I gasped, shivering.

What was *wrong* with me?

The man in my living room was a druid, a rogue, a murderer, and a wanted criminal. I shouldn't find him attractive. I shouldn't want to kiss him, make out with him, or rip his clothes off him. I was smarter than that.

I finished showering, twisted my damp hair into a bun, and wrapped myself in my fluffy blue bathrobe. Cracking the door open, I peered out. Zak sat on a kitchen chair, slouched tiredly and looking at something on his phone.

Ensuring my robe was tightly closed, I stepped into the main room. "You can have the shower if you want."

His eyes came up. They met mine, then drifted slowly downward. There wasn't much skin to see, but I had no doubt he was imagining my naked body beneath the thick layer of terry towel. I waited to feel fury at his boldness.

Instead, slow heat roiled through my lower belly.

"Sure," he said as though he hadn't taken a good twenty seconds to reply while he mentally undressed me.

I strode into my room and slammed the door. When I turned toward my bed, I came up short.

A white feline sat primly on the foot of the bed. He lifted a paw, licked it, and casually swiped it over one ear, all without breaking eye contact.

Ríkr, I murmured silently.

Saber, he replied, drawing out my name. *Having fun, dove?*

I cleared my throat. *Not really, but it isn't your business anyway, Ríkr.*

Protecting you is my business. He rose to his feet and stretched, back arching. *I do delight in watching you and the druid circle each other like territorial cats, but drop your guard too far and—*

I won't, I interrupted. *I don't trust him any more than you do.*

He flicked his tail side to side. *I must disagree. I would certainly never allow the druid to—*

"Don't finish that," I growled, accidentally speaking out loud.

—in my mouth—

"Not listening!"

Trying hard to block out his voice, I hastened to my closet. Dressing in boy-short-style underwear, a sports bra, sweats, and another oversized t-shirt, I picked up my discarded jeans and transferred my switchblade into the pocket of my sweatpants. Then I slipped my fingers into the other pocket and withdrew the golden locket I'd taken from Arla's office.

Zak was gone and the shower was running when I emerged from my room. Taking the locket to the kitchen sink, I scrubbed it with disinfectant, then washed my hands. Water splashed noisily from behind the bathroom door, and I glanced at it, my lower lip caught between my teeth.

Tearing my gaze away, I turned—and paused. A black backpack leaned against the table leg. He'd forgotten his bag.

I picked it up. As I carried it to the coffee table, Ríkr trotted out of my room. He watched me shamelessly empty the druid's belongings onto the tabletop.

Violating the druid's privacy by examining his possessions, my familiar observed. *I approve.*

I sorted through the items. Clothes. A single towel. A bare-bones bag of toiletries containing a toothbrush, toothpaste, razor blade, and other essentials. Ríkr prodded a bar of pine-scented brown soap with one paw.

Picking up the knife, I unsheathed it and studied the ten-inch blade with a serrated section of steel. A weapon but also a tool.

More interesting was a tangle of leather ties, each one knotted around a colorful crystal. Two leather wrist bracers held more gems. The Crystal Druid indeed. They were artifacts, I knew—objects containing an arcane spell. I had no way of knowing what the magic did.

Stuffed in the bottom of his backpack was a bundle of sturdy leather. I undid the tie and unrolled it, discovering an alchemy kit. Together, Ríkr and I examined the collection of potion bottles, dried herbs, powders, liquids, a mortar and pestle, measuring instruments, drafting paper in a tight roll, pencils, and thick markers for creating arcane circles.

So he didn't merely *use* alchemic potions. He was a full-blown alchemist. Di-mythics—double-gifted magic users—were few and far between. How much training and discipline did it take to master two completely different magics?

I studied Zak's assorted belongings, then tugged his backpack closer. If he was an alchemist, he should have a grimoire—a book recording all the alchemic recipes he knew. I unzipped the bag's front pouch to find the trail map he'd taken from me, along with a notepad. Scrawled on it were descriptions of where he'd found animal and fae bodies and what he'd discerned about them.

Setting those aside, I turned his bag over. On the back was a short zipper—a pouch intended for a wallet or passport. I tugged it open.

"You," a male voice growled, "are trying really hard to make me lose my temper, aren't you?"

I looked up. The bathroom door was open—the shower silent—and Zak stood in the threshold, my purple towel wrapped around his waist. Water glistened on his skin, droplets running down the planes of his chest and ridges of his abs. Broad shoulders, tapered waist, all hard muscle. A fine trail of dark hair ran down from his navel and disappeared under the low-riding towel.

It took me a good long moment to force my gaze up to his face. His dripping hair hung over his forehead, but it did nothing to hide the fury in his eyes.

I arched my eyebrows, then rezipped the hidden pocket without opening it. While he glowered from the bathroom doorway, I methodically replaced each item in his backpack in the same order I'd removed it. When everything was packed away, I closed the bag, carried it across the room, and held it out.

Holding his towel with one hand, he grabbed a strap and pulled it away from me. "You don't look even slightly ashamed."

I said nothing, not bothering to pretend.

Shaking his head, he stepped back into the bathroom and shut the door in my face.

Returning to the sofa, I sank down in my spot and whispered to Ríkr, "Thanks a lot for the warning. Why didn't you tell me he was done showering?"

My familiar gave me a feline smirk, then transformed into a hawk and flew through the wall, vanishing from sight.

Five minutes later, Zak returned, fully dressed in worn navy jeans and a lightweight, long-sleeved black shirt that clung to his torso. His hair was roughly combed back from his face, and his green eyes flashed with muted anger as he looked at me reclined on the sofa, a gold chain tangled over my fingers.

He sat on the opposite end of the sofa and set his bag beside him—on his far side, as though I might lunge for it if it were within my reach.

"Will you *finally* tell me how that farmer's palomino died?" he asked irritably.

I leaned back, the locket swinging from its chain. "Its heart was gone."

His mouth hung open for a second, disbelief replacing his anger. "What do you mean, *gone?*"

"Stolen with fae magic. Not that the human vet realizes that. The killer is stealing their victims' hearts."

Muttering a curse, he slumped into the cushions. "That's terrifying."

I didn't mock him for admitting the killer frightened him. Any sane person would be scared. A fae that could steal your heart without wounding you—possibly without even touching you—was the stuff of nightmares and horror tales. Considering four deer had died seemingly within seconds of each other, the killer's power had little to no restrictions. How did you defend against that?

Cross paths with this fae, and you'd die.

"Do you know of any fae with an ability like that?" I asked.

"Not off the top of my head, but it gives me something to ask other fae about."

I balled up the locket chain and tossed it to him. "I found that under my coven leader's desk chair. Open it."

He pried it open and peered at the two tiny photos.

"The woman is my coven leader's daughter, Laney. The man is Jason Brine, also a witch. He and Laney had a whirlwind romance before he disappeared."

"Disappeared?"

"Arla—my coven leader—was a rehabilitation supervisor for the MPD. Convicts join the coven until their parole is complete or they violate the conditions and get dragged back to a correctional center."

"He was a convict?" At my nod, Zak's gaze slid across my face. "And are you a convict as well?"

"Yes."

"Crime?"

"Murder."

His eyebrows rose slightly—mild surprise, as opposed to the horrified repulsion most people felt upon learning they were sitting beside a murderer. "Lallakai said the other witches accused you of killing the coven leader."

My fingers curled into fists. "I didn't kill her."

"But your coven thinks you did."

"So does the MPD," I told him flatly. No point in hiding it now. He could put the pieces together on his own. "I'm a convicted murderer, I have a bad reputation, and I had motive since she was in charge of my parole. Plus"—I puffed out a breath—"I discovered her body."

I could feel his gaze, but I didn't look at him. I didn't need to see him weighing this new information and putting together all the things I hadn't said—and all the reasons I'd first sought him out after finding Arla dead.

I waved at the locket. "Anyway. Jason."

"What about him?"

"He didn't finish his rehabilitation. He decided to cut and run six months ago, ditching Laney. But the photo in that locket is recent—less than four weeks old. Her hair in it is blond, but she only bleached it last month. Before that, it was brown."

He lifted the locket close to his face, eyes narrowed. "Their faces were cut from the same photo. You can see her hair on his shoulder, and his arm is around her."

I nodded. "So Jason is back, and he's either trying to win Laney over with gifts, or they're already together again."

"And you think Jason is involved with the fae killer?"

"He liked to brag about his conquests. His whole MO was calling rare, dangerous fae and making black bargains." In witch vernacular, a black-magic witch was one who made deals with fae that involved violence, death, or betrayal. "Apparently, he did this for hire and made a lot of money."

"And got himself arrested while he was at it," Zak murmured, studying the photo. "There are a few different ways to call fae, and using a crossroads makes all of them easier. If Jason is after a fae that's difficult to lure out of the fae demesne, it makes sense he'd come here to do it."

"So we can assume he showed up here four weeks ago, or less, and reconnected with Laney. They took a photo together and made this locket."

"And we can assume that around two weeks ago, he successfully called a deadly fae to the human plane," Zak murmured, continuing the narrative, "and the fae's been stealing hearts and leaving trails of dead bodies on the mountainside since then."

"Arla found out somehow. Maybe she found the locket and asked Laney about Jason—or she saw Jason visiting Laney. Or something. Whatever she found out, the fae killed her because of it."

"Jason could be controlling the fae."

"Maybe." I tugged on a lock of my bangs. "Does Laney know Jason came back here to set a killer fae loose?"

"And does she suspect that her boyfriend might have murdered her mother?"

Remembering Laney's crazed accusations, I frowned. "She really thinks I did it."

"She could be in denial," Zak suggested, rubbing his jaw. "Or maybe Jason isn't involved. If he is, she might have answers, but approaching her will be difficult. We don't know how close Jason might be, or how the fae targets its victims. If we draw her—or his—attention, we could end up face to face with this fae before we're ready."

"Laney already wants me dead," I mused. "If she could send that fae after me, she would have by now. But we still need to know what the fae is and how it kills before we put ourselves in Jason's crosshairs."

Zak nodded. "I think another visit to the crossroads is warranted."

My eyes lost focus as I thought back to my last visit. "The kelpie told me he knows the creature you're seeking. I didn't get the feeling it was a bluff."

"Hmm. All right, I'll start with him."

"*We* will."

His mouth twisted. "Last time I suggested we work together, you attacked me. You might remember. It happened an hour ago."

I ignored that. "I get off work at four tomorrow. Meet me here."

"You want to waste an entire day at work?"

"I, unlike wanted fugitives such as yourself, need my job." When he gazed at me expressionlessly, I sat forward. "Don't even think about going without me. You're here for fae favors, but *I'm* about to get charged with murdering my own coven leader. I have way more on the line than you do."

"Speaking of which, the MPD knows where you work. Going there is a risk."

"They won't arrest me in front of a bunch of humans. And I'm trying *not* to look suspicious by missing work and vanishing for an entire day."

Which I'd already done and shouldn't repeat.

He grunted. "Where's your phone?"

"Why?"

"Just give it to me."

I had to get up to grab it off my bed. Dropping back onto the sofa, I held it out. He took it, tapped on the screen for a moment, then passed it back. A new text message was open, the recipient's number already added.

"That's the MPD's crime hotline," he informed me. "Report that you saw me in this area."

"Are you serious?"

"Obviously."

"Don't screw with me. The MPD won't let me off the hook for Arla's death just because a wanted rogue walked through my neighborhood."

He rolled his green eyes toward the ceiling. "No, and I don't plan to take a fall for you or anyone else. But you need to change the trajectory of the MPD's investigation, and this is the fastest way to do that. The agent in charge of my bounty won't ignore a tip if you describe me."

"But how is involving *another* agent going to help?"

"You're already their prime suspect, so it can't hurt, can it?"

Grumbling, I turned my attention to my phone and, after a moment's hesitation, typed out a description of a dark-haired, green-eyed druid armed with alchemy and crystal artifacts riding a fae stallion. I showed the message to said druid.

"That'll do. Send it."

Hoping I wasn't making a stupid mistake, I hit send, then pushed to my feet. "I suppose you want to sleep on my sofa again."

His gaze was heavy on my back as I walked over to the fridge. "Unless you want to share your bed."

"Come near my bed and I'll cut off your balls."

He snorted quietly, amused rather than intimidated, and warmth flushed through me. An intense flashback—him shoving me into the wall, our mouths locked as his tongue aggressively stroked mine—hit me and I sucked in a silent breath.

When I pulled Dominique's casserole dish out of the fridge, his voice rumbled behind me. "Are you going to share that?"

"No."

"You're just going to eat in front of me?"

"Yes."

"I brought you lunch."

My jaw clenched. I shoved the dish in the microwave, opened the cupboard, and stared moodily at my small stack of mismatched dinnerware.

Growling under my breath, I pulled out two plates. Damn druid.

20

HE WAS WAITING *for me in the alcove, a dark shadow with the hood of his jacket pulled up.*

I didn't know how he could stand to wear a coat in this weather. We'd first met on a rainy June night. Tonight, we were on day six of an August heatwave. Even now, shortly after midnight, the balmy warmth was oppressive, and I wore shorts and a loose black tank top, the straps of my red bra peeking out.

Slipping into the alcove, I leaned against the opposite wall. He pushed his hood off, his dark hair mussed. His face was clear of bruises, and it struck me—not for the first time—that he was really good looking.

We studied each other, the muffled voices from within the building filling the silence.

"Did you manage it?" I asked.

Nodding, he withdrew a small object from his pocket and held it out. I took the tiny vial and held it up to the dim security light. A faintly green liquid sloshed inside the half-empty glass vessel.

"How much will it take?"

"A few drops," he answered. "It smells minty, so put it in something with strong flavor."

"Like coffee?"

His mouth curved up. "Coffee is perfect."

An answering grin flashed over my face. It seemed strange to smile while we discussed murdering my aunt, but I couldn't suppress my elation. Her death meant freedom from fear, pain, and misery. Freedom from a future that held nothing but suffering.

Her death meant a new future. That was scary too, but I wouldn't be alone.

I tucked the vial deep into my pocket with my switchblade. "What will happen when she drinks it?"

"Numbness in her face, then violent trembling, then convulsions and unconsciousness, then death. It'll start in less than a minute, and she'll be dead in ten." He shifted his weight. "I had to look it up. Never actually seen someone poisoned with it."

I gulped down slight nausea. "Did Bane notice anything when you stole it?"

"No." He grimaced. "Maybe. He was watching me this afternoon. He might suspect I'm up to something, but he'll never guess what. He has no idea about your spell. Did … did you bring it?" he asked hesitantly, as though afraid of my answer.

"Of course." I patted the front of my shirt. "I never take it off."

He relaxed. "You wear it all the time?"

"Yeah. My parents gave it to me, remember? To protect me."

His gaze drifted across my chest, then back up to my face. "What happened to your parents?"

My throat tightened. "They were helping search for a missing hiker in the mountains north of our home. They knew the area really well … but they never came back. Their bodies were found a few weeks later. It looked like an animal attack, but no one was sure what kind of animal."

"Probably a fae, then," he murmured.

I nodded, my hand closing in a fist over the pendant under my shirt. "What about your parents? Bane isn't your dad, is he?"

His face twisted in revulsion. "We're not related." He was quiet for a moment, his gaze sliding away from mine. "I don't remember my parents."

Cold tinged my veins. "Nothing?"

"Just … my father's name. That's it." He pushed his shoulders back. "Will you be okay without your artifact?"

"Yeah, I'll be fine. There are no fae in the city to bother me."

"Not many," he agreed.

A twinge of hesitation stilled my hand, but I forced myself to reach for the chain around my neck. I tugged it up until the pendant came free—a dark brown river stone etched with a swirling design.

"That's it?" he breathed.

"Yep." I lifted the chain over my head. My neck felt naked without the slight pressure of the chain.

I held it out.

The boy took it with reverent hands. He ran his fingers across the etching, his eyes losing focus. "The magic in this is really powerful." He looked up at me, and his mouth fell open in sudden disbelief. "You're—why didn't you say you were—"

A drunken shout shattered the humid quiet. Someone was outside, near our alcove, too close.

The boy pulled me into the darkest corner of the alcove. We huddled in the shadows as another slurring voice called out. Scuffing, uneven footsteps. Laughter. A door slammed, and silence fell.

For a long moment, we didn't move, then let out relieved sighs in unison. His breath stirred my hair, and I shivered, aware of his warm hands gripping my upper arms, the chain of my pendant pressed against my skin.

Tugging the chain from his hand, I lifted it over his head, settled it against the back of his neck, then tucked the pendant beneath the collar of his shirt.

"Tomorrow night," I whispered, my hand resting on his chest over the hidden pendant, "we'll meet across the street in the alley. Ruth and Bane will be dead. We'll be free."

"Free," he repeated, his eyes closing. "What time?"

"I'm not sure. It'll depend on when Ruth has her after-dinner coffee."

He nodded. "I'll wait for you."

"I'll wait for you too." My fingers pressed into his chest. "All night."

"And then we'll leave this city together."

"Together."

His eyes met mine, and my heart jolted with sharp anticipation. He leaned down. Our lips brushed. My hand slid over his collarbone, fingers curling around the back of his neck. His mouth melded against mine.

Soft, slow kisses. So slow, because urgency pounded in both of us and we couldn't surrender to it. Fear ran through our blood, but we couldn't acknowledge it. Desperation choked us, but we had to keep breathing.

We kissed until I parted my lips and he tasted me. Heads tilting. Kisses deepening. My fingers slid up into his hair. His hands ran up my arms, then pulled me against his chest.

A door slammed nearby and we both jumped. Nervous. Edgy. Our eyes met. We didn't speak, no words needed. Parting from each other, we slipped out of the alcove. It took only a few tense minutes to sneak into the attic.

It was hot, stuffy, and even more humid than the air outside. In the corner farthest from the muffled voices leaking up from the den, he shrugged his jacket off and set it quietly on the dusty floorboards.

I was in his arms an instant later. Holding him. Kissing him. Our slow, hesitant pace broke. My hands ran up and down the front of his shirt. He caressed my back. Movements faster. Mouths locking. Breath coming fast and hard.

I couldn't stop touching him. Couldn't stop kissing him. Couldn't stop myself from sliding my hands under his shirt and touching his hot skin.

"Do you want to?" he whispered against my lips.

"Yes."

"You sure?"

"Yes."

Then he was kissing me harder. Then his hands were slipping under my tank top.

I peeled his shirt off, stroking and exploring his chest, lean but hard with muscle, my pendant hanging from his neck. And he pulled my shirt over my head, caressing my breasts, pushing up my bra, cupping me in his warm hands.

Then we were sinking down onto the scant padding of his jacket, our limbs entangled, our panting breaths and soft sounds hushed. Quiet need. Feverish desire. His mouth tasting me everywhere. My hands touching him everywhere.

Tomorrow, my life would change. But tonight, I was changing.

A stranger whose name I didn't know, his hot breath on my skin, kissing my belly as he tugged my shorts down my hips. A boy who'd somehow, so quickly, become more important than anyone else in my life. We would escape together, survive together. Be together.

My arms wound around his neck, my fingers gripping his hair as I arched up into him, pressing our bodies together, feeling his warmth and weight and presence. My heart pounding. Blood rushing. Vivid, awakened, alive.

I'd never surrendered to pain, to fear, to despair. But tonight, I would surrender to him—surrender everything.

My past, already hanging around his neck.

My present, electric with desire under his hands and mouth.

And my future, waiting to begin.

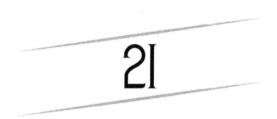

21

I WOKE UP READY to commit murder for a second time.

My body ached with unsatisfied need, ignited by that damn druid. Rolling over, I grabbed my phone and turned off the alarm, the vague memory of whatever dream I'd been having dissolving away to nothing. Zak's rough, primal attention last night wasn't as easy to forget.

And that ticked me off even more.

Seething, I stormed to the bathroom, ignoring the man on my sofa, who watched me pass with groggy confusion. When I emerged from the bathroom, the coffeemaker was percolating, but Zak was back on the sofa, an arm over his face to block out the light.

By the time I completed my morning chores in the stable and got ready for work, my temper had cooled. I told Dominique my truck had broken down, and she offered to loan me their old Ranger.

At the clinic, I smiled cheerfully at my coworkers, then busied myself preparing for our first procedure of the morning, a cruciate ligament repair for a Labrador. Ríkr, lazy as ever, picked an out-of-the-way corner and went to sleep.

The morning dragged despite the hectic lineup of surgeries, my thoughts rotating between the fae killer and our plans to revisit the crossroads, and the MPD agents circling ever closer, goaded by whatever Laney might have reported after our encounter last night. It got harder and harder to smile when my coworkers spoke to me, and I knew I needed to get out of the clinic to settle myself.

Checking that my wallet was in my pocket, I was halfway to the back door when a voice called to me.

"Saber!" Hailey waved from the short hall that connected to reception. "Can you come to the front?"

"I'm going for lunch," I called back, my hand on the door.

"Someone's asking for you."

I paused. It couldn't be Zak bringing me another lunch. He had no way to get here, and besides that, Hailey wasn't nearly giddy enough for him to be my visitor.

Ríkr? I asked silently. *Who is it?*

His sleepy thoughts mumbled into my head. *Who? Where?*

You're a big help, I complained as I hovered at the door, debating whether to duck outside. Just as I decided that was the safer bet, Nicolette appeared beside Hailey, a suspicious frown on her lips.

I forced a smile. "Coming!"

Reluctantly abandoning the door, I strode toward them. They moved aside, and I slowed as I approached reception. At the nearer end of the long desk, Kaitlynn was reviewing paperwork with a middle-aged couple, their obese pug sitting at their feet. An elderly woman sat on a chair in the waiting area with a cat carrier on her lap. And at the far end near the exit …

Laney smiled vapidly at me, her blond hair styled in beach waves and her designer purse under her arm.

My lips thinned. I wasn't sure if this was better or worse than the MPD agents I'd expected. Hoping she wouldn't make a scene in front of human witnesses, I cautiously approached.

Her eyes glinted meanly behind her oversized sunglasses. "Look at you," she hissed, "going about your day like you're *so* innocent."

I said nothing, waiting.

She curled her lips in a sneer. "If you'd just confessed to the coven last night, maybe we would've put in a good word for you with the MPD, but now it's too late."

A good word? More like additional condemnation. "Too late how?"

"The MPD is arresting you tonight. They've even brought in a bounty hunting team to take you down, like a rabid animal."

A surge of adrenaline tightened my gut, but I kept my expression clear. "How do you know that?"

"I told the agents that you threatened to kill the coven." She raised her chin, attempting to glare down at me even though I was taller. "How does it feel knowing you're living your last hours of freedom right now?"

"Feels like I should skip town before they arrest me."

"Don't even bother. With a bounty on your head, you're doomed no matter what you do." She hitched her purse up on her shoulder. "I just wanted to see your face when you realized you won't get away with killing my mother."

Did she really have no idea how Arla had died? Did she not suspect Jason, her convict boyfriend, in the slightest?

"Well, now that you've warned me, I probably *should* run. Maybe into the mountains," I added in a thoughtful tone. "No one would find me there. I'll head north. Up Summit Trail."

She inhaled sharply, her shoulders rigid. "Summit Trail? Why would you go there?"

I gazed at her silently, and her face tightened.

"I—I'll tell them that's your plan," she threatened.

"Will you? What happens if the MPD follows me up Summit Trail?"

"You ..." She stepped back. "You're a murderer. You're a killer."

I gave her my real smile. "I am."

Jaw clenching, she whipped her hand out, her palm striking my cheek with a loud *smack*. Gasps rang through the room as everyone's attention snapped toward us.

"Rot in hell, you psychotic bitch!" she screamed. Whirling on her heel, she shoved through the door and ran outside to her silver Prius.

I watched her go, my cheek throbbing. Why had she come here? Denied my confession, had she wanted to bask in my pending arrest instead? To see my reaction? To get in a little personal revenge before the MPD made their move tonight?

As her Prius sped away, the car parked in the spot behind hers was revealed: a black sedan with a man leaning casually against it. He wore a dark suit, his face turned toward the clinic. Tall, trim, older, with brown hair cut short and dark-rimmed glasses.

Cold spilled through my limbs.

"Saber?"

I started, surprised to find Hailey and Kaitlynn on either side of me, their faces full of concern.

"Are you okay?" Kaitlynn took my arm. "Come on. I'll get you an ice pack. Do you want us to call the police?"

The police? That would only complicate things more. I stared through the window at the MPD agent. Would he come inside and confront me in a building full of potential human casualties?

Where there was one MagiPol agent, others must be close by. Were they covering the clinic from all sides, waiting for the right moment to strike? They thought I had magic that could steal people's hearts from their chests. That was the only reason they hadn't moved on me yet—but when they did, they wouldn't hold back.

I waited, seconds ticking past, but the agent didn't step away from his vehicle.

The MPD was hunting me, and if Laney wasn't bluffing, then my time was almost up.

"Saber?" Kaitlynn prompted.

"No," I said quickly. "No police."

"You should press charges." Taking my arm, Hailey tugged me into the hallway that led to the staff room. "She assaulted you."

As we left the reception area behind, Nicolette's shrill voice floated after us. "But what did Saber do to her first?"

I STOOD AT the clinic's back door. I'd changed out of my scrubs and into a pair of jeans and a racerback tank top—my spare clothes from my locker. My phone was in one pocket, my switchblade in the other, and the keys to Dominique's truck were in my hand.

My shift was over and I couldn't hide in the clinic any longer. The agent watching the building from his car was still out front, and Ríkr had found another man in a suit watching the back, where the old Ranger was parked. If Laney was to be believed, there would also be an ambush waiting for me at home.

Pretending to follow my regular routine was no longer an option.

Ready? I called to Ríkr.

And eager, my familiar replied, his telepathic voice coming from the direction of the rooftop.

Be careful, I warned him. *You don't know what magic or weapons that agent has.*

I'm always careful, dove.

I scrunched my nose skeptically. *Then let's do this.*

Keys ready, I threw the rear door open, revealing a small parking lot that ran behind the strip mall. The second agent loitered near a dumpster, wearing a matching suit to the other agent but compact and slender in build, with dark hair buzzed close to his scalp, except for a short, mohawk-like strip down the center.

He jerked straight at my appearance, his sunglasses turning toward me—and he completely missed the white hawk plunging out of the sky above him.

Ríkr struck with the full speed of his dive. Lucky for the agent, we'd decided against inflicting grievous wounds, so the fae used his body weight instead of his talons.

Shouting in alarm, the man staggered, arms whipping up to shield his head as Ríkr's wings beat at him.

I sprinted toward the truck, unlocked the door, and leaped into the driver's seat. The engine shuddered to life. As I slammed it into gear, the agent flung his hand out. Crystalline shards formed over his fingers and shot outward in an arc.

A kryomage.

Ríkr dodged the counterattack with a sweep of his wings, grabbed the man's sleeve with his talons, and yanked his arm backward, pulling him off balance.

I stomped the gas pedal. The truck peeled out, and I sped past Ríkr and the agent. Rubber squealed against pavement as I turned onto the main road, the flash of my familiar's wings disappearing from my rearview mirror.

Gripping the steering wheel, I joined the heavy traffic heading west toward Vancouver. If I was being followed, I wanted the MPD to think I was fleeing to the big city.

My tension increased with each kilometer I drove, my heart drumming a slow but forceful beat against my ribs. I was nearly vibrating as I stopped the truck at the last traffic light before the Lougheed Highway. Just as I was debating whether to go back, I felt a brush of familiar fae power across my senses.

I cranked the window down, and a moment later, a white hawk zoomed into the truck and landed on the passenger seat. He ruffled his feathers, then shook his whole body, spraying water droplets and tiny ice crystals in every direction.

"Are you hurt?" I asked urgently.

Injured by a mere ice magician? Ríkr gave me a deeply displeased stare. *I am insulted.*

I rolled my eyes. "You've recently been bashed by a bear fae and captured by a pixie. How should I know what you can handle?"

His offended air increased. *A human's magic is no challenge. My kin require more finesse.*

"I see," I murmured, though I didn't really get it.

The traffic light changed, and I directed the truck onto the highway, driving west into Burnaby. There I turned north, met up with Highway 7A, and headed back east toward Coquitlam. Navigating my way through the town, the traffic dense with the evening rush hour, I headed not toward the rescue but toward Quarry Road.

Ten minutes later, I pulled the truck into the same small gravel parking lot where I'd called Pierce after my first visit to the crossroads.

Climbing out, I stretched the tension from my legs as I looked around. A few unfamiliar cars were parked nearby, but the lot was abandoned. Ríkr took off into the trees where he could keep watch.

I waited, my discomfort tightening into frustration.

"Where is he?" I muttered angrily. "He's supposed to—"

My phone vibrated against my hip, and I snatched it out, expecting a message from a certain tardy druid—but the message wasn't from him. It was a text from an unknown number.

> This is the lead investigator on the
> Ghost's bounty. I'm following up on your
> hotline tip. We need to chat.

My brow furrowed. He wanted to "chat"? That didn't seem like the right word for an interrogation about a notorious rogue and his dead-or-alive bounty.

My phone pinged again and a second message appeared beneath the first.

> BTW, saw you're the primary suspect in a
> murder. That's exciting.

Exciting?

A third ping.

```
I'll be there ASAP. Don't skip town, k?
```

Don't skip town? Did he somehow know I was evading arrest at this very moment?

The soft energies of the forest rippled, and the serenade of songbirds quieted with the thump of approaching hooves. Tilliag appeared between two trees, his neck arched and a druid astride his back.

I shoved my phone into my pocket. "You're late."

The stallion pulled up beside me and Zak reached down. His arm clamped around me, and he hauled me up onto the horse. Before I could snarl a protest, Tilliag launched into a bouncy trot that had me scrambling to get my legs into position. Zak's hands drew me back against him as I found my seat.

"Before you pull your knife on me," he said into my ear, "I'm only late because I had to maneuver around the six bounty hunters who showed up at the rescue."

So Laney hadn't been bluffing.

"Why didn't you leave sooner?" I demanded as Tilliag trotted onto the wide gravel path of Minnekhada Trail. "I warned you they might come."

"I figured you'd prefer I not leave any evidence that I'd been in or around your home." He pulled a small backpack off his shoulder—one I recognized as mine. "I also grabbed a few things for you. Food, water, change of clothes."

I awkwardly pulled it on. "What about Dominique and Greta?"

"They left before the bounty team moved in. The MagiPol agents probably tricked them into leaving."

A sick feeling gathered low in my gut. "We have to find Jason Brine and the killer fae. If we don't …"

I'd never be able to go home.

"We will." He reached around me to take handfuls of Tilliag's mane. The fae equine pushed into a canter, his hooves thudding against the hard-packed gravel and trees flashing by as we raced toward the looming summit of Mount Burke.

Soon, we would be at the crossroads. And very soon, we would finally learn what sort of monster was stealing the hearts of fae and leaving so much death in its wake.

22

DAPPLED SHADOWS danced over us as Tilliag trotted along the dirt trail. The tireless stallion had cantered until the steepening slope had forced him to slow. He kept up the quick pace for another seven or eight kilometers, then slowed to a purposeful walk as the terrain grew rougher and roots and rocks cluttered the narrowing path.

I relaxed into the horse's gait, trying to ignore Zak's warm hand on my waist, his other hand resting casually on his thigh. He moved so seamlessly with his mount that I almost forgot he was there.

Almost.

My gaze lifted skyward, and I spotted a flash of white wings—Ríkr gliding on air currents above us. Humming a thoughtful note, I skimmed the dense forest, the air heavy with heat and pine scent—actual pine, not Zak's soap.

It wasn't until I'd shifted my vision to the fae demesne that I spotted them: two black wolves weaving through the trees on silent paws, their scarlet eyes occasionally glancing our way. That was three of Zak's four fae accounted for. Where was Lallakai, the beautiful but deadly eagle?

I refocused on the earthly forest, the mists of the fae realm fading from my vision. "You have four familiars? Two vargs, Lallakai, and Tilliag?"

The stallion's left ear flicked toward me as he listened in.

Zak adjusted his seat, his hand pressing into my hip for a moment. "Tilliag isn't my familiar, not in the traditional sense. He promised me ninety-nine days of service as repayment for a debt."

A temporary alliance? Interesting. "What about the vargs?"

"They're familiars by the common definition."

"Do you not like the common definition?"

"It's a witch idea. Druid relationships with fae don't fit into simple little boxes like 'familiar' and 'not a familiar.'"

"How would you describe your relationship with the vargs, then?"

"Companions. They've been with me for over twelve years. The pack used to be five …" A pause, and when he spoke again, his voice was rougher. "But I lost three of them recently."

"Lost them?"

"I made a stupid mistake, and they paid the price."

Part of me was glad I couldn't see his expression. I didn't want to sympathize. "Do these two have names?"

"Why not ask them?"

I bit the inside of my cheek.

"The larger one is Grenior. The smaller one is female, and her name is Keelar. You don't interact with many fae aside from Ríkr, do you?"

"Not really." I shifted my hips, wishing Zak weren't so close behind me. The temptation to lean back into him wouldn't go away. "I rarely see other fae, and they don't approach me. Probably because they can tell I'm too weak to be useful."

"Having weak spiritual power doesn't make you useless. Ríkr would attest to that, or he wouldn't have tied himself to you."

I grunted in dubious agreement.

"How did he end up as your partner?"

Normally, I would never have answered that question, but Zak already knew my biggest secret—that I was a convicted murderer. "I was offered 'rehabilitation' when I was eighteen. The MPD sent me to Arla, but instead of meeting her like I was supposed to, I went exploring."

"Taking your parole seriously, I see."

"I'd been stuck in a concrete box for over two years. I was dying to run barefoot through a meadow and roll in wildflowers and shit."

He coughed. "I can't really picture that."

"Next time I'm released from prison, I'll invite you along." I shifted my hips again. "Anyway. I ran into Ríkr that day. He followed me around for a few hours, being annoying, then just … never really left. When I met Arla the next day, she asked if he was my familiar and he said yes—just to shock her, I think. He gave me his familiar mark about a week later."

Zak made a thoughtful noise. "That's all? He took a liking to you?"

"Guess so. Whenever I ask why he sticks around, he says I make his life more interesting."

A muffled snort.

"Shut up."

"My life's also been more interesting. Repeated threats, assaults—"

"Shut up," I repeated in a growl. "What about you and Lallakai?"

"We go way back. I was fifteen when I first met her, but we didn't form an official relationship until I was seventeen."

"*Official* relationship?" I repeated. "Meaning what, exactly?"

"She's—"

His mistress. Ríkr swept out of the trees in sparrow form and landed on an overhanging branch a few yards up the trail. *And he is her obedient consort.*

My eyebrows shot up. "Is that what it sounds like?"

Yes, Ríkr said promptly.

"No," Zak snapped. "It isn't."

Really? Ríkr's wings flashed as he took off, transforming back into a hawk in mid-flight. *Does she not sup upon your vibrant druid power like a queen sampling the sweet favors of her handsome young lover? Is that not the price you pay for her protection?*

Zak had gone rigid, and Tilliag flicked his ears in annoyance.

I waited for the druid to deny Ríkr's assessment, but he said nothing. Perhaps he couldn't deny it. Druids, like witches, had no offensive or defensive magic—not inherently. We relied on magical gifts, favors, and protection from benevolent fae instead. If Lallakai was protecting him, she would require payment, and what better to demand than free rein to consume the alluring spiritual energy the druid exuded?

Tilliag gave his hindquarters a rough bounce, jolting Zak out of his rigid stance. He slid into my back, then righted himself, muttering under his breath.

Both his hands were on my waist now.

"Where are you from?" I asked abruptly, searching for something else to focus on.

"I used to live north of Vancouver."

That wasn't quite what I'd meant, but his phrasing distracted me. "Used to? Where do you live now?"

"Wherever I want."

His unfriendly tone didn't stop me. "Does that mean everything you own is in your backpack? Is that why you wanted to use my laundry?"

"I'm into minimalistic living."

"Funny. Why don't you have a home?"

"I'll spill the whole tragic tale of my past if you spill yours first."

That was a hard pass on my end. "One question, then."

"What?"

"You *are* going to leave when this is all over, right?"

"Thanks for the sympathy," he said sarcastically.

"You don't want sympathy."

He was silent for several moments. "No, I don't. I want to go back and kill the person who took away my home."

His home had been *taken*? "Why don't you?"

"I should have said, 'Kill them *again.*'"

"Oh." I hummed a few notes. "Did it help?"

"What?"

"Killing them."

"Yes and no."

When he said nothing more, I nudged him in the ribs with my elbow.

He grunted. "Do you really want to hear how I murdered someone? Most people find the topic uncomfortable."

"I'm a murderer too, remember?"

"Not the same kind."

"How do you know?"

"Because I've killed many times." His voice roughened again. "So many times I've lost count. People who deserved it. People who probably didn't deserve it. Sometimes I tortured them before I killed them. The blood on my hands will never wash clean, and it's been a long time since I cared."

I listened to the thud of Tilliag's hooves. "I never regretted it. The person I killed. I only regretted getting caught. I'm more careful now."

"More careful? Have you been killing farmers and burying them in the pigsty?"

"Not killing them, but I like making them bleed." I hummed softly. "Before Harvey Whitby, the last animal abuser to cross my path I put in the hospital. The two before him I bankrupted. I blackmailed another into selling his farm and moving. The one before that I framed for extortion. He's in jail. Oh," I added, "and there were the teen boys who tortured a cat. They're all missing a finger so they'll never forget what I did to them."

Zak swore quietly. "You managed all that without getting caught? *While* being closely monitored by your coven and the MPD?"

I shrugged.

"All right." He exhaled. "I'll admit it. You're a bit scary."

I didn't realize I'd laughed until I felt him tense with surprise.

After a moment, he murmured, "When I come across sick bastards who abuse fae or hurt kids, I just kill them."

A strange feeling tightened my gut. "I thought you were a kidnapper."

"In the strictly legal sense, I am. But I couldn't just leave those kids for the next trafficker to pick up, and I don't care what the MPD accuses me of. They've never been worried about the accuracy of the charges."

"You …" My mouth bobbed open. "You were *saving* kids?"

Amusement threaded his raspy voice. "If you'd rather think of me as a child-napping, fae-whoring rogue, feel free."

I snapped my mouth shut, reeling on the inside "Whatever. Just know that if you ever betray me, I'll slit your throat."

"Noted."

———

THE EVENING SUNLIGHT sparkled on the waters of Dennett Lake. My thighs and calves ached from overuse, and I was glad when Zak decided to take a short break before continuing on to the bushwhacking portion of our trek. I'd done a lot of riding, but no horse could maintain a grueling pace like Tilliag could.

With wobbly knees, I veered toward a fallen log by the trail's edge. The picnic areas with weathered wooden tables and rusted firepits were abandoned, and a busy chipmunk searched beneath them for forgotten crumbs.

I dropped onto the log, its bark worn smooth by hundreds of hikers using it as a bench. Slinging my small pack off my shoulders, I dropped it at my feet and dug out a bottle of water. While Zak retrieved water from his own backpack, I downed half the bottle, then poured some on my face. The cool liquid rushed over my cheeks and off my chin, splattering my shirt.

It was too hot and humid for this shit. No wonder we were the only idiots out here.

As I investigated the bag's contents to see what else Zak had grabbed for me, he gazed toward the lake. His focus moved up to the summit, and he turned in a slow circle as though to pinpoint a distant sound he could barely detect.

"Do you sense that?" he murmured.

I squinted, searching for anything out of the ordinary. "Sense what?"

His frown deepened. He peered down at me for a second, seeming to debate something, then grabbed a handful of Tilliag's mane and pulled himself onto the stallion's back.

"What are you doing?" I asked sharply.

"Something is off, but I don't know what. I need to stay focused, and you're a distraction."

I shot to my feet. "You are *not* going without m—"

He turned Tilliag westward. "Last time you set foot in the crossroads, you got separated from your familiar and almost walked into a kelpie's jaws. Just wait here. I'll be back in an hour or two, hopefully with answers."

"Zak—"

Tilliag launched into a trot. I ran after the stallion, spitting with fury.

"Why did you even bring me out here?" I yelled.

"Just trying to keep us both alive," he called as Tilliag broke into a fast canter. "Try not to stab me when I get back."

"I'll stab you in the heart, you piece of shit!" I screamed pointlessly as the stallion and his rider cantered the length of the lake and disappeared into the forest at the far side, cutting toward Summit Trail.

"Bastard," I snarled. "Ríkr! Follow him!"

With a sweep of hawk wings, my familiar landed on a nearby boulder. *I regret I must decline.*

"What? Why?"

The druid is not alone in sensing a malevolent power that was not present here before. His blue eyes scoured the summit. *Fae the likes of which you do not know skulk in the tides of the crossroads' magic. The danger is great.*

"I can handle myself."

He clicked his beak. *Still, I would not abandon you for a better reason than spying upon the druid.*

Spinning on my heel, I marched back to my bag, zipped it up, and slung it over one shoulder. If Zak wouldn't take me to the crossroads, I'd go myself. It wasn't like I didn't know the way.

I strode away from the log.

Would you care to hear a riddle? Ríkr asked from his boulder. *What shape does a druid upon his horse make when chased by a witch upon her feet?*

"Shut up, Ríkr."

Circles, he informed me. *He will ride there and back before you can catch him, dove.*

My angry steps slowed. "That bastard left me behind."

He did, so save your strength so you might maim him upon his return. His tone softened. *We are safer here, and he will be more efficient without a ward to guard.*

Halting, I stretched out my senses. Tension threaded the hot, still air, and the soft lap of water against the pebbly shore was the only sound. I couldn't detect anything more, but I was a terrible witch.

I swore again. Shoulders slumping, I walked back to the log and dropped onto it. Ríkr was right. Zak would reach the crossroads long before I could catch up to him. Chasing him would only waste energy, and it was too damn humid for a high-speed hike up a mountain peak.

Heaving a sigh, I opened my backpack again. Zak had tossed in a box of granola bars and a bag of trail mix from my kitchen. I whiled away twenty minutes picking all my favorite nuts from the trail mix. My knee bounced with irrepressible impatience.

I hated being idle. Too long with nothing to do and my brain went into overdrive. Obsessive, anxious thoughts fought for dominance—Jason Brine and his killer fae, Laney and her visit to the clinic, the MPD agents and their bounty hunting team at the rescue, Zak ditching me and how that made me so furious I could scream.

With nothing better to do, I emptied the backpack and repacked it. As I tucked the granola bars away, the soft clink of a chain caught my attention. I dug into the very bottom of the bag and pulled out the golden locket from Arla's office. Zak must've packed it to keep it out of the MPD's hands.

I popped it open. Jason Brine's tiny face grinned at me, his head shaved and chin covered by a brown beard; he was surprisingly handsome, with angular features and a charismatic air. Laney beamed in her photo, happier than she ever looked when I was nearby. Did she love him?

My scattered thoughts turned to our conversation this afternoon. I wasn't sure whether to believe her claim that she'd come to witness my reaction to the news that I was about to be arrested, but her reaction to my mention of Summit Trail had been interesting. She must've known I was hinting at the crossroads. Did she suspect something? My gut still said she wasn't involved in her mother's murder.

I stuck the locket in my back pocket and stretched my legs out. Minutes ticked by. My gaze drifted across the summit on the far side of the lake, the crossroads beyond it. Tantalizingly close, yet too far to easily reach. Zak could go to hell for abandoning me here.

With unbearable impatience scraping at my self-control, I slid off the log to the ground, crossed my legs, and attempted to meditate. It took a solid ten minutes before my mind calmed and my sense of time slid away.

I meditated until the sun's golden light faded and shadows deepened across the landscape. Pushing to my feet, I stretched my limbs. It'd been close to two hours now. If Zak didn't return soon, nightfall would beat him here.

At least night would alleviate the oppressive humidity. I scrunched my toes in my hiking boots, my feet unpleasantly hot.

Leaving my backpack beside the log, I walked to the shore. A low, flat boulder jutted out into the lake, and I sat on the far end, pulled my boots off, rolled my jeans up above my ankles, and stuck my feet into the cold water.

A sigh slid from me. Much better.

I glanced toward the sunset. Had Zak learned anything at the crossroads? Had Balligor revealed what he knew of the "creature" we were seeking? If he didn't find anything, I wouldn't be able to prove my innocence to the MPD. They'd keep hunting me.

With a metallic clink, a snow-white squirrel appeared beside me, his pale blue eyes stern. A golden locket hung from his mouth.

Drop something, dove?

"Oh." Taking the locket, I balled up the chain and reached for my pocket again, intending to ensure it was tucked away properly this time.

Ríkr heaved a squirrely sigh. *And if you drop it again? Put it somewhere safer.*

"Like where?" When he gave me a long look, I grimaced and unlatched the chain, then looped it around my neck. "Better?"

He didn't answer, his blue eyes turning toward the lake. His fluffy tail quivered. I looked down at the water, my feet submerged to my ankles. The water was slightly murky, the pebbly bottom a mosaic of browns. It was maybe two feet deep.

My skin prickled, tension winding my tired muscles tight. Ripples ran across the surface. A shadow slid across the water.

No.

A shadow slid *beneath* the water.

Saber! Ríkr yelled, leaping skyward as he transformed into a hawk.

The lake's quiet energy burst, the surface of the water exploded, and a huge shape launched from the frothing waves.

I threw myself backward. White wings flashed. Jagged teeth, a jaw opening wide. A wave splashed over me, drenching me, blinding me. I rolled off the boulder and landed on my feet in the shallows. Sloshing backward onto the shore, I grabbed for my switchblade with one hand while frantically rubbing the water from my eyes with the other.

My vision cleared.

My heart stopped.

A hulking black creature, covered in rotting vegetation and algae slime, stood in the shallows on four legs. Its bulky, vaguely horse-like head turned toward me, its long muzzle full of curved teeth that pointed in every direction.

White wings, stained with crimson blood, hung from the kelpie's monstrous jaws.

23

THE KELPIE SWUNG its head, spitting the small fae from its mouth. The hawk tumbled across the rocky shore, a lifeless heap of bloody feathers.

"Ríkr!" I screamed.

The kelpie turned back to me, water and slime dripping off its huge form. It was easily twice the size of the creature that had burst out of the pond at the crossroads, and I couldn't tell how much bulk was rotting seaweed and how much was flesh, bone, and muscle.

We meet again, pretty one.

The familiar voice hissed into my mind, and I reeled back another step. Balligor? The same kelpie as before? How was he so much larger?

I scanned the fae's massive form for an obvious weak spot, my fingers tight around my switchblade, but its four inches of steel had never felt so insignificant. Ríkr hadn't moved, not even a twitch.

Balligor slunk closer, his front legs shaped like a cat's with dragonish feet, his hind legs like a horse, and a lizard's tail. His mouth opened, splitting the sides of his long snout, his teeth stained with Ríkr's blood.

You smell so sweet, pretty one, he purred, towering over me, twice the mass of a large draft horse. *But so little power. Perhaps your flesh will satisfy me instead.*

I stepped backward, pebbles digging into my bare feet. Fear, sharp and unfamiliar, flooded my body.

A shame the druid did not approach the water. His long black tongue snaked out of his mouth. *Not a glance toward me, the arrogant fool.*

Zak had sensed danger, but not its source. Ríkr hadn't realized where the malignant energy he'd detected was emanating from either. They'd both thought it was coming from the crossroads. They'd both thought this spot was safer.

His power … his power is so potent. Balligor licked his chops. *So irresistible, pretty one. You cannot imagine.*

He was almost on top of me, but I hadn't noticed him move. Just as I'd ended up too close to the pond last time, distance around this fae was not what I perceived.

His head lowered, and hot breath that reeked of sulfur and swamp bathed my face. *I would much prefer the druid to you.*

"Th-then …" I was stammering. Trembling. I so rarely felt fear that I couldn't contain it. "Then let's make a deal."

A deep laugh gurgled in his throat. *A deal, pretty one?*

"You want the druid. I can get you the druid."

Can you?

"I know where he went."

Rocks crunched under the fae's feet as he circled behind me, his foul breath making my throat convulse with nausea. *He went to the crossroads. But that does not help me, pretty one. There is too little water there, and my form is not enough to defeat him. I need him to come here.*

Did larger bodies of water increase his strength—and his size?

"I'll bring him here," I said.

Hot, moist air washed over my back, and a rough tongue ran up my arm from elbow to shoulder. *Will you, pretty one?*

"I—I just—need … something to lure him here." I fought my fear, fought for clarity. "Something convincing. He's searching for a creature. You mentioned it before."

The kelpie slathered his tongue over my skin a second time. Was he deciding that eating the weak witch he'd already caught was preferable to bargaining for a chance at the druid?

"Tell me something about the creature," I told him breathlessly, "and I'll convince the druid to come here to look for it. He'll walk right into your reach."

The creature … Balligor gurgled a laugh. His claws scraped the pebbled shore as he circled in front of me. Water lapped at my heels. I was right at the edge of the lake. When had I moved toward the water? Or had the water moved closer to me?

A shadow of Death. The fae lowered his head, and a pale eye gleamed from beneath the matted vegetation draping his face. *He appears with the sun's retreat, and no weapon does he need to claim his prey. Nameless animals cannot resist his call, and their spirits fly to his ever-hungry mouth.*

"His call?" I whispered.

Balligor was so close that his huge head filled my vision. *Fae and humans, our spirits are bound to our names. We can resist his* call—*but not always. Some lose their minds to terror. Some to rage. He will pursue his chosen prey relentlessly until they give up their name to him.*

My breath rushed through my clenched teeth.

Names have power, pretty one. Give him another's name, and he will call their life away, regardless of distance or defense. The fae reared back with a wet gargle. *Humans are such fools to give their true names to any who ask. No fae is so reckless.*

"That—" I gulped for air. "That should be enough to lure the druid here. I'll tell him that the killer fae is—"

No, no, pretty one. Balligor's massive jaws cracked. *My lure is already set.*

"What?"

His tongue slid out and I recoiled before it touched my face. *I can taste the druid on you. He will come to the water's edge …*

Powerful claws closed around my ankle.

… for you.

He wrenched my leg out from under me and I pitched backward. As I slammed down, I snapped my switchblade out and drove it into the fae's clawed hand. His painful grip spasmed but he didn't let go.

I yanked the blade out and stabbed again.

Hissing, Balligor grabbed me by the neck. Sitting back on his haunches, he lifted me into the air. I rammed my blade into his inner wrist. He snarled, squeezing my throat, cutting off my air.

I twisted my blade, digging it in, searching for something besides flesh. The tip ground across bone. I shifted the knife up and felt it catch on a tough, sinewy band. Black spots flashed in my vision, my lungs screaming. Grabbing my knife with both hands, I wrenched it out of his wrist, tearing through tendons and—

His enraged bellow rang out as I fell. Water splashed as the fae staggered, his arm outstretched and his fingers gaping open in an awkward claw shape.

The median nerve in the wrist. Sever it to cripple the functionality of the hand and forearm.

Shoving up, I bolted away from the lake. Thundering footsteps shook the ground, and a hand seized the back of my shirt, dragging me into the air. Gaping jaws opened wide as Balligor swung me toward his mouth.

But I could still hear thundering beats.

Hoofbeats.

Magic flashed, and a whip of golden light snapped around Balligor's upper jaw, yanking it sideways.

I crashed onto the top of his slimy snout and bounced off. Plunging down, I landed on my back at the water's edge, the air rammed from my lungs and my diaphragm seizing. The fae's thick legs splashed feet away, but I couldn't move.

Black fur. A canine face appeared in front of me.

Hold on to me, a low female voice growled inside my head.

I forced myself up and slung an arm around the varg's shoulders. She dragged me through the shallow water, away from the kelpie's stomping feet. My lungs finally unlocked, and I gasped for air.

Balligor roared furiously.

Twenty feet along the shore, the colossal fae swung at Zak and Tilliag. The blow struck the stallion in the shoulder, throwing him off his legs. Zak leaped clear of the falling horse and landed in a roll. As he came up, the kelpie's claws flashed toward him.

Zak's whip vanished and an amber shield formed from the same semi-transparent light, flaring out from his forearm. He thrust it up, and Balligor's claws slammed against it. The power of the strike should have crushed a human's strength, but Zak held against it.

"*Impello*," he snarled.

A ripple of air burst off him, and the kelpie jolted as though struck by an invisible fist. Zak whipped a potion off his belt and flung it. The glass shattered against the fae, and Balligor recoiled as thick brown smoke billowed from the splattered potion.

The druid darted backward, reaching for one of the crystals hanging around his neck. "*Ori vis siderea!*"

A swirl of purple magic engulfed his hand. He flung it in the kelpie's face. Balligor balked at the magic—then whipped his thick reptilian tail out. It slammed into Zak, hurling him off his feet.

The fae wolf supporting me shot away, and I splashed onto my hands and knees. A second varg ran out of the underbrush, and the canine pair charged the fae's rear as he bore down on Zak.

Another flash of magic. A burst of gray smoke from a potion. A bright explosion of fire.

But it wasn't enough.

The fae wolves tore at the protective layer of vegetation covering the kelpie. Tilliag charged but couldn't get close as Balligor whirled. His tail smashed the vargs away. His swinging arm knocked the stallion to the ground. And with his slimy armor protecting him from Zak's potions, he grabbed the druid by the throat and lifted him into the air, jaws opening wide.

Zak pulled the ten-inch knife from its sheath on his thigh and slammed it down into the fae's mouth. The steel point burst through his lower jaw.

Roaring, Balligor slammed Zak into the ground with bone-breaking force. Pinning him by the chest, the fae laughed wetly.

So weak, Crystal Druid, he taunted. *You are a disappointment to your reputation. You think that pitiful human magic can hurt me? Where is your arsenal of fae magic?*

The sunlight dimmed. Shadows rippled across the lake, and the earth shuddered beneath buzzing power.

"Where indeed," a female voice purred.

With a dark shimmer, Lallakai stepped out of the fae demesne, her emerald eyes glittering. Her knee-length raven hair swirled and her hips swayed seductively as she sauntered toward the kelpie.

"A crucial oversight, swamp scum, that you would forget to whom the Crystal Druid belongs." Her red lips curved up. "An error which will cost you your life."

Balligor snarled. *Shadow witch. I will never—*

She raised an elegant hand. Phantom wings flared wide on either side of her. Black power writhed up from the ground, and she cast her hand sideways. The dark magic swept out in arching blades.

Blood sprayed. Balligor staggered backward, a strangled gargle escaping him as his protective vegetation fell away and his blood splashed the shore. Roaring, he lunged toward her.

Lallakai waved her hand again. Another swirl of shadow blades ripped across the kelpie. He staggered, snarling. Another graceful gesture, and a third wave of shadow magic tore into him.

Bellowing, he whirled toward the water. As he fled, she pointed a sharp black fingernail at his back. The air burned with power as shadows spiraled around her arm, then shot from her finger like a spear. It pierced his neck at the base of his skull, and he crumpled into the three-foot-deep water.

On my hands and knees at the lake's edge, I could only stare.

Turning, Lallakai looked down at Zak, lying at her feet. "My dearest stubborn druid, when will you give up this foolish pride?"

Zak, a hand pressed to his ribs, said nothing.

"Rumors of your weakness will spread. More fae will try for you." She sank gracefully to her knees at his side. "You need me, my love. As desperately as ever. Why will you not let me help you?"

Her tone was sweet, caring, sad. It raised my hackles more than if she'd hissed vile threats.

She brushed her talon-like nails over his cheek. "How many wounds will you take? How many battles will you lose? You could already have replenished your lost magic if you would but rely on me again. Like you once did."

If it hadn't been so quiet, I wouldn't have heard his hoarse reply.

"You want me to give you too much, Lallakai."

She cupped his cheek. "You already gave yourself to me. You belong to me."

"If you want mindless obedience, bind me with magic and feed off me like a leech."

Shadows coiled around her, the air vibrating with her anger.

I pushed to my feet, water splashing noisily. Lallakai raised her emerald gaze to me as I stooped to pick up my switchblade, the steel glinting among the brown pebbles. Retracting the blade, I tucked it in my pocket, then turned and limped away.

The Lady of Shadow and her druid said nothing else as I moved down the shore, hardly feeling the sharp rocks under my bare feet. The same sharp rocks dug into my bruised knees as I knelt.

Carefully, gently, I turned Ríkr's body over and straightened his bloodstained wings.

A pale blue eye cracked open. *You're alive, dove.*

My heart lurched. "That's my line."

It would take more than a bite from a kelpie to end me.

"You look about three seconds from death."

Looks … are deceiving.

A short, shaky laugh escaped me. I pulled him into my arms, gathered him gently to my chest, and curled my body around him, letting the razor-edged terror that I'd lost him slip quietly away.

24

"THAT'S THE BEST I can do," I told Ríkr, knotting the last bandage. His hawk form was more gauze than feather.

Allow me a day's recuperation, he mumbled, *and I will be a spritely and delightful companion once more.*

I didn't point out that he'd be lucky to walk under his own power in a mere day. Winding the roll of gauze up, I tucked it into Zak's alchemy kit, open on the ground beside me. I hadn't realized it was also a first aid kit.

The druid sat nearby, slouched against a tree trunk with his eyes closed and his hand on his ribs.

I capped a small bottle—a potion he'd instructed me to drip onto Ríkr's wounds to speed healing—and tucked it back in the cloth kit, then spent a few minutes inspecting the soles of my feet. Scraped up but not bleeding. This was the last time I'd take my shoes off anywhere but in my own apartment.

Crossing to the boulder at the water's edge, I collected my hiking boots and socks. Balligor's body was a massive, reeking heap in the water. I returned to the shade where Zak waited, though the shade wasn't necessary anymore. A soft orange glow radiated from behind the western slope of the mountain, all that remained of the fading sunlight.

Sinking down beside the druid, I tugged a sock onto my foot. "How did it go at the crossroads?"

He sighed without opening his eyes. "Pointless. The whole area was abandoned."

"Too bad." I pulled on my other sock. "Seeing as you ditched me here so my useless witch weight wouldn't slow you down, you probably don't want to know what I learned about the fae killer while you were gone."

Zak cracked his eyes open. "You learned something? From Balligor?"

I nodded, still too irritated that he'd ditched me to feel smug. "He said the killer can devour its victims' spirits—which must include their hearts too—by 'calling' them. Animals have no defense, but if you have a name, you can resist. Trying to resist might make you go mad with rage or fear, though."

He sat up a bit straighter, wincing with the movement.

"If the killer knows your name," I continued, stuffing my foot in my boot, "you have no defense. It can devour your spirit even if you aren't nearby. That's probably how Arla died. Jason told the fae her name so it would kill her."

He swore. "That means he can have the fae kill anyone whose name he knows."

"And that means it's extremely unlikely Laney knows about the fae or its powers. If she did, she'd already have given it my name." Shoes on and tied, I turned to the alchemy kit. "Do you need anything before I pack this up?"

"Vitality potion. The purple one. And the gray one with bubbles."

I pulled out an amethyst-colored potion, uncorked it, and held it out. Keeping a hand against his ribs, he took the vial and downed it like a shot. I found a fizzy gray one, my nose wrinkling at its astringent odor. "What's this?"

"Pain killer."

A heavy-duty one, I suspected. I passed it over and he tossed it back.

"Are your ribs broken?" I inquired grudgingly, not really wanting to know how badly he was hurt.

"Bruised. I think." He scrunched his eyes. "The pain killer will help. My main issue right now is the aftereffects of the strength potion I took before fighting Balligor."

I'd been surprised the huge fae's blows hadn't crushed him. Lips pressing thin, I folded the alchemy kit up, then checked on Ríkr again. He was dozing, his breathing steady despite his terrible wounds.

Balligor had almost killed us all, but Lallakai had slain him with so little effort. I glanced down the shore to where the Lady of Shadow was ambling along the waterline, her long hair fluttering in the breeze—though I couldn't feel a breeze, only sticky humidity. She didn't seem concerned about the battered state of her druid.

She and Balligor had both talked about Zak's lack of magic. My gaze turned to his right forearm, his scarred druid tattoos hidden against his flat stomach as he held his ribs.

My eyes narrowed. I seized his wrist and pulled his arm up. Blood smeared his hand from scrapes on his palm.

As I retrieved the gauze again, I bit my inner cheek against the question fighting to get out. I didn't want to ask, but I couldn't hold it back any longer. "Why did you save me?"

"I've done that a few times now."

"I'm aware." I poured disinfectant on a gauze pad and wiped the largest scrape clean. A faded rune—a spell of some kind—was tattooed across his palm, now damaged and useless. "You're a self-confessed murderer and the most wanted rogue in Vancouver. You have a million-dollar bounty on your head." My eyes lifted to his. "Why are you going out of your way to keep me from dying?"

He looked away, leaning his head back against the tree trunk. Eyes distant, shuttered, hazed with shadow.

"Have you ever lost everything?" A soft question, his voice low and raspy. "Ever had a moment when you realized everything that matters to you is gone, you fucked up, you lost it. And all that's left are the worst parts of your life and the worst parts of yourself."

I gripped his hand, his skin warm and palms calloused, and breathed silently through my nose to calm the seething emotions his words had awoken. "What does that have to do with saving me?"

His green eyes slid to mine, exhausted down to his core. "Do you ever want to be someone else?"

All the time. Every day.

But I wouldn't admit that. "You still haven't answered my question. Why did you save me?"

"I haven't decided yet."

That he was repeating an answer I'd given him didn't escape my notice. "Bullshit."

"Truth. I saved you from that bear fae because I'm not completely heartless, and because I wanted information from you. But beyond that, I don't know. I've always worked alone. I don't know why I accepted your help with all this, or helped you, or stuck around. I don't even know why I'm telling you this right now. It's not like me."

I squinted at him.

His chest rose and fell with a deep, slow breath. "But I don't want to keep doing things the way I always have, so … here we are."

Cursing under my breath, I returned my attention to his hand. This man was incomprehensible. He was a murderer who saved children. He was a rogue who wanted to bring a killer to justice. He was the druid consort of a deadly darkfae while holding her at arm's length. He was powerful but had lost some or most of that power.

I just didn't understand him.

Thoughts churning, I scrubbed the mud off his hand, then dug the small piece of gauze between his middle and ring fingers. It rubbed across rough skin. I peered at the gap between his fingers, expecting to see another scrape—but it wasn't a cut. Not a recent one.

It was a scar.

My body froze, every muscle locking. No air in my lungs. No heartbeat in my chest.

And utter chaos inside my head.

Memories were flooding my brain, rushing in like a burst dam, sweeping away everything else. Memories I'd seen only as disjointed glimpses for the past ten years. Memories I'd thought were gone forever, lost to my trauma-fueled amnesia.

I was fifteen again, sitting in a stuffy attic.

I was holding my switchblade. I was swinging it down, stabbing it into the floorboards. A dark-haired boy snatched his hand away. Blood ran from between his fingers.

"Saber?"

The deluge continued, relentlessly pouring every lost memory into my consciousness until I was shaking and gasping, my sightless eyes staring into a past I'd never wanted to relive.

"*Saber?*"

Hands were on my shoulders, shaking me. I blinked, and green eyes appeared before me. Zak. His voice sounded again, distant, echoing with words that couldn't penetrate the madness screaming through my skull.

My newly whole memories flashed and spun, over and over. My switchblade stabbing downward. The boy snatching his hand away. His bemused expression as he'd watched it bleed. Dark hair. Fair skin. Eyes …

Green eyes.

For the first time in a decade, I remembered the boy's face. It was there, in my mind, clear as the first night I'd met him. Tousled hair and straight nose and full lips and those beautiful, unforgettable green eyes. I'd fallen in love with those eyes. Fallen in love with *him*.

And I was staring into those same eyes right now.

A scream burst from my throat. Hoarse, agonized, inhuman. All the broken pieces inside me writhed and whirled in a maelstrom of slashing pain, of shattered hopes, of crushed innocence.

My knife was in my hand and slashing toward him.

He flung his arm up. The blade caught it, dragging across flesh. Blood spilled down.

"You bastard!" I screamed. "*You bastard!*"

I lunged for him. We tumbled across the grass, his gasps of pain the only sound I heard. Strength I'd never known powered my limbs. Adrenaline. Rage. Brutal, animalistic bloodlust.

Saber!

I wanted to kill him. I *would* kill him. He needed to die—right now, right this second, before his presence, his very existence, tore me apart even further.

Saber!

My blade flashed as we wrestled, and he couldn't overpower me. I was too strong, and he was exhausted, injured. He was bleeding. He would die. He would—

Saber! Ríkr yelled inside my head.

A sharp pull on my hair wrenched me off him and threw me backward. I landed on my ass, knife clutched in my hand.

Lallakai towered over me, her emerald stare piercing. Zak was half sprawled behind her, propped up on his elbows, bloody and breathing hard. My knife had reached him. More than once. I couldn't tell how many wounds or how deep.

Not deep enough.

His eyes were wide, disbelieving, stunned. He stared at me as though he'd never seen me before. As though I were a ghost come to life after ten years in the grave.

Careful, Saber, Ríkr hissed warningly, struggling to stand where I'd left him under the tree.

I pulled my feet under me and stood, unable to look away from Zak. "You *bastard*."

"No."

My hand tightened around my switchblade at his guttural denial.

"No," he rasped again. "You're not her."

I drew my arm back.

"You can't be her."

I took aim.

"She was—"

I flung the blade. It spun in a perfect arch, straight for his throat.

Lallakai's hand flashed out. A splatter of blood. Elegant fingers curled around the blade she'd caught in midair, and she cocked her head, her crystalline eyes gleaming.

My chest heaved. Emotions, sensations, sights, scents, sounds—the memories, so agonizingly fresh, were boiling through my subconscious, and my eyes burned. No. No, I wouldn't. I couldn't. Inexcusable. Unforgiveable. I wouldn't. I would never let him see me cry.

Whirling, I sprinted for my bag. I grabbed it, scooped Ríkr up with my other arm—and I ran. Ran hard. Ran fast.

Zak didn't call out. He didn't make a sound.

My feet pounded against the hard-packed trail. Trees whipped by, the shadows deep. I was screaming inside. Pain, rage, hate, agony, anguish. Loathing. For him. For me. For being a fool. For letting him in. For trusting him.

And I'd made the same stupid, unforgivable mistake *twice*.

My chest was on fire. My legs were giving beneath me. I kept running until I knew I was out of sight, out of earshot, out of reach.

I collapsed to my knees in the middle of the trail. Clutching my backpack and Ríkr's feathered form. Whole body shaking, trembling. The broken shards of my heart and soul spinning and spinning, grinding and slashing.

I curled in on myself, tears streaming down my face as the memories I'd repressed for ten years rose up and buried me in the darkest, coldest night of my life.

25

THE SMELL *of percolating coffee clouded my head with jittery nerves. I could hear it from the kitchen, that odd, sharp burbling noise only coffeemakers made.*

Aunt Ruth sat in her favorite armchair, the floor lamp beside her casting a warm glow over her brown hair as she studied something on her laptop screen. Her reading glasses, propped on her slim nose, reflected a white spreadsheet.

Before she could notice my gaze, I bent over my notebook, a thick calculus textbook beside it on the coffee table. Sitting on the floor hurt my back, the tight waist of my designer jeans cutting in my stomach, but Ruth liked to see me working.

Her ward must be smart. Must be polite, demure, perfect.

Ruth didn't think I was any of those things. I was stupid, rude, pathetic, weak. But I had to look perfect or it would reflect poorly on her. Not too perfect, though. I couldn't look better than Ruth, or I'd pay even worse for that.

The coffeemaker let out a loud gurgle, and I scribbled random numbers across my homework. Tonight was the last night. I wouldn't have to be afraid after this. In no time at all, she would be dead and I would be far from here, alongside the boy I'd fallen in love with.

Tonight, I would finally learn his name.

Excitement buzzed through me, and I understood why he'd wanted to wait. The small, sweet pleasure of learning his name was so easy to focus on. It calmed me. It reassured me.

Ruth closed her laptop lid. I struggled not to tense as she rose, straightened her cashmere sweater over her slim hips, and walked into the kitchen. The clink of a mug. The clatter of the carafe sliding off the hotplate.

My nerves buzzed, adrenaline spiking. I'd slipped the poison into the carafe shortly after she'd started the coffeemaker. Her drink was already tainted. All she had to do was swallow a few sips.

I hoped I'd added enough. The minty smell had been so strong. I didn't want her to catch a whiff of it.

Ruth reappeared, a steaming mug in her hand. She set the mug on the end table beside her armchair and sank down. Pulling her laptop onto her thighs, she opened it and tapped in her password. The spreadsheet reappeared, reflected by her glasses.

I hid my shaking hands in my lap as I pretended to read my textbook. She studied her document. Her hand lifted. She picked up the mug and lifted it to her lips.

Paused.

Looked at me.

"Rose, did you complete your food journal for the day?"

She refused to call me by my first name, always using my middle name instead.

"Yes, ma'am." Did my voice sound too thin?

She lowered her coffee mug a few inches. "And you kept under a thousand calories?"

"Yes, ma'am." My aching stomach confirmed it. She always found out when I lied. "Nine-hundred and seventy calories."

"Good. I won't have an obese whale in my house. Left on your own, you'd eat like a heifer with her first calf."

"Yes, ma'am."

Her attention returned to her laptop. She lifted the mug back to her lips and blew on the hot coffee. I forced my gaze to my textbook, watching from the corner of my eye.

"Rose," she murmured, still focused on her spreadsheet. "Tell me, what are your plans for the future?"

Startled, I looked up. "The future?"

"Yes, stupid girl. Answer my question."

"I—I'd like to go to veterinary school. They're competitive, but my grades—"

"Veterinary school? Please. Who would put the life of their pet in your incompetent hands? Any idiot can pass a test, but even an animal doctor needs at least half a brain, which is far more than you possess."

Not responding was disrespectful, so I forced out another "yes, ma'am."

Drink the coffee.

"Real intelligence," she continued, the steaming mug in her hand, "is more than memorization or basic math."

Just drink it.

"It requires deductive ability. Logic. Reasoning. An innate cunning, if you will."

One sip. Just one.

"You, however." She lifted the mug to her mouth. "Your ability to reason your way through a problem is utterly crippled."

The mug tilted. She swallowed a large gulp.

My stomach dropped with a mix of terror and elation. I gripped the edge of the coffee table, terse, waiting. Less than a minute, he'd said.

"For example." She took another large gulp. "When someone deceives you, you're hopelessly dense."

I stared at her face. The first symptom was numbness. How would she react?

Pushing her laptop aside, she stood, mug in hand, and crossed the spacious living room to stand beside me. Her cold brown eyes gazed down at me.

"Poison, as an example."

My brain stuttered. My limbs seized.

"Did it occur to you that a deadly poison isn't likely to smell like peppermint oil?"

Paralyzed, I stared up at her as something inside me turned as brittle as newly frozen ice.

"Did you even question it?" Laughing, she upended the coffee mug over my head. Scalding liquid splashed over me. "Did you test the so-called poison first? Did you use your brain at all?"

The mug swung down, shattering on top of my head. I jolted sideways—then her foot slammed into my side. As I fell over, she picked up my heavy calculus textbook, snapped the sturdy cover closed, and raised it over me.

"Stupid—traitorous—whore."

The book hit me. Again. And again. I curled into a ball, arms shielding my head.

"After I took you in. Paid for the best education. Bought you a wardrobe of beautiful clothes. Made your ugly face passable. Fed you."

The blows rained down. It didn't stop. Wouldn't stop. I couldn't breathe. It hurt, hurt too much, hurt like I was dying.

"After all I've done for you, you'd try to kill me? Ungrateful bitch."

She kept ranting but I couldn't hear her. Couldn't fight her. Couldn't stop her. Couldn't do anything but cower and shake as she beat me. On and on, the worst beating she'd ever given me. It wouldn't stop, wouldn't end, and my entire world became pain.

Slowly, distantly, I realized it was quiet.

No more blows. My thoughts were fuzzy, my stomach twisting. The taste of vomit in my mouth. Slowly, agonizingly, I turned my head.

Ruth was back in her armchair, tapping on her laptop, her hair smooth and expression undisturbed.

I pushed myself up, arms shaking, and spat the bile and blood from my mouth. Choking back a whimper, I crawled toward the kitchen.

"Your bedroom is the other way," Ruth remarked, not bothering to look up from her screen.

I kept crawling toward the kitchen.

"Are you running away?" She snorted. "Go ahead, then. Find your little boyfriend. Get it out of your system before you come crawling back."

In the kitchen doorway, I levered myself to my feet. Every gasping breath sent spears of agony through my ribs. I staggered into the kitchen.

"Beg for my forgiveness," Ruth called after me, "and I might reconsider selling you to the Wolfsbane."

Her cruel laughter followed me out the patio door.

I couldn't take a bus looking like this, and I didn't have my wallet anyway. So I walked. What else could I do? I had nothing but the clothes on my back and … and the switchblade in my pocket. Always in my pocket. I liked to play with it. I would spin it and flash it around like I was so tough.

But I was too much of a coward to use it. Not on Ruth.

I walked. I stopped. I cried, and I walked more. Minutes to hours. The night crept by. It hurt so much. Every step hurt, but I kept going, because we'd promised.

Something with our plan had gone wrong, something awful, but he would be waiting for me. We'd figure it out. He'd help me. I wasn't alone.

I wasn't alone.

I wasn't alone.

The streets were quiet, the deep of night holding the city in its spell. I staggered to the crime den, the hated building where we'd first met, then turned toward the opposite sidewalk. Limped across the road. Stepped into the dark alley.

Empty.

I staggered all the way to the end before stumbling back. Sinking down to sit on the dirty asphalt, I leaned gingerly against the wall and stared out at the street. Waiting. We'd promised.

A raindrop plopped on my head. Another hit my nose. Patter, patter. The rain fell, soaking me in seconds, and I tucked myself into a tight ball. No jacket, but the cold water numbed me a little to the throbbing, burning, stabbing pain that was everywhere.

I waited.

Dizzy. Nauseous.

I waited.

Tired. Cold.

I waited.

Hurting. Hurting so much.

My face was buried in my arms, legs pulled up to my chest, raindrops drumming on my head, when I felt the shift. The sour, tainted energies of the city swirled as someone more than human approached.

I lifted my head.

He stood ten paces away. Long jacket, hood up. Face in shadow. Watching me like he had that first night, so still, so ominous.

Then he moved. Slow strides. Closer, closer. Three feet away, he stopped again. I couldn't see his face through the shadows of his hood. My heart throbbed in my chest, rain running down my face.

His hand slid from his pocket. A chain hung from his gloved fingers. He tossed it down.

A clatter on the pavement. My river-stone pendant lying on the wet, muddy ground. Raindrops splattered on the rune carved into its face.

A deep, ugly crack split the rune.

My eyes wouldn't move from that crack. Couldn't move. Couldn't believe what I was seeing.

I dragged my stare up to his shadowed face.

He turned and walked away.

The soft rain became deafening thunder in my ears. My vision fractured. His dark silhouette receded farther and farther. He didn't stop. Didn't pause. Didn't look back. Then he was gone from my sight.

From my life.

From my future.

Sitting in the rain, I shuddered. Whole body. Violent. Shaking as the brittle parts of me broke apart. The shards cut me, cut deep, punishing me for my weakness, my naivety, my stupid, stupid hope.

I sat there as I was sliced apart from the inside. Sat there until the pain crystallized into something else. Until the shards started to grind against each other in my chest.

Not anger. Not rage. Not hate. Something colder and deeper and utterly unquenchable.

Uncoiling, I pushed to my feet. The pain was distant. My fear had disappeared.

I stepped over my broken pendant, the last vestige of my past, and walked away. Walked all the way back to the grand house with its manicured lawn and expensive furnishings, where Ruth waited in her armchair.

When dawn broke, I was sitting on the living room floor. I was still sitting there hours later when the front door clattered, when the housekeeper's horrified scream rang out, when she vomited in the doorway.

And I was still sitting there, drenched in Ruth's blood, my christened switchblade in my hand, when the police arrived to arrest me.

26

TEN YEARS LATER, I was shattering inside once more.

Deep blue dusk draped the mountainside, the shadows beneath the trees already dark as night. I'd recovered enough composure to resume walking, but I could barely make out the path and my boots scuffed unsteadily against the uneven ground. My backpack hung from one shoulder, Ríkr cradled in my arms.

Saber? he ventured cautiously.

I said nothing. Human emotions were difficult for fae to comprehend. He couldn't comfort me, and I didn't want to be comforted anyway.

The return of my fractured, missing memories should have made me feel whole for the first time in a decade. Instead, I felt more broken. The grinding in my chest wouldn't stop. It was like a voice screaming in my ear to react, to lash out, to destroy the source of my pain—but I couldn't. To reach Zak, I would have to get past Lallakai, his two vargs, and a fae stallion. He was too well protected.

I would find a way. Once I was calmer. Once I had centered myself. And when I next faced him, I wouldn't merely kill him. I would get answers first.

I wanted to know *why*.

The boy who'd won my teenaged heart. Who'd given me a fake poison. Who'd taken my only treasure, my parents' precious artifact, and destroyed it. Who'd offered me hope, then left me for dead. The boy who'd betrayed me.

I had one answer now: the boy from my past had been a druid, not a witch.

It made perfect sense, and I blamed my fifteen-year-old self's inexperience and naivety for failing to guess the truth. No one feared a witch the way the other criminals at the den had feared Bane. On top of that, he and his apprentice had both possessed multiple familiars when most witches were lucky to have one.

But I'd been a young, stupid girl. Druids were rare, so rare, they'd said. Druids died young, they'd said. You'd be lucky to ever meet a druid, they'd said.

Had he intended to trick me from the start? Had he been thinking of betraying me when we'd first kissed? Had he been planning to destroy my only treasure while we'd made love with it hanging around his neck? Had he laughed at my idiocy while he'd picked out a harmless herbal extract to give me instead of a poison?

I'd been so stupid.

The near-full moon peeked above the treetops, but its light wasn't enough to illuminate the path. Cradling Ríkr in one arm, I swung my bag off my shoulder and dug into it for the flashlight Zak had so considerately packed for me. The thought made me want to smash the bag's contents on the ground.

Saber, Ríkr whispered, this time in a tone of warning.

I stilled my movements—and I heard it. The distant *duh-duh-dun, duh-duh-dun* of a cantering horse, growing steadily louder.

Whirling back the way I'd come, I braced myself. The beating hooves grew clearer. I bared my teeth in anticipation, ready for another round even though I had no weapon.

A dark shape appeared around the bend in the trail. Tilliag's acid-green eyes gleamed as he slowed to a trot, blowing loudly as he approached.

There was no rider on his back.

Standing stiffly, I watched as the stallion halted a few feet away. He surveyed me, then turned his head, presenting the side of his neck. Something glinted in his mane—my switchblade, tied to his long, coarse hair with a piece of twine.

Take it, the stallion ordered.

I hesitated, then stepped closer. A quick tug on the twine undid the knot, and my switchblade fell into my hand. My fingers curled tightly around it.

"You came all this way just to give me my knife?"

Tilliag snorted. *The druid bid me to take you to safety.*

Every muscle in my body went rigid.

How noble of him, Ríkr muttered.

"Not happening," I told Tilliag sharply. "Go back to him."

The horse flattened his ears. *I will either carry you or accompany you.*

I turned on my heel and marched away. Hooves thudded after me.

"Go away, Tilliag."

Another snort. *I agreed to this task.*

"I won't ride you."

Then walk. I dislike carrying humans.

Wrapped in my arms, Ríkr's vivid blue eyes narrowed with displeasure. *Your disdain for humans is undermined by your obedience to one.*

Tilliag ignored that.

I stomped another few yards. "Is this a pathetic attempt by Zak to soothe his guilt? Making sure I get home safely won't fix shit."

Going home wasn't an option anyway. The MPD's bounty team was probably still waiting at the rescue, and I hadn't learned anything that would convince them of my innocence. I needed the fae killer or Jason Brine, and my chances of finding either by myself were nil, especially with Ríkr injured.

I make no effort to understand the minds of humans or druids, Tilliag told us haughtily. *Zak did not explain his thoughts when he gave me this task.*

Not mere obedience, Ríkr remarked. *Blind obedience.*

I am paying my debt to the druid, Tilliag shot back. *It matters not why he bid me to do this.*

"I don't want Zak's help," I snapped. "So you can go."

He blew into my ponytail. *You are slow.*

I sped up, though I couldn't keep up the pace. "Where is Zak? Is he walking back?"

He went on to the crossroads.

"What? Why? We came to interrogate Balligor, but he's dead."

Tilliag stopped to grab a mouthful of long grass from the edge of the trail.

Chewing the long blades, he ambled after me. *Zak seeks the heart thief and the witch who called it here. He must kill one or the other before the heart thief learns his name or yours.*

I resisted the urge to look toward the dark summit.

What foolhardy hubris has convinced him he is a match for this heart thief? Rikr asked, putting words to the question I was too stubborn to ask. *He could not defeat a kelpie. The heart thief will most certainly take his life.*

If the thief does not know Zak's name, the stallion replied, *he can resist its call.*

"Or it'll try to suck out his soul without his name and drive him mad," I growled. "It's stupid and risky."

Tilliag trotted a few steps to catch up to us. *I would return to him to speed his search, but I must accompany you. You are slow,* he added pointedly.

Rikr canted his avian head. *The return to civilization is a fair distance to walk, dove.*

I huffed out a furious breath. "*Fine.* I'll ride."

Crouching, I opened my bag and slid Rikr inside it. He sighed aggrievedly as I zipped the top partially shut, then slung it carefully over my shoulders.

Ears perked eagerly, Tilliag presented his side to me. I grabbed a handful of his mane and hauled myself up. The moment I was settled, the stallion launched into a trot.

I squinted at the dark path, then up at the moon. Horses had superior night vision to humans, and being a fae, Tilliag could probably see even better. That didn't make the ride more comfortable, though.

My thoughts stretched ahead to my next move. Head into town? Hide in Vancouver? If I could avoid capture until morning, I could buy camping gear and disappear into the wilderness for a couple of weeks. Or should I stay closer? Hope like a fool that Zak would catch the fae killer or Jason Brine?

No, I wouldn't count on him. I wouldn't trust him with *anything*. I should have known when I'd first spotted him riding out of the fae demesne and mistook him for a terrifying wraith that he was too treacherous for anything but a knife in the ribs.

Even if he'd saved my life more than once.

"Betrayer," I muttered.

Tilliag's ears swiveled back toward me.

Do you intend to kill him? Ríkr asked.

"Yes."

Tilliag arched his neck, his trot going bouncy. *The druid is not as powerful as he once was, but I do not think you are strong enough to slay him.*

"What would you know?" I growled.

Exactly so, Ríkr added, backing me up. *A lynx may kill the lion should she crave it more.*

A dismissive snort. *Arrogant, you and your witch. I knew it from the moment I first beheld you both.*

"And I knew from the first moment I saw you and Zak that you two were trouble," I shot back. "Riding down that road like Death itself. I should've turned back right then."

The stallion looked at me with one eye. *Of what road do you speak?*

"Quarry Road. I saw you and Zak riding down it right before the gunshot. I was hiding, so neither of you saw me until the bear fae's attack later."

He trotted in silence for a moment. *We traveled no roads that night. I ran the trails among the trees.*

"But I saw you." I frowned. "A dark rider on a black horse. Who else could it have been?"

We took no roads, the stallion insisted.

An icy prickle ran along my spine, and as I shivered, a melody whispered in my mind. Soft, haunting notes.

A dark rider on empty roads.

Words slipped from my lips, lilting to a forgotten tune. "*On empty roads, in places dark … hoofbeats race, fair souls to mark.*"

Tilliag slowed to a walk, his ears turning toward me.

"*The dark rider comes, when the cold night falls.*" My voice trembled, the notes warbling. "*The dark rider speaks, when deep his voice calls. The dark rider kills, when he knows your name. And your soul the Dullahan will claim.*"

Tilliag stopped in the middle of the trail. I sat upon the stallion's back, silence all around us. The melody looped in my head, and I could hear my father's low voice as he sang the second verse in a spooky tone, his blue eyes sparkling with mischief.

"*Do not weep, do not pray.*" I was shivering. "*But bar your doors til dawn of day. The dark rider comes, when the cold night falls.*"

Balligor had said the fae killer appeared at night. He called for the spirits of his victims. And if he knew your name, he would steal your life away.

"*And your soul the Dullahan will claim,*" I whispered.

The Dullahan. More commonly known as the headless horseman. The old Irish myth spoke of a black rider who carried his head under his arm, riding through the countryside at night. Any who saw him died, for he would call their name and steal their soul.

And I had seen him.

A dark rider upon a black steed, appearing from the mists of the fae demesne. I'd been afraid. Me, who rarely felt fear, had climbed into a ditch to hide from his gaze. I'd instinctively known he was something terrible, something deadly.

But when I'd seen Zak astride Tilliag shortly afterward, I'd chalked up my response to an overreaction.

The Dullahan. Tilliag's ears were pressed flat to his head, his hooves planted on the trail. *That creature has never been seen in these lands.*

"The crossroads," I croaked. "Does the crossroads connect to Ireland?"

I do not know.

"Ríkr, do you know?"

I am not certain, my familiar whispered, *but it links to a land across the great sea where many ancient fae of human legend dwell.*

"Then that's what Jason did. He called the Dullahan here and set him loose."

Set him loose, dove? Ríkr repeated softly. *A being such as that cannot be controlled or contained. It is a hand of Death.*

Balligor's taunt rang in my head, and I muttered his words to myself. "Knowing Death will not protect you from it."

Protect …

I hummed under my breath, the notes rising and falling as I stretched my memory. Another verse. Wasn't there another verse? I dredged up my father's face, his expression a goofy exaggeration of menace.

"*Darkest death,*" I sang, "*face him ne'er without pure gold his stare to sever.*"

My hand closed around the locket hanging from my neck. A gold locket. Jason had given it to Laney. As a romantic gift— or as protection? And … Farmer Whitby. A gold watch on his wrist. His gunshot had drawn the Dullahan's attention, but the fae hadn't killed him—because he'd been wearing gold.

"Zak doesn't know." I gripped a fistful of Tilliag's mane, the locket engulfed in my other hand. "He doesn't know that gold can ward off the Dullahan. He doesn't have anything to protect him, and the Dullahan could come through the crossroads at any moment."

The stallion spun on agile hooves, facing back the way we'd come.

Wait! Ríkr barked, squirming helplessly in my backpack. *Saber, why go to his aid? Why expose yourself to the Dullahan for a man you despise?*

Arching his neck, Tilliag danced on the spot, waiting for my response.

I bit the inside of my cheek. The sharp grind in my chest, the burning need for vengeance, hadn't abated. But … but …

Scrunching my eyes shut, I snarled, "That bastard owes me an explanation. I won't let him die before I get it—and then I'll kill him myself. Let's go!"

Tilliag sprang straight into a gallop. With thundering hooves, he raced toward the mountain's summit and the crossroads where the Dullahan would soon appear.

If the specter of Death wasn't already on the hunt for his next heart.

27

I DIDN'T DARE bring Ríkr into the crossroads when he was injured and helpless. On Summit Trail, high above the crossroads, I hung my backpack in the upper branches of a tree, Ríkr tucked inside.

He wasn't pleased about being left behind. I'd be hearing about it for weeks—assuming I survived.

Down in the valley, I gripped Tilliag's mane as the stallion picked his way through the crumbling ruins and draping vines of the crossroads. The place was eerie during the day. At night, it was outright unsettling.

In the darkness, the previously crimson blossoms blushed a pale pink, radiating a ghostly luminescence that lit the moss-covered ground. Mist drifted through the shadowy, ethereal trees, obscuring everything more than a dozen yards away, and I didn't dare call Zak's name aloud.

"Do you sense him?" I whispered to Tilliag.

It is difficult to sense anything, the stallion replied, his ears swiveling nonstop. *I cannot even detect others of my kind.*

Watching his twitchy ears and stiffly arched neck, I hoped his nerves were steelier than the average horse. I didn't want to get thrown at the first unexpected noise.

We ventured deeper. I recognized none of the mossy paths from my first visit, even though I had an excellent memory for directions. The intersecting trails twisted in nonsensical tangles, the weather-worn pillars with their alien architecture forming unfamiliar patterns. Even Balligor's small pond was nowhere to be seen.

The crossroads changed depending on the power feeding it, Ríkr had warned me when we'd first come here.

No signs of life disturbed the curtains of vines. Had all the fae that frequented the crossroads fled, knowing a killer stalked this place at night? How many, like Balligor, recognized the Dullahan's work?

I touched the locket around my neck, tucked under the front of my shirt to rest against my heart. I'd been checking it obsessively since remembering my father singing the Dullahan's song. He'd always been a singer. So had my mother. All the folk tunes and old ballads I knew, I'd learned from them.

"*Darkest death, face him ne'er ...*" I whispered again. "*Without pure gold his stare to sever.*"

I hoped the lyrics were accurate, or I'd just ridden to my death for the sake of a man I wanted to murder with my bare hands.

Banishing the thought, I stretched my senses out, hoping to distinguish his presence—or *any* presence—but all I could feel was the ancient, inhuman power of this place. It shimmered across my mind like a haunting caress.

Tilliag halted. His muscles quivered as he raised his head, ears turning, tracking a sound.

A soft thudding.

Hoofbeats.

I clutched Tilliag, and we waited motionlessly as the sound grew louder. My nerves tightened, fear skittering up and down my spine.

The rhythm of hooves grew closer. I couldn't tell which direction it was coming from, and my fear deepened into terror. I quaked on Tilliag's back, air rushing through my nose as I fought the rising hysteria. Unnatural. Unreal. This fear wasn't real. I didn't spook this easily. A mere sound couldn't make me tremble.

Except I *was* trembling.

The thudding was soft, ominous, everywhere—then it grew quieter. Fainter. Receding.

Gone.

Tilliag and I waited in silence, and when the sound didn't return, I exhaled harshly. The fear in my gut waned, and I unclenched my hands to shake out my aching fingers. Tilliag blew out a loud breath and tossed his head.

Neither of us commented on how we'd both frozen in terror.

Checking that the gold locket was still around my neck, I opened my mouth to speak.

The scent of death, Tilliag said suddenly.

"What?" I hissed.

I have scented death, he repeated, raising his head to test the air, his upper lip curled. *It is close.*

"Where?"

He started forward, nervousness clinging to him. I ducked strings of luminescent vines, scanning the crumbling ruins that protruded from the earth like stony stalagmites, covered in lichen and moss. Shadowy, semi-transparent trees towered around us, the mists of the fae demesne drifting among them.

A faint whiff of something foul reached my nose. My gut turned over.

Were we too late?

Tilliag's ears perked forward. He broke into a trot, the moss muffling his hooves as he rushed through a stone archway and into an ancient courtyard surrounded by crumbling pillars.

He pulled up short.

Across the small courtyard, the dark shape of a man was slumped against the farthest pillar, his dark clothes blending with the deep shadows.

Without thought or planning, I swung off Tilliag's back. My feet landed silently on the moss, then they were racing forward, carrying me to the fallen man without my command. My lungs strained, empty of air.

My body rushed toward him even as my mind screamed that I didn't care, didn't care, didn't care. I wanted him dead. I wanted it. He should be dead. He deserved to be dead.

So why couldn't I breathe?

I slid to a stop beside the slumped man and dropped into a crouch, reaching for the hood hiding his bowed head. I shoved it back—and squirming white maggots spilled from the fabric. At the sight of the man's sunken eye sockets and bloated flesh, the stench of decomposition hit me. I lurched away and slipped, almost falling.

This wasn't recent death but old death. This wasn't Zak.

I hated the treacherous relief that swept over me.

Covering my nose and mouth with my hand, I squinted at the corpse. Similar in build to the druid, but shorter. Bald. A thick bristle of brown hair on his rotting chin.

I didn't know much about decomposing bodies, but I knew the life cycle of a fly. The maggots infesting the corpse were fat from gluttonous feeding. The man had been dead for at least a week, probably closer to two.

I stretched out my hand. Flicking away maggots, I lifted a gold locket off his chest. It wasn't the same as the one I'd found in Arla's office; this one was oval-shaped. But when I flipped it open, I found identical photos in the tiny frames.

"Jason Brine," I whispered.

A hand closed around my arm.

I jerked away from the unexpected touch, glimpsing a human-shaped shadow reaching out from behind the pillar where Jason's corpse lay. The person wrenched me toward them—then threw me into the darkness between stony columns.

I pitched forward, hands outstretched, but I didn't meet ground where I expected to. There was no ground. Hidden by the shifting mists, the terrain dropped away in a steep slope. I slammed down on the moss elbows-first, tumbling, careening, unable to stop. The shadows and mist spun, trees flashing past.

The fall lasted only seconds before I rolled to a shuddering halt, sprawled facedown with my entire body screaming.

Behind and above me was the scuffing sound of someone half running, half sliding down the steep hillside. Head reeling with dizziness and pain, I pushed myself up onto my knees and twisted around.

A woman slid the last few feet down the slope, her blond hair pulled into a braid over one shoulder. Recognition was still ricocheting through me when she raised her hand, palm up.

Faint sapphire light. A fae rune on her inner wrist. Blue sparkles filled her hand, almost like glitter.

She flung the magic in my face.

My entire body went numb. I slumped back to the ground, a faint moan slipping from me as a terrible weight settled over my limbs and compressed my lungs. My muscles had turned to straw, my mind fuzzy with the fae magic she'd thrown at me.

Crouching, Laney leaned over me, her lizard familiar perched on her shoulder. Gold earrings framed her face. A tangle of gold chains around her neck. Her wrists jangled with gold bracelets. She'd decked herself out in the precious metal.

Somewhere above, an equine scream shattered the stifling silence. Tilliag, voicing his anger. No horse could make it down that slope. He'd have to find another way—unless he planned to abandon me and search for Zak instead.

That would make sense. He owed me nothing.

"Summit Trail." Laney's mouth twisted, her eyes red-rimmed from crying. "If you hadn't said that, I'd never have realized it. I thought Jason had failed. After I dumped him for his obsession with his stupid plan, did he go running to you instead?"

I couldn't answer her. My arms twitched as I struggled to move them. She grabbed my ponytail and wrenched my head around so my face pointed toward hers.

"I bet you thought it was just great. The perfect way to kill my mom and get away with it. No one would ever guess." She angrily wiped away a tear. "I was so stupid, wasn't I? I didn't even realize what had killed her, even though Jason told me all about this fae monster."

More tears ran down her cheeks. "You murdered my mom. *Murdered her.* Now you'll pay for her life with yours." She released my hair, letting my head thunk against the hard ground, and rose to her feet. "You know the urban legend that you can summon Bloody Mary by calling her name three times? Well, it works on some fae too. Jason told me."

Pivoting, she faced the dark mist. "Dullahan!"

Her high-pitched shout echoed through the phantom trees. My limbs shuddered as I fought to move.

"L …" I gasped airlessly.

"Dullahan!"

"L … ney. St … p."

She sneered down at me, then threw her head back and screamed, "*Dullahan!*"

Quiet stillness settled over us in the wake of her cry. She put her foot on my shoulder, pressing down until the joint threatened to pop. "I figured you'd show up after what you said. Did you kill Jason too? He was wearing gold, so it wasn't the Dullahan, was it?"

The air was thick with humid heat, clogging my lungs.

"No one will ever find your body up here," she muttered, nerves creeping into her voice. "You'll die just like my mother did. That's better justice than anything the MPD would do."

My throat worked as I strained to speak. "Didn't … kill her."

"Why are you denying it? You even came to our house to check she was dead!" She stomped on my shoulder, and a sharp, agonizing *crack* split my collarbone. "Who else could have done it? *Jason?* He was already dead! No one else knows about the Dull—"

She jerked back from me and spun toward the dark forest. Her familiar poked his head over her shoulder again, staring in the same direction.

A soft, almost inaudible rustle stirred the shadowy underbrush.

"Dullahan?" she called, fear weakening her voice. "I'll give you her name. It's Saber Rose O—"

With a flash of gold, a thin line of light flew out of the darkness and snapped around Laney's throat. It went taut, yanking her off her feet. She slammed down. Her familiar tumbled across the moss, hissing angrily.

"The *Dullahan*?" a voice rumbled. "I should've realized it. I didn't know the headless horseman stole hearts, though."

Shadows coiled around Zak's legs as he strode out of the trees, his golden whip in hand. His eyes gleamed with iridescent fae power; Lallakai was possessing him.

With a flex of his arm, he tightened the whip around Laney's neck. "You must be the daughter of the coven leader. Nice of you to join us."

"Druid—" she choked, shock twisting her face.

"Be a good girl and stay right there. Or …"

From the shadows swirling slowly around him, his two vargs slunk into view. They circled Laney, muzzles ridged and fangs flashing. Her familiar cowered in place, pressing against the ground. Zak flicked his hand, dissolving the lasso spell, but Laney didn't move, her terrified eyes darting between the two fae wolves.

Zak swept toward me, and I could do nothing as he approached—but even if I could've moved, I probably would've stayed motionless anyway.

Tilliag had said I wasn't strong enough to take on the druid, and I finally saw why.

Power electrified the air around him with savage potency. His unnaturally bright eyes pierced my skin as they moved across me. Shadows clung to him, and markings I'd never seen before, black feathers in the pattern of wings, swept down the heavy muscles of his shoulders and upper arms and flared up the sides of his neck, edging his jaw.

The Crystal Druid. *This* was the man with a reputation of power, even among fae.

Against Balligor, he'd been a strong, cunning fighter. Now, his power scarcely seemed mortal, and he wasn't even using it. He was merely existing with it. Merely exuding it, like the building static before a thunderstorm unleashed its torrent.

He crouched beside me. His fingers touched my chin, gentle as he turned my face toward him. After a moment of study, he pressed his palm to my forehead. A rush of cold air swept over me and my vision darkened.

I blinked, and my vision popped back in. Strength flooded my limbs, Laney's fae spell vanishing.

I could move again, but I didn't. His hand remained on my forehead as his eyes searched mine. Mine searched his.

"Why did you come back?" he asked softly.

"The Dullahan. The only defense against ..."

My throat tightened, cutting off my words. My entire body began to tremble, my skin cold, gooseflesh rushing over my arms despite the humid heat. Terror slid through my veins like icy sludge, clogging my suddenly racing heart.

Zak's pupils dilated with the same fear. His gaze lifted toward the dark trees.

A sound. Quiet. Growing louder.

Hoofbeats.

This time, I knew it wasn't Tilliag.

I pushed up on my elbows, the sharp pain in my collarbone barely registering. Zak was crouched beside me. Laney was on her hands and knees a few yards away, the two vargs flanking her. All five of us faced the trees as the darkness deepened, as the glow of the flowering vines dimmed, as the shadows shivered to life.

He came from the trees, passing through the semi-transparent trunks as though they didn't exist. His towering black steed danced across the moss with muted thuds of its huge hooves, its nostrils flaring and eyes burning like hot coals embedded in its skull.

Astride its back, the Dullahan's ghostly figure was draped in tattered black fabric, his hood drawn up. I couldn't see his eyes but I felt his gaze—felt it press down on my soul like the hellish touch of Death himself.

28

I TREMBLED AS the Dullahan examined us. Though he was called the headless horseman, he seemed to have a head. What he didn't have was a face—there was nothing but empty darkness inside his hood.

His focus settled on Zak. The druid's spiritual power was honey to fae, drawing them like bees to a flower.

The Dullahan *inhaled*—that was the only way to describe the way all the air sucked toward him. His monstrous steed stamped a hoof, steam rushing from its nostrils as it grunted deep in its chest.

Your name.

The voice wasn't sound but sensation—words in the form of jagged claws tearing through my very soul.

Give me your name.

My body went rigid, unadulterated terror obliterating my senses. Cold sweat drenched me, my skin burning, the fire tempered by a single cold spot against my chest.

Speak your name to me.

With whimpering yelps, Zak's two vargs bolted into the trees. Laney cried out as her fire salamander fled with frantic, scuttling steps. I wanted to run too, but my legs wouldn't hold me. A step away, Zak bent over, clutching his head, eyes squeezed shut as he panted.

The Dullahan's deadly attention was fixed on the druid. *Lady of Shadow, Night Eagle, Lallakai. Give me your true name.*

The feather tattoos running down Zak's arms blurred. Phantom wings lifted off his shoulders and unfurled from his back, stretching wide. A shadowy form overlaid his body as the black eagle pulled away from him. Lallakai's emerald eyes gleamed as her curved black beak opened.

Her enraged shriek split the night air as she brought her wings down, propelling herself upward. She swept her wings down again, and blades of shadow slashed toward the Dullahan.

The darkness crawling around him surged up into a swirling barrier. The eagle fae's attack met it and fizzled away to nothing.

Lallakai, give me your true name.

She let out another piercing cry—then beat her wings. Rising into the air. Higher. Even higher, the mists of the crossroads hazing her broad feathers. Her silhouette dimmed, then disappeared.

I stared upward. She ... she'd fled?

Beside me, Zak gazed skyward with wide, disbelieving eyes. His mistress, his guardian, had abandoned him.

Druid.

His limbs stiffened. His eyes went blank, pupils dilating wide, the little color in his face draining away.

Druid, give me your name.

His mouth opened, his throat working as though fighting a compulsion to obey. A hoarse rasp escaped him.

Lunging for him, I clapped my hand over his mouth before he could speak—but could the fae drag his name from his mind? The locket on my chest was like a spot of dry ice, freezing against my skin. It was doing *something* to protect me, but Zak had nothing.

Druid.

Even I felt the crushing power of the Dullahan's call. Zak shook, his eyes rolling back. He needed protection. He needed gold.

My gaze swung to Laney.

She'd scuttled toward the dense trees, quivering like a frightened fawn, her glassy stare locked on the Dullahan and his black steed—but when she felt my attention, her gaze shifted.

For an instant, our eyes met.

"Her!" Laney yelled, pointing at me. "Take her! Her name is Saber—"

My hand clamped harder over Zak's mouth, but he wasn't the person I needed to silence.

"—Rose—"

Zak's eyes rolled toward me, bright with horror.

"—Orien!"

The Dullahan's invisible stare turned my way—and his full attention slammed over me. I sagged into Zak, my hand slipping off his jaw.

Saber Rose Orien, give me your life.

The claws that had torn through my soul now pierced my chest. They closed tight, my heart lurching desperately, my limbs convulsing. The power ripping through my innards *pulled*—but the locket seared my skin, impossibly icy, and the Dullahan's magic slid away as though unable to get a proper grip.

Zak flung his hand out.

Silver liquid spilled from the vial in his grasp, flying in a wide arc. It splattered across the moss, and smoke boiled up from the points of contact. A stench like burnt oil and rusted iron clogged the air.

The Dullahan's steed threw its head back, hooves stamping as it snorted. The gray smoke thickened, obscuring its form, and Zak grabbed my arm as he shoved to his feet. I staggered up beside him.

The black equine leaped through the coiling smoke, eyes rolling and mouth gaping.

Zak threw me clear as the horse rammed him, knocking him down. I fell, rolled, and scrambled up on shaky legs. Zak had staggered up too, one of the crystal artifacts on his chest glowing. His hand lit with a golden glow as he cast his whip spell at the horse's face. The equine reared, front hooves kicking out.

He couldn't fight the Dullahan, so he was attacking the fae's mount—but that wouldn't protect him for long.

Whirling on my heel, I sprinted toward Laney.

She yanked something from her boot and lunged to her feet. An eight-inch utility knife flashed, her fingers clutching its handle. I pulled out my switchblade and pressed the trigger. Four inches of steel popped out with a click. Behind me, the Dullahan's steed screamed furiously, its hooves thudding against the ground.

I didn't wait for Laney to posture, to threaten, to brace for attack. I rushed in, silent and determined.

Fear widened her eyes, and she slashed clumsily. I caught her wrist with one hand, and with the other, I thrust my short blade down into the top of her thigh. She screamed as her leg buckled. I shoved her down, rammed my knee into her sternum, and twisted her knife out of her hand. Flinging it away, I pressed my knife to her ribs.

Tears of agony streamed down her contorted face. "Just kill me already."

"I'm not going to kill you." Keeping my knife on her, I grabbed the tangled chains on her chest and yanked them over her head. "And I didn't kill Arla either."

Druid.

The weight of the Dullahan's voice slammed down, almost driving me into the ground.

Give me your name.

I shoved off Laney, stumbling weakly, my legs threatening to buckle. Gold chains in hand, I left the witch where she lay and ran toward the shadow-enshrouded Dullahan and his mount, Zak somewhere beyond them. I couldn't see the glow of his whip spell.

Druid, give me your—

"I know his name!"

Laney's crazed shout rang out, ten yards behind me, and my running steps faltered. I spun, halfway between her and the Dullahan.

As she pushed up onto her knees, bitter triumph and stark anguish competed in her expression. "That man is Zakariya An—"

Her eyes widened, that blend of triumph and guilt frozen on her face—triumph that she would extinguish the life I was trying to protect, guilt that she'd failed to protect her mother's life.

She blinked slowly. Her hand lifted, fingers fluttering around the handle of my switchblade, embedded in her throat. Blood bubbled around the wound. She sagged backward, sitting on her heels.

I lowered my arm, still able to feel the blade leaving my hand. Still seeing it flash, spinning end over end in a perfect arc, before striking her throat.

She collapsed onto her front, limbs jerking. Awful wheezes and gargles filled the otherwise silent woods.

I turned away from her. The Dullahan, atop his huge mount, watched the woman with his invisible gaze. Air rushed around us with the creature's slow inhalation, as though he were savoring the welcome arrival of death.

Behind the black steed's long legs, Zak was on his knees, a hand pressed to his head and his shoulders heaving. I peeled a long chain from the tangle I'd taken from Laney and crumpled it into a ball.

The Dullahan's hood turned as he refocused on his preferred victim. *Druid, Zakariya—*

Zak went rigid, the creature's call hitting even harder now that he knew part of his name.

—give me your—

"Here!" With my shout, I flung the necklace beneath the horse. It landed on Zak's knees.

I dropped two more chains over my neck, and clutching the last one, I dove toward the glint of steel on the ground—Laney's knife. Snatching the handle, I ran toward the Dullahan as I wrapped the gold chain around the blade. The horse's head swung my way.

Feet flying across the mossy ground, I leaped at the black horse. My grasping fingers caught a handful of the ragged fabric hanging from the Dullahan's thin body, and I hauled myself up as the horse skittered away.

My arm drew back. Swung down.

I drove the gold-wrapped knife into his chest. It plunged in as though sinking into hard clay instead of flesh.

Then clawed fingers closed around my throat.

At the touch of the Dullahan's hand, I had a moment, just a moment, to realize how utterly stupid I'd been to think a mortal weapon could harm this being. How utterly stupid I'd been to think I could survive him when so many had perished, when even powerful fae fled his presence.

Because the moment he touched me, the full force of his soul-rending power deluged me. My limbs seized. My heart stopped—literally stopped, succumbing to the storm raging through my body and spirit. The icy weight of gold around my neck disappeared. Nothing could protect me with the creature's touch on my skin.

This was how Jason had died. This was why his locket hadn't saved him.

Give me your life, Saber Rose Orie—

Zak lunged up on the Dullahan's other side, grabbing the horse's mane for leverage, and looped the gold chain I'd thrown him over the creature's hooded head.

The Dullahan's arm snapped toward him, impossibly fast—but he didn't grab Zak by the throat.

His black-clawed fingers plunged into the druid's chest, disappearing inside his body. Holding me by the throat and Zak by the chest, the Dullahan lifted the druid close to his shrouded face as he inhaled. The mind-crushing pressure of his power shifted to the druid.

If you will not give me your heart, then I will take it.

In my blurred vision, I glimpsed a line of gold glinting against dark fabric. My limbs trembled. I was weak—but I'd always been weak. I was defeated—but I never gave up.

I grabbed the chain Zak had dropped around the Dullahan's neck and pulled. The gold links snapped taut, and for an instant, nothing happened—then the chain *slid*.

Slid like a wire cutting through clay.

Slid right through the Dullahan's neck.

The resistance on the chain disappeared and I fell, landing hard on my back, the gold chain clutched in my numb, quaking hands. A thud sounded as Zak hit the ground on the horse's other side.

The Dullahan sat atop his unmoving steed, a dark figure with no head. The horse's ears were flattened, its fiery orange eyes rolling, its legs straight and stiff.

Air rushed through the clearing. The Dullahan inhaling.

But he had no head. No face. No mouth.

He inhaled—then he howled.

The bellowing cry slammed me down as the creature's power exploded out of him in a wild, uncontrolled tidal wave. The mists of the crossroads writhed, the semi-transparent trees rippling, the vines and their flowers withering and dying.

A dark shape plunged out of the dark, misty sky.

Black wings spread wide, Lallakai plummeted—a beautiful woman with streaming black hair and the phantom wings of her eagle form. A blade of black power arched from her hands, and as she met the headless Dullahan, she drove it through the creature's chest.

Her momentum hurled the Dullahan off his mount, and together they crashed to the ground. The black horse leaped away, galloping into the mists.

Lallakai pinned the Dullahan to the ground with her blade. Black flames raged around the two fae—two wielders of shadows and darkness. She drove it deeper into him, and his clawed hands twitched and jerked toward her weapon. Her emerald eyes blazed brighter, and the twisting darkness around them swirled into a tight maelstrom, sucking into her black sword.

The Dullahan convulsed, then sagged—and sagged more, his black robes sinking to the ground as the Night Eagle's power devoured his body, his very essence. The spinning darkness faded. Lallakai pulled her weapon from the ground and straightened, her wings arching off her back. The Dullahan's dark garments were empty, the ragged fabric pooled on the moss.

The headless horseman was gone.

I slowly pushed into a sitting position. A few yards away, Zak lay on his back, his chest heaving with rough breaths and one hand gripping the front of his shirt where the Dullahan had sunk his hand into him.

His shirt wasn't torn. No blood. Though the creature had held him off the ground with his phantom grip, he hadn't damaged Zak's flesh.

Fae magic was terrifying.

Lallakai opened her hand. Her shadow blade faded away like dark smoke, and her phantom wings furled against her back and melted into nothing. She turned, studying her gasping druid, then looked at me, her beautiful face unreadable.

With a rough cough, Zak pushed onto his elbows, then sat up as though so exhausted he could barely manage that small movement. His weary green eyes lifted to mine. I could see the questions in his gaze—why had I come back to warn him, why had I tried so hard to save him, why had I killed a woman to protect him?

I stared back at him, too tired to answer his unspoken queries.

Especially since I had no answers.

29

WITH A BOISTEROUS NEIGH, Whicker cantered the length of the paddock. Prancing and blowing excitedly, the big gray swerved toward me. He lipped at the strange object I wore—a white sling holding my left arm—and I patted his neck reassuringly. He trotted off again, delighted to stretch his legs after so much time in a stall.

It was strange to be back at the rescue.

I hadn't planned to return, not with an MPD ambush waiting for me, but on our way down the mountain, Zak's phone had gone off. He'd checked his messages, tapped out a reply, then informed me I was clear to go home.

He'd refused to explain how he knew that, but I'd gone along with it anyway. After all, had there been agents waiting, I would've made sure they arrested the notorious Crystal Druid instead of me. Lucky for the both of us, there'd been no sign of agents or bounty hunters on our return.

But it was still strange that the MPD had suddenly backed off, and I didn't trust it. I didn't feel safe. I couldn't relax.

Leaning against the paddock fence, I lifted my gaze to Mount Burke, its rounded peak hazed with clouds stained pink by the setting sun in the west. Almost forty-eight hours had passed since we'd killed the Dullahan at the crossroads.

Forty-eight hours since I'd killed Laney.

As Whicker frolicked around the paddock, I wondered, for the thousandth time, what was wrong with me. Why I made such self-destructive decisions. Why I seemed so determined to ruin my life.

Instead of leaving Zak, whom I hated, whom I wanted dead, to fend for himself against the Dullahan, I'd gone after him. Instead of escaping while the Dullahan was focused on him, I'd tried to help. And instead of letting Laney call out his name, I'd killed her.

Before we'd left the crossroads, I'd located Balligor's pond and thrown my switchblade and Laney's knife into its murky waters, but I knew disposing of the murder weapon wouldn't be enough. I was already the prime suspect in Arla's murder, and most of my coven had witnessed my and Laney's confrontation at her house.

Now Laney was missing. It was only a matter of time before I became the prime suspect in her disappearance.

I'd already packed my things. At the first sign of the MPD's return, I would flee into the wilderness and disappear. I should've already run for it, but I couldn't bring myself to leave. This was the only place that'd felt like home since my parents' death. I couldn't bear the thought of losing it.

Especially now, mere days after recovering my missing memories. I was still raw, still bleeding inside. I'd never

forgotten that I'd killed my aunt, but reliving the whole thing—
the building hope, the crushing failure, the soul-tearing
betrayal, my violent retaliation …

Lost in the past, I was still staring at the clouds, now dark
and dusky, when Whicker walked over to nose at my pockets.
Shaking myself, I clipped a lead line to his halter and led him
back into the stable, his hooves clopping on the concrete aisle.
I settled him in his stall, checked on Whinny and the other
horses, then locked up.

The weather was still humid, though not as unbearably hot
as it'd been two days ago. I breathed in the scents of night,
squinting toward the glowing lights of the house as I debated.

I am hurt, dove.

"You're fine," I replied without looking away from the
house.

I am most wounded.

"You're *fine*."

With a flash of white fur, a blue-eyed cat leaped onto the
mounting block beside me. *I nearly perished, yet you can't trouble
yourself to ask after my wellbeing even once.*

I shot Ríkr a withering look. "I asked plenty yesterday, and
all you did was complain that I was smothering you. Weren't
you the one saying how you're a fast healer and you'd be fine
with a day of sleep?"

He slanted his ears sideways. *My assurances should comfort
your concern, not erase all worry.*

"Oh really." I waved at his unblemished fur with my good
hand. "And the fact you look perfectly healthy again also
shouldn't erase my worry?"

Hmph. He jumped off the wooden block, his tail lashing.
Such a cold heart.

"Don't pretend that isn't your favorite thing about me."

I do adore your viciousness. Never change, my lovely dove.

I turned away from the welcome lights of the house. "Not planning to."

Aside from a single visit to my apartment to grab a few changes of clothes and pack my getaway bag, I'd been sleeping in the house since returning from the crossroads. Zak was in my suite, and wherever he was, I didn't want to be.

Seeing him would mean confronting him about our past and his betrayal ten years ago. Despite my claim that I wanted an explanation, part of me wanted to just stick a knife in him and be done with it.

I strode toward the stable's rear door. Ríkr watched me go but wisely didn't follow.

Pushing the door open, I started up the stairs, my senses stretching ahead of me. I knew Zak was there. Ríkr was right that the druid's energy spread out from him like a slowly expanding wave, claiming more and more land the longer he stayed in one place.

It set my teeth on edge, his essence suffusing *my* home. At least I couldn't sense the sharper buzz of Lallakai's power; she'd been guarding him closely since returning from the crossroads, but she must be off somewhere else right now.

I stopped at the suite door, my good hand drifting toward my pocket—but my trusty switchblade was gone. I was unarmed, and I hated that too.

I hated everything about this.

Jaw clenched, I threw the door open and swept inside. The main room looked more or less untouched except for the blankets folded on the sofa, a pillow stacked neatly on top. My bedroom door was shut, as I'd left it, but the bathroom door was open, light spilling out into the dimly lit main room.

At the thump of the door shutting behind me, Zak stepped into the bathroom's open threshold. Black jeans hugged his legs and clung to his lean hips. He wore no shirt, leaving the sculpted muscles of his torso on display. Strips of white gauze were taped to his lightly tanned skin.

His hair was damp from a recent shower, his jaw clean-shaven and his green eyes sharp as they met mine from across the room.

I glanced from the bandages—around his left bicep and right forearm, over his right side just below his ribs, and a square on his left pectoral—to the roll of medical tape he held. I didn't remember the Dullahan injuring him like that.

A brief memory replayed in my head: a crazed scream erupting from my throat as I lunged for him with my knife.

Right. *I'd* injured him like that. Those were knife wounds.

I raised my chin, daring him to look for nonexistent guilt in my expression or body language. I didn't feel guilt. He'd deserved that and more.

My gaze moved over his face. The sight of him, the understanding of who he was, ignited the fires of hatred, regret, and self-loathing from that night ten years ago. His betrayal tore at me, as fresh as if just yesterday he'd walked away from our promise, leaving me beaten and broken in the rain.

He leaned his shoulder against the doorjamb. "You're back."

"I didn't go far," I replied, my voice husky with the emotions I was battling.

"I know. I saw you." He waved toward the window overlooking the pasture, then turned his attention to my sling. "How's your shoulder?"

Answering him calmly, casually, was almost impossible, but I forced the words out. "Cracked collarbone. When are you leaving?"

"I need to collect the fae favors owed to me. After that ..."

"After that, you'll leave and never come back."

He pushed off the doorframe and stepped into the main room. "Will I?"

"You will," I snarled. "Or I'll gut you and feed your entrails to your own vargs."

"Really." He was advancing toward me with slow steps, a jaguar stalking his quarry. "Do you want me dead? Or do you just want to hurt me?"

"Both. Pain, then death."

He drew closer, too close, but I had no way to stop his approach.

"I find that hard to believe," he rumbled.

"Did you already forget who gave you those wounds?"

"You did ... but they weren't even close to lethal." His broad shoulders filled my vision, and my traitorous feet stepped backward. "Shortly after you knifed me, you risked your life to save me."

I stepped back again and my back hit the door.

"Strange thing for someone who wants me dead to do, don't you think?" He stopped, barely a foot of space between us, his stare pinning me. "Why did you save me?"

My heart drummed behind my ribs, my innards churning, sharp edges grinding. I wanted to hit him. I wanted to make him bleed.

But what I most wanted was for him to speak the words that would repair the broken pieces inside me. The words that would fix all the ways he'd shattered me. The words that would let me lay my past to rest forever.

Except words like that didn't exist.

Nothing he said would fix me. Nothing he said would change what had happened between us. And the thought of hearing his inadequate explanation or weak apology—or worse, no apology at all—was more than I could take. He'd already destroyed me once. Learning why he'd done it might destroy me again.

Zak's eyes darkened, and he asked again, "Why did you save me, Saber?"

"So I could kill you myself."

His jaw tightened—and Ríkr's voice sounded in my head.

A black vehicle just pulled into the yard. Three males are getting out.

My eyes widened, and so did Zak's as he also heard my familiar's warning. I leaped away from the door, colliding with his chest in my rush. The MPD. It was the MPD. They were here for me. I'd expected more warning. I'd expected to have time to get away.

"Out," I gasped, shoving past Zak. "Need to get out!"

He caught my good elbow and spun me to face him. His hands gripped my upper arms, stopping my urgent movement.

"Saber, calm down."

"*Calm down?*" I half shouted, fear transforming into fury. "They're here to arrest me! I'm not going back to that. I'm not!"

"I know, and you won't. They won't arrest you. You're going to talk to them."

The men are heading for the stable, Ríkr told me urgently.

"Are you fucking kidding me?" I wrenched against his hands, sharp pain lancing my collarbone. "Let me go!"

He held on tighter. "Listen to me, Saber! You texted the hotline like I told you to, right?"

"Yes, but—"

"Then trust me and—"

"*I'll never trust you again!*"

Ríkr's voice lashed my mind. *They're coming up the stairs.*

Zak swore. He released my shoulders—then grabbed the sides of my face and pulled my face up.

His hot mouth met mine, hard and urgent. As swiftly as he'd kissed me, he pulled back, leaving me stunned.

A loud bang shook the door a few feet behind me.

"Just open the door, Saber. It'll be okay, and if it's not, I'll kill those agents myself." He released me, strode to the bathroom, and shut himself inside, the door closing with a soft click.

A fist hammered on the apartment door a second time.

"Saber Orien?" an older male voice called.

Panic swam through my head. In a daze, I turned to the door. I no longer had time to run for it, which meant … which meant I had to once again trust the boy who'd betrayed me.

With a shaking hand, I turned the bolt and swung the door open.

30

TWO MEN in dark suits stood in the doorway, and only one thing about them registered: the silver MPD badges hanging from their necks on fine chains, the etched pentagrams in their centers glinting like winking eyes.

Horror closed over me like a wave of suffocating water. I was fifteen again, sitting in a precinct holding cell as MPD agents towered over me, condemnation in their pitiless stares.

The men stepped into my home, the older one leading the way. He was tall, his hair cropped in a simple style. Wire-rimmed glasses sat on his nose, a folder under his arm. His partner, the agent Ríkr had attacked, was younger than me, with a bronzy-taupe complexion, short mohawk, and flinty gaze.

"Saber Orien?" the older one demanded sternly, his attention shifting to the sling I wore.

"Yes," I whispered, searching for my usual fearlessness—but I was unarmed and injured, and they were in my home, in my space.

"I am Agent Harris." He gestured to his partner. "This is Agent Park. We're here to—"

"Hey, do I not even warrant an introduction?"

The question floated from behind the agents, and with it, a third man stepped around the other two. Unlike them, his athletic six-foot-tall frame was clad in a casual jacket and jeans, his brown hair tousled and his face youthful and almost naively open.

His blue eyes met mine, bright with curiosity—and lurking beneath that amicable openness was a sharp perception that warned of cunning.

"I'm Kit," he said, flashing me a bright smile. "Agent Morris, actually, but call me Kit. I'm—"

"Not working this case," Agent Park hissed.

"—the lead investigator for the Ghost's bounty. I texted you a couple days ago."

This guy was an MPD agent too? *And* a lead investigator?

New fear pierced me. The agent in charge of the Ghost's bounty was in my home—and so was that very same rogue he hunted. Zak was hiding in my bathroom, one casual search away from discovery. I would be charged with murder *and* harboring Vancouver's most wanted criminal.

Agent Harris cleared his throat. "Miss Orien, we're here to discuss the death of Arla Collins, leader of your coven and your rehabilitation supervisor. Where were you on the evening of June seventeenth?"

"Here," I replied tersely. "Until I went to Arla's house to talk to her about my rehabilitation."

"Where she found her coven leader's body," Morris cut in as he strolled past me into my living room, his hands clasped behind his back. "Which we all know already."

"This isn't your case," Agent Park snapped again.

"It will be," Morris said cheerfully, pivoting to face the other two agents. "The coroner has already ruled Arla Collin's death as an attack by a non-human, non-mythic entity. Aka, a fae. And your suspect saw *my* suspect in this general vicinity. My suspect, as you may recall, happens to be an exceptionally powerful druid known for wielding some pretty intense fae magic."

Agent Harris pushed his glasses up his nose. "You have no proof that the Ghost was involved in this—"

"Not yet, but you have no proof that Saber here can steal people's hearts out of their chests either. So if you wouldn't mind hurrying up and asking her all those redundant questions about where she was on which night, I'd like to ask her about the actual scary mythic murderer and where he might be right now."

The senior agent flexed his jaw. His young partner glared daggers at Morris.

Jerking around to face me again, Agent Harris pulled a sheet of paper from his folder. "I am hereby serving you a summons to appear for questioning at the Vancouver precinct within seventy-two hours. We will complete your interrogation there, without any"—he shot a fresh glower at Morris—"interruptions. You are not to travel outside the greater Vancouver area before then."

I took the paper, fighting not to crush it in my fist.

"We will see you soon, Miss Orien." Agent Harris turned away. "She's all yours, Agent Morris."

Morris grinned at their backs as they strode out. He followed them to the door, stuck his head across the threshold as though to ensure they were actually leaving, then firmly shut the door. Turning around, he leaned back against the wood, his eyebrows arched.

"So," he drawled, "where's he hiding?"

My teeth snapped together, but before I could respond, the bathroom door behind me clicked. I whirled around, my stomach dropping as Zak appeared, now wearing a shirt. He surveyed the agent across the room.

Morris gave a dramatic bow without stepping away from the door. "You summoned me, oh dastardly druid?"

Zak snorted. "Took you long enough to show up."

"I'm a busy guy. And you have no idea how many baseless tips about random dudes in hoods I have to sort through every week. I'm not exactly hanging on the edge of my seat waiting for them." He shrugged. "I'm here now. That's what counts. You mind filling me in on *why* exactly I'm here?"

"I want you to make sure those two idiots figure out that Laney Collins, daughter of the victim, was involved with Jason Brine, an ex-con, and he's the one who unleashed the fae killer responsible for all the deaths in this area in the last two weeks."

"Ah." Morris rubbed a hand through his hair. "Hasn't Laney Collins been missing for the last two days?"

"You'll find her and Jason Brine's bodies north of Mount Burke at the fae crossroads." Zak's green eyes gleamed. "Laney's body has, unfortunately, been mauled by scavengers. But her dental records and belongings will confirm her identity."

Her body had been mauled? How did he know that? Unless he'd ensured her corpse would be too damaged for the cause of death to be determined.

"Ooookay," Morris muttered. "And am I steering the investigation in that direction because it's what actually happened, or because it's what you want the MPD to *think* happened?"

"Everything I've told you actually happened, and I'll leave it to you to fill in the missing pieces."

"How generous." Morris considered that for a moment, then smirked evilly. "I can't think of any other agents I'd have more fun upstaging than Harris and Vinny."

Zak's smirk was even more evil. "Knock yourself out."

I couldn't hold my tongue any longer. "What *the hell* is going on with you two?"

Piercing green eyes and almost-as-vivid blue eyes fixed on me. Neither man said anything.

"Please," Morris said after a moment, pushing away from the door, "tell me you've seen *The Dark Knight Rises.*"

I stared blankly at him and he sighed.

"Okay, well, just wait to show up for your summons until the very last minute. I'll need those seventy-two hours. And Zak, keep a low profile until this is done." He arched an eyebrow. "Actually, keep a low profile forever. It'd make my life easier."

Zak grunted in an amused way, and Morris slipped out the door, closing it quietly behind him. Silence fell over my suite, and I kept on staring at the door, my head spinning.

Now I knew why Zak had told me to send that hotline tip and involve the agent in charge of his bounty. And I knew how Zak had determined it was safe for me to return home. The Ghost had a reputation for being untouchable, but I hadn't suspected how far he'd gone to ensure he'd never be arrested.

And thanks to him and his pet agent, I'd escaped arrest too. For now.

"Saber," Zak said quietly.

No. Not happening. I was off balance, dizzy, floundering. I couldn't deal with him and his betrayal and the answers that terrified me. Not right now.

I yanked open the door Morris had just closed, rushed down the stairs, and marched out into the humid night air. As I rounded the corner of the stable, the taillights of the agents' car receded down the long drive. I watched until they'd disappeared, then turned to the farmhouse, its windows lit invitingly.

Paper crinkled, and I realized I was still holding the MPD summons. I folded it up and tucked it in my pocket. Seventy-two hours. Was that enough time for Agent Morris to prove Jason was the perpetrator and I was innocent?

My hand drifted to my chest, where the golden locket had lain. Jason, and Laney, and most likely Arla as well, were the only people besides me and Zak who'd known about the Dullahan. And they were all dead. I had killed Laney. The Dullahan had killed Jason and Arla.

But Arla ...

I pressed my fingertips into my sternum. Jason could have given Arla's name to the Dullahan, but he'd died at least a week before her. Why would the creature wait over a week to take her life? Laney couldn't have done it; she hadn't realized the Dullahan was on the loose until I'd mentioned the crossroads to her, and she'd been convinced to the very end that I was responsible for her mother's death.

Who else had known Arla was involved, even peripherally, in the Dullahan's appearance?

Humming the eerie melody of the Dullahan's ballad, I drifted toward the orchard, hoping the night air and scent of leaves and young fruit would clear my mind. The trees closed around me, neat rows with broad branches that hid the dark sky.

"*And your soul the Dullahan will claim,*" I sang under my breath.

"Little witch."

At that purring voice, I turned sharply. Lallakai leaned against the trunk of a plum tree, her long hair swept over one shoulder. Her emerald eyes glinted in the darkness as she smiled at me.

My jaw tightened. "What do you want?"

She stepped away from the tree, hips swaying. "Merely to thank the witch who saved my druid from certain death."

"I didn't do it for you or for him."

"No?" She sauntered toward me, stroking the mass of hair resting on her shoulder.

I held my ground as she stopped indecently close. She was slightly taller than me, and I stretched my neck to glare into her flawless face.

Her eyelids lowered halfway, a coy look. "Did you save him for your own sake, little witch?"

"What about you?" I shot back. "You abandoned him."

"Out of necessity." She pushed the long length of her hair off her shoulder to fall down her back. "The Dullahan's power was driving me into a rage, and had I lost control, I might have struck down my own beloved druid."

I remembered the mindless ferocity of the bear fae and couldn't call her a liar, especially since she'd returned to finish off the Dullahan with powerful magic neither I nor Zak possessed.

Lallakai's cool fingers touched my face, catching me off guard. She stroked my cheek, her pupilless eyes filling my vision.

"As I said before, little witch," she crooned throatily, "your power is surprisingly sweet. A treat for any fae. Your shapeshifter companion has enviable luck to have claimed you all for himself."

"Ríkr didn't *claim* me."

"No? Then I'm free to have a taste?" Her hand curled around the back of my neck, and her other hand slid over my waist, pulling me against her soft curves. Her silky lips brushed my ear. "May I taste you, little witch?"

She phrased it as a question, but her grip told me refusal wasn't an option. I had no weapons and one arm in a sling. With no better option, I curled my good hand into a fist.

A cold breeze, as though someone had switched on an air conditioner, washed across my hot skin.

I warned you, vulture.

The low snarl slid through my mind, and Lallakai turned, pulling me with her.

A white coyote with azure eyes stood between two trees, his fur so pale it appeared bluish in the darkness. His hackles were raised, his lips pulled back to show his fangs. It was the largest form I'd ever seen Ríkr take.

"Ah," Lallakai breathed, her talons pricking the sides of my throat, dangerously close to my jugular. "Your threat surprises me, shapeshifter. Surely you realize that a pitifully weak creature such as yourself can make no claim against anything I desire?"

Release her. Ríkr's low voice roiled through my head like an arctic wave. *I will not warn you again.*

My heart raced as I tried to think of a way to escape Lallakai's hold before Ríkr had to take drastic action. He was no match for any of Zak's fae companions, especially not this one. Should I call for Zak? Would he hear me?

"So commanding," the Night Eagle mocked. "I quake with fear."

The coyote's muzzle ridged with fury. A chill breeze swirled through the orchard.

Lallakai pulled me into her and her mouth brushed along my cheek. "Come now, shapeshifter. I will tarry no longer. If you wish to stop me, show your power."

Ríkr snarled.

"No?" Her wet tongue flicked against the corner of my mouth, but I couldn't move with her sharp nails at my throat. "Then I shall enjoy her—"

Pale blue light exploded through the orchard on a wave of subzero cold.

The blast of icy luminescence threw me back, blinding me. Lallakai's hand slipped from my neck, her talons scraping my skin, then she grabbed my shoulder and yanked me toward her again, pain blazing through my injured collarbone. My vision blurred, then cleared.

The air was sparkling.

Tiny crystals of frozen moisture drifted between the trees, shimmering like glitter. Ice covered the ground, jutting upward in jagged, glassy spikes. Thick fractals coated the trees, icicles hanging from the branches, every leaf frosted in white. A bone-deep chill saturated the air, as though I were standing not in a summer orchard but on a mountaintop in January.

"I told you, Lady of Shadow, that if you touched her again, I would shatter your flesh into a thousand shards."

I knew that low, clear-toned voice. I'd heard it inside my head every day for the past seven years—though never dripping with such primeval menace.

His voice was unmistakable, but the creature standing before me wasn't Ríkr. His eyes were pale blue, exactly the same, but …

But he stood taller than me.

But his shoulders were broad, his skin pale and smooth, his ice-white hair hanging in long locks around his face.

And his arm was outstretched, his fingers curled around Lallakai's throat.

I stared at his face, too flawlessly beautiful to be human. Cheekbones too sharp, full lips too pale, jaw too smooth. Faintly luminescent azure markings ran up the left side of his face, disappearing beneath the elegant but aggressive black headpiece that covered his forehead. Short, straight antlers that gleamed like pure gold rose above his head.

No human countenance could appear so calm yet so utterly deadly at the same time.

In that flash where arctic cold had descended on the orchard, he'd closed the distance between us, his exotic garments of white, black, and metallic gold fabric swirling around him from the swift movement. He had a lethal hold on Lallakai—but she merely smiled, the ancient malevolence rolling off her as strong as his.

"Ah," she cooed playfully. "Greetings, Lord of Winter."

The temperature in the orchard dropped further, the jagged ice thickening.

"Your masquerade as a feeble shapeshifter was most entertaining." Her emerald eyes glittered with challenge. "But I'm afraid I will have to intervene before you destroy the girl entirely. My druid is rather attached to her."

Ríkr smiled a gentle, murderous smile. "And I, Lady of Shadow, will entomb you in an ocean of ice for daring to lay your gluttonous hands upon *my* druid."

SABER'S STORY CONTINUES IN

THE LONG-FORGOTTEN WINTER KING
THE GUILD CODEX: UNVEILED / TWO

I thought I was a useless witch whose only weapons were a switchblade and a mean disposition.

I thought Zak was a rogue druid with waning power and an alluring aura that's impossible for me to resist.

And I thought my fae familiar was a harmless shapeshifter who chose me because I'm "mildly interesting."

But nothing is what I thought. Nothing is what it seems.

Including me.

I need answers, and I need them fast—before I sink any deeper in the quagmire of secrets I've fallen into.

The Crystal Druid's. The Winter King's.

And my own.

www.guildcodex.ca

ABOUT THE AUTHOR

ANNETTE MARIE is the best-selling author of The Guild Codex, an expansive collection of interwoven urban fantasy series ranging from thrilling adventure to hilarious hijinks to heartrending romance. Her other works include YA urban fantasy series Steel & Stone, its prequel trilogy Spell Weaver, and romantic fantasy trilogy Red Winter.

Her first love is fantasy, but fast-paced adventures, bold heroines, and tantalizing forbidden romances are her guilty pleasures. She proudly admits she has a thing for dragons and aspires to include them in every book.

Annette lives in the frozen winter wasteland of Alberta, Canada (okay, it's not quite that bad) and shares her life with her husband and their furry minion of darkness—sorry, cat—Caesar. When not writing, she can be found elbow-deep in one art project or another while blissfully ignoring all adult responsibilities.

www.annettemarie.ca

SPECIAL THANKS

*My thanks to Erich Merkel for sharing your exceptional
expertise in Latin and Ancient Greek.*

Any errors are mine.

THE
GUILD CODEX
UNVEILED

A vigilante witch with a murder conviction, a switchblade for a best friend, and a dangerous lack of restraint. A notorious druid mired in secrets, shadowed by deadly fae, and haunted by his past.

They might be exactly what the other needs—if they don't destroy each other first.

THE
GUILD CODEX
SPELLBOUND

Meet Tori. She's feisty. She's broke. She has a bit of an issue with
running her mouth off. And she just landed a job at the local magic
guild. Problem is, she's also 100% human. Oops.

Welcome to the Crow and Hammer.

THE
GUILD CODEX
DEMONIZED

Robin Page: outcast sorceress, mythic history buff, unapologetic bookworm, and the last person you'd expect to command the rarest demon in the long history of summoning. Though she holds his leash, this demon can't be controlled.

But can he be tamed?

DISCOVER MORE BOOKS AT
www.guildcodex.ca

THE
GUILD CODEX
WARPED

The MPD has three roles: keep magic hidden, keep mythics under control, and don't screw up the first two.

Kit Morris is the wrong guy for the job on all counts—but for better or worse, this mind-warping psychic is the MPD's newest and most unlikely agent.

DISCOVER MORE BOOKS AT
www.guildcodex.ca

STEEL & STONE

When everyone wants you dead, good help is hard to find.

The first rule for an apprentice Consul is *don't trust daemons*. But when Piper is framed for the theft of the deadly Sahar Stone, she ends up with two troublesome daemons as her only allies: Lyre, a hotter-than-hell incubus who isn't as harmless as he seems, and Ash, a draconian mercenary with a seriously bad reputation. Trusting them might be her biggest mistake yet.

SPELL WEAVER

The only thing more dangerous than the denizens of the Underworld ... is stealing from them.

As a daemon living in exile among humans, Clio has picked up some unique skills. But pilfering magic from the Underworld's deadliest spell weavers? Not so much. Unfortunately, that's exactly what she has to do to earn a ticket home.

A destiny written by the gods. A fate forged by lies.

If Emi is sure of anything, it's that *kami*—the gods—are good, and *yokai*—the earth spirits—are evil. But when she saves the life of a fox shapeshifter, the truths of her world start to crumble. And the treachery of the gods runs deep.

This trilogy features thirty stunning, full-page illustrations.

GET THE COMPLETE TRILOGY
www.annettemarie.ca/redwinter